Catacomb

Cat's Crusade
Book 2

Nik Morton

ROUGH
EDGES
PRESS

Catacomb
Paperback Edition
Copyright © 2023 (As Revised) Nik Morton

Rough Edges Press
An Imprint of Wolfpack Publishing
9850 S. Maryland Parkway, Suite A-5 #323
Las Vegas, Nevada 89183

roughedgespress.com

Paperback ISBN 978-1-68549-239-7
eBook ISBN 978-1-68549-238-0

With love to Jennifer, Hannah, Harry, Darius, and Suri
Thank you to James Reasoner and Jake Bray for
believing in the character, Cat

cat•a•comb (ˈka-tə-ˌkōm\)

n.

1. a subterranean cemetery of galleries v
   tombs—usually used in plural
2. something resembling a catacomb
   a. an underground passageway
      passageways
   b. a complex set of interre'
      the endless catacombs of ι

Ananke

The name of a primordial deity in Greek mytho.
the personification of necessity and fate. She was
present when the universe began, with her consort,
Chronos (time). She was said to rule over fate. Being the
mother of the Fates, only she could control their
decisions.

Catacomb

Prologue

Dogs of Law

Summer, 2013—Vauxhall, South London

"Rippon's death certainly seems bizarre," Detective Inspector Alan Pointer remarked over the rim of the Delft coffee-cup. He should have known better but sipped the aromatic hot black liquid anyway, then grimaced. The Superintendent's secretary had sugared it again. "All he did was rub suntan lotion on himself in his garden—and a couple of hours later, he's dying before his poor family's eyes." Bizarre was an understatement: it was a gruesome case, skin peeling off; the man's flesh disintegrating into body-fluids.

"Let me explain, Alan." Superintendent Keith Thurston scratched his bald head.

Pointer had joined the National Crime Agency in April when it replaced the Serious Organized Crime Agency. Thurston used his first name; they'd been round the block together for several years. When accompanied by anyone else, of course, it was DI

Pointer. Now, he teepled his plump fingers, an old mannerism. Implicit in his tone was "Are we sitting comfortably? Then I'll begin!" So he began: "Some years ago a group of Birmingham chemists discovered a method getting plastics to disintegrate automatically when thrown away."

after but that was a long time back; I thought it practical, lack of funding for research...?"

Thurston nodded, setting his sallow cheeks trembling. "The invention involved dyes which, when added to plastics, caused them to break down under the action of sunlight's ultra-violet rays."

"Though this was before the ozone layer depletion crisis? Now, they'd disintegrate even faster than planned, I guess." The irony was lost on Thurston.

"Correct. The Swedes and Canadians have been working on it, too, but only the British version works when subjected to direct sunlight. Well, I say British, but it isn't quite. The firm now dabbling in it is French-Swiss—Ananke. Their founder, Loup Dante bought the rights—the fate of so many British innovative firms and inventions—and hired the scientists."

"So commodities on window-sills are safe?"

"Yes. To start with, the self-destruction time could be varied from three months of summer sunshine to three years. They toyed with calling it Ecodream! Now, though, if applied in the right proportions, this stuff could turn plastics to dust in three hours!"

Pointer didn't like where this was leading: Rippon, the Incredible Melting Man. But it was time for his "It's only effective on plastics, surely?"

Shaking his head, Thurston mumbled, "Was, Alan, was... But the military got interested..."

Bloody typical!

"As you're aware, any major scientific discovery has the Defense people looking for ways utilizing these inventions. Often, it's the other way around, isn't it? A military invention has civilian use—look at GPS, for example."

Pointer nodded while trying to maintain bearings in Thurston's lengthy and rather ring explanation. "Intensive research came up with adaptation for use on human tissue and metals. And only glass and rubber are really impervious."

Of course the suntan lotion had been in a glass

Thurston went on, "It can assume any color; we s call it a dye, though." He shrugged. "But without th action of sunlight, the stuff's harmless."

Well, in for a penny: "And the formula's been stolen?"

A reluctant nod. "As well as a large sample of the dye, yes."

Pointer's mouth had gone dry, but he had no desire to resort to the coffee. "How on earth did Rippon come to possess the adulterated lotion in the first place?"

"A good point. Rippon was the Under Secretary responsible for Science and Research Coordination. He used to entertain scientists regularly at his Belgravia home. Keeping in touch, he called it. The four suspects all visited Rippon last week when they reported the formula and sample missing."

"I see," Pointer said. "A few minutes in Rippon's bathroom and the lotion could've been treated. It was just his bad luck the weather turned hot and Rippon had time to bask in his garden."

"Whoever planted the deadly sample must have

been aware of the forecast—hot weather for two weeks. That's the length of our summer, normally, isn't it?" Pointer wasn't going to get into a discussion about the weather and climate change. "I suppose that money's the motive?"

"Yes. Our lab discovered the bottle's label had a " on it: Payment of £2 million for the return of formula and the sample."

"And the means of communicating our response?"

Thurston sipped his coffee. "The culprit had no way of knowing when the sample would take action. He or she waited for the announcement and then sent the demand to the Home Office. They passed it to the Director-General and he dumped the file on me pretty damned quick, I can tell you!"

"When's the deadline, sir?"

"We must give our decision in tomorrow's *Times* and await further instructions. The alternative given isn't pretty—an unspecified town's water-supply will be treated with the stuff at..." and he squinted at his desk-clock/calculator, "...seven tomorrow night."

"This puts the current bout of consumer terrorism in the shade." No pun intended. "We've less than twenty hours."

"Imagine," Thurston said, shaking his head, staring at his open file.

Pointer was no slouch at imagining the worst scenario and had already done so: a whole town, washing and cooking, then going out to work in the sunshine. Sunshine was rare enough in these islands, but to make it a killer defied belief. Bloody typical of the defense establishment! A boon to mankind, to abolish waste, and they have to meddle with it, turning sunshine into a killer far more effec.. than cancerous melanoma.

We could pray for rain, Pointer t.. ..ght without enthusiasm since he'd viewed the forecast..

Thurston stood up, paced the tire.. ..et and scowled at the streaks of pigeon-pollution.. ..ening the windowsill outside. "Well, Alan, I want y.. ..o to their Research Establishment—Pethewray Poi... ..ie Devon coast. The security dossiers of the.. suspects, courtesy of the Minister himself, are c desk." He jutted his chin at the teak furniture in Pointer had difficulty identifying it as a desk. 1 dockets were red, and as Pointer picked them up the. India-tags clinked on the polished surface. Thurston swerved round, and Pointer smiled: the desk was unscathed. "All have been involved with the project since MOD took over. And they're the only ones who've had access to the formula and the dye samples and also visited the poor sod Rippon in his home."

POINTER ELECTED to drive down in his battered old Citroen—he profited a little more on expenses. Detective Sergeant Carol Basset occupied the passenger seat, working through the dossiers. She usually drove Pointer around but was happy to let him take the strain. It had proved a strange yet rewarding partnership; they'd worked together even before NCA was established, and they were comfortable with each other's work methodology. Partly due to their surnames, partly because they made a good and rather tenacious team, many in NCA referred to them as "the dogs of law". Pointer was not

keen on celebri[ty] a term that had been demeaned in
recent years, [bu]t he couldn't argue with that definition.
Carol reck[oned] d it was a hoot. He always thought of her
as Caro[l] it traditionally he referred to her as "Sergeant" er than "Basset" when in public.

he way on the road Pointer couldn't get rid of
[ni]ghtmare vision of a sunny ghost-town succumb-
[H]ad they recently passed through it? Were those
[tra]ppers he'd seen back there destined to die by the
[su]n's glowing rays? Death held no sting for him now,
but this latest threat made him shudder.

Twenty checkered years with the Force meant he'd
seen his fair share of misery: widows prostrate, rape
victims in catatonia, unrepentant murderers demanding
lawyers, psychotic killers in straitjackets, orphaned children in traumatic shock, mutilated children and their
bereft parents: the list was endless. And the Grim
Reaper hadn't left him unscarred, either. Eileen had
foolishly opened a mysterious parcel addressed to him
during the Kyle terror-gang investigation. There wasn't
much of the house standing when the bomb-blast's
dust-clouds subsided. Courtesy of extremists, not your
run-of-the-mill underworld villains. Society of late
seemed to breed a lot of extremists; some began as so-
called activists but over time they became extreme. It
was as if the thin veneer of civilization was being
scraped away by incursions from the State, self-interest
groups, interfering self-aggrandizing do-gooders, reli-
gious zealots, lawmakers who didn't understand human
nature, and of course politicians and the judiciary who
didn't live in the real world. Eventually, they caught the
bastards responsible for the bomb, though their subse-
quent absurdly lenient sentences didn't remove the

profound emptiness she'd left behind. They'd bought this car on their tenth wedding anniversary.

When a number of the city's villains he'd helped put inside actually paid their respects at Eileen's funeral, he had almost gone to pieces. Stupid, really, they'd been too close, loved too deeply, so when he was left alone, he was just that—alone. They had no friends, only acquaintances and colleagues; they'd been regarded as "that couple joined at the hip". Everyone did their best, offering well-meaning platitudes.

Christ, he thought, I'd better get rid of the car. I can't face this self-pitying catharsis every time I drive long-distance!

"You're very quiet, sir?" Carol said.

"Sorry, I was thinking."

"That's my job. You make the arrests."

Pointer laughed, tears streaming, vision slightly blurred, but not dangerously affected. He glanced quickly at her, but she was looking at the dossier. Hastily, he wiped his eyes and cheeks with the back of a hand; there was hardly any wobble as he steered one-handed.

The clock was ticking.

UNDER THE SEEMINGLY BENIGN sun Pointer parked in a layby, a small distance before the next rise which concealed all but the radio antennae of the Pethewray Point establishment.

"We're early," he said. "The Research Director isn't expecting us till 9am."

"Fancy a look around, sir?"

"Indeed." He opened the door and got out. "Time for a little relaxation, before the fray," he said, feeling guilty since the time was running out.

Leaning on the other side of the car roof, Carol said, "And time to brush off the clinging cobwebs of memories, if nothing else."

Sometimes, he was sure she was a mind-reader.

Breathing in the salty air, he walked across the weather-beaten prickly-yellow gorse, Carol silent by his side. Fields gently climbed toward the cliff edge a half-mile away, where he could glimpse the shale rooftops of a couple of cottages. Circling gulls squealed plaintively.

The warming sun highlighted the Ministry of Defense notices surrounding the isolated village of wired-off Nissen huts and prefabricated offices. Scaffolding framework stalked to the rear of the place; drills stuttered loudly on the faint breeze. It was in places like this, on the edges of solitude, where his senses came alive; the opposite of sensory deprivation—city-life surrounded the body, permeated the skin and mind: only here could he seem to function as a human being.

He blinked away morbid thoughts and turned to Carol. "Time to go, Sergeant."

A ROYAL MARINE sentry was on duty at the red-and-white striped entrance barrier. Over on the left was a huge billboard advising anyone who cared that Trenwith Contractors were working on the site.

Their hastily acquired passes were in order. The crease-proud sea-soldier seemed amused by Pointer's travel-weary fawn suit. Eileen had always badgered him to get a new one—but then new cases kept cropping up. The Marine barely gave Carol a glance; she was Pointer's bag-lady, stout and stern-faced, wearing a pinstripe trouser suit.

Above the builders' raucous din, the Marine directed them to a uniformly characterless gray-and-brown prefab building, its numerous windows blinking.

Sweat made Pointer's shirt cling to his body as they crossed to the swing doors.

Once inside, he was relieved that his shirt quickly dried with the flow of cool air-conditioning.

The elderly receptionist eyed the passes, then her pen placed a tick against their names in her register and then she stood. "This way, please, Sir, Miss."

She led them along a stark fluorescent-lit corridor that echoed to her Scholl footwear. At the elevator's double doors, she informed them, "Room 303 is directly opposite the doors on the second floor."

The elevator deposited them and Pointer depressed the buzzer of the door marked *A. Pescod, Director of Research* in white on red Dymo-tape.

A younger, attractive blonde female secretary answered and led them into the "inner sanctum" as she called it.

The builders' noise wafted through an open window which doubtless put a strain on the air-conditioning, contributing to global warming; still, it was only taxpayers' money.

Rising from behind his utilitarian desk, the Director grimaced at the sound. His gray hair was closely cropped, his eagle eyes a deep speculative brown, eyebrows pencil-thin. There was something vaguely Teutonic about him; the set of prognathous jaw and bracing of martinet's shoulders; his fleshy fish-pouting lips were paradoxically uncompromisingly stern. All he needed was a monocle. Shining false teeth smiled innocuously.

In Pointer's business, you're careful concerning first impressions. He was particularly careful now. "Pointer, sir. Alan Pointer. And this is Sergeant Carol Basset."

"I'm Adrian Pescod, the headman of this outstation," he said, making what seemed like a superfluous statement of the obvious. A soft, warm hand. He nodded to Carol. "Take a seat—I won't be a moment." Stretching backwards, he shut the window, lowered the venetian blinds, the slats rattling. "That infernal racket! I'll be glad when they've done!" His shoulders sank into his rotating leather chair.

"A new extension?" Carol asked, taking the lead, as usual, fishing for ice-breaking conversation to make the interviewee relax.

"Sort of." He gave her a smile. "Our old lab's a bit outdated. This new one they're working on will probably be the most advanced in Europe—*when* it's finished!"

"When we came in I noticed a contractor's billboard—?"

"Ah, yes." Pescod blinked, adding quickly, "Oh, don't worry about security—they've all been thoroughly screened, checked way back to the details of which hand the midwife used to smack their backside!" He chuckled, obviously pleased with his choice of words and imagery.

"My job's not security, Mr. Pescod, but detection. But if you'll recall, Philby, Blake and Fuchs, among others, all had security clearance."

The Director froze. "Yes, you're right of course—I suppose you can't be too careful." He lapsed into an uneasy silence. Then, abruptly: "What kind of maniac would make such a threat?" The alarm in his eyes seemed genuine enough. "They're paying up, I trust?"

"No. The threat could be construed as a terrorist act. You know it's not government policy to fund terrorism."

"But it might not be terrorists."

"Indeed, that's why we've been called in. It could be an organized crime group seeking to boost its coffers."

"I thought that kind of thing was only in fiction!"

"It's far from fiction, sir," Carol said. "Organized crime is serious business."

"Sergeant Basset is right. And we mean 'business'. Their effects ripple through into almost every town's high street."

"That's not too comforting. I must lead a sheltered life here... But the ransom and the deadline, it's—"

Pointer raised a calming hand. "They're hoping the sergeant and I can get somewhere before the deadline. Tell me, are the others aware that a threat has been made and a deadline set?"

"No, I only learned about it from the Home Office a short while ago. Do you suspect anyone in particular?" Pescod asked in a stage-whisper. "From the dossiers, I mean..."

"Too early to say," Carol offered.

Pointer pursued another tack. "I was told only four people—Fisher, Erskine, Carter and Lodge—besides yourself—had access to both formula and samples at any one time. Is that correct?"

"Yes and no," Pescod responded. "At the outset, I had overall control. But now that the team's advances have gone ahead to such a degree, I've given them free rein." He added hastily, almost defensively, "It says I can delegate as such in my Terms of Reference."

"I don't doubt it," Carol said.

He glared at her, and added, "With regard to this particular project, Professor Fisher had control. He was —is—the lead."

Pointer leaned back in the chair. "I see. Now, I'd like to use somewhere for an interview room, if possible. Have you an office or something suitable spare?"

"The old lab isn't being used at the moment." Pescod grimaced pointedly. "No formula or samples to work on, you see..."

THE INTERVIEWING ROOM wore inhospitable grays and greens. The retorts and beakers lounged empty, the Bunsen burners were conspicuously dumb. Bottled alkaloids and acids lined the tiered shelves of a locked glass cabinet. The big wooden workbenches were spotless, unlike those at Pointer's old crumbling Secondary Modern School; no carved initials and penned protestations of eternal love, indelible for posterity. There were a number of computer screens and towers.

A booming voice in the corridor distracted him.

Professor Fisher stooped to conquer the doorway, agitatedly brushing his thinning dark hair with a hand. His forty-eight years appeared distinguished with graying about his large ears.

"I'm Detective Inspector Pointer, and this is—"

"I know." Fisher twitched his bent rugger nose and ignored Pointer's proffered hand. His whole demeanor was singularly antagonistic, even to the set of his broad shoulders. He glared at Carol.

She didn't flinch, simply smiled at him, holding the dossiers to her chest. Taking the lead from her, Pointer decided to remain cool: no time for his Irish forefathers' blood to boil. "Alright, Professor. How important is the formula to another country?"

"Or a terrorist organization?" Carol added.

"Priceless!" Pivoting round, hands remaining awkwardly in his white coat's voluminous pockets, he added loudly, "This is one of the greatest breakthroughs we've had! Rubbish that will vanish with sunlight! Think, man, what it could mean. We're adapting it beyond plastics—the absolute destruction of all waste— not just plastics. Ecologists will be ecstatic! Conservationists will be forever grateful!"

"I understand, Professor," Pointer said, icily, the stark vision of some unsuspecting township disintegrating before his eyes, like paper exposed to nitric acid. Tidy, efficient. "But I'm not here to discuss the discovery's merits." He couldn't avoid the harshness of tone. Time was running out, and it was getting to him. "I have reason to believe that one of your team has stolen the formula and samples—have you any ideas?" Get the suspects to talk about each other: it works, sometimes.

Fisher's steady blue-gray glare intensified. "My people were hand-picked by me and any suspicions like that are reflected on my judgement—"

"Not necessarily," Carol interjected.

He glared at her again. "Listen, Inspector," he boomed, "I didn't want this witch-hunt—but I agreed in the project's interests. That's all." The project first, people second. Pointer had met his sort before. "Do you realize how many hours the team has spent on this? Months, Pointer!" He pointed rudely; he found that a lot, people pointing at him, as if emphasizing his name. "Do you understand?" he snapped. "I don't intend destroying any careers!"

Barely concealing his anger, Pointer sighed; it didn't help, the adrenalin was already in his bloodstream and would be anxious for release or the odd artery to clog. He needed a stress-buster but settled for grating his teeth. "Are all of your team here today?"

"Of course—well, excepting Fay Lodge—she's ill. What with all this security mumbo-jumbo, none of us have had the chance to visit her!"

ERSKINE WAS SMALLER and narrower than Fisher and looked much older than thirty-seven.

"You're Professor Fisher's partner?"

Behind his bifocals, Erskine's weak egg-blue eyes leapt as though he disagreed with an aspect of that statement. "So I'm led to believe," he replied in a soft whisper, sitting opposite Pointer and his sergeant.

"Oh?"

He rubbed the side of his aquiline nose, removed his glasses and squinted, first at Pointer then at Carol. "Why should I confide in you?"

"Our job's usually collation," Carol explained gently. "Marrying loose ends and forming an overall picture. Really, anything you say might help."

Erskine's brow wrinkled, creasing well up to the

bald pate. Thatch-colored hair bristled in unruly tufts. "The empirical approach?"

"You could say that. Who do you feel is responsible for the formula's disappearance?"

The little medicine man rubbed his ear agitatedly. "Oh, Fisher, naturally."

Perhaps Pointer should have been surprised. "Why do you say that?" he demanded, leaning forward.

"It's no secret we dislike each other, you know..."

"No, I didn't," Pointer lied.

"Well, it goes back to University days—different backgrounds, different ethics, really." He sighed, shifting on the chair's edge. "Fisher always seemed to get the better of me, throughout my school life and even in our chosen field of science. I know it's corny, a cliché, even. I'm as competent as he is, but I'm not cut out to snivel and drool over the top brass—it isn't my way. At least Fay appreciates me for what I am—honest." He hunched his shoulders expressively. "But what's the use? By suggesting Fisher, I'm casting suspicion my way."

"Not necessarily," countered Carol; she liked that phrase.

"Oh, I know how you people work... Still, I'm not afraid of prying eyes." Implying that someone else was, of course. Subtle.

A SUBTLE PERFUMED aroma tantalized Pointer's nostrils. Still in her thirties, with little make-up and deep brown hair, she looked very attractive. "And you're Mrs. Carter?" He detected a hint of rouge and light brushing of coral lipstick.

Her husband had been lost about four years ago during maritime research off Florida. Odd, how Pointer invariably pictured widows as forlorn creatures, eyes reflecting sadness. Yet few were: and Irene Carter most certainly wasn't.

"Now, let me see," Pointer said, "you work with Professor Erskine?"

"Usually." Her voice was deep, very contemplative, as if each word was carefully weighed. "But—Miss Lodge and I—we often fluctuated between projects." She produced a slow feline curve to the corners of her mouth. "We're a team, really. Close."

Pointer managed to veil his skepticism. "And do you like working with Erskine?"

Fleetingly her large nutmeg-brown eyes clouded. Evidently, she had been offended: the simple omission of "Professor"? Or something else?

"Well, do you?" Carol pressed.

"Yes," she replied curtly.

"This is where Professor Erskine works, is it?" Carol asked.

Carter gazed around the laboratory, seeming to linger beyond casual recognizance, as if savoring the texture of the highly-polished wood, the gracefulness of the glass pieces. "It is," she answered in a barely audible whisper. *With the exception of Fisher who probably didn't know the meaning of the word, everybody I'd interviewed so far had whispered. Why?*

At that moment, Pointer noticed Carol gesture at another workbench, with everything neatly filed away, spotless and clean.

"Fay Lodge's?" Pointer guessed.

The light in Irene Carter's eyes went out. "Fay?" Sourness entered her gaze and tone. "She's supposed to be sick..."

"Supposed to be?" Carol echoed.

Irene lifted her slim shoulders, as though the movement explained all. "Yes. But I doubt it. It's not the first time..." She sneered. "Plenty of late nights, that's our Fay. She's more likely suffering from a hangover..." Then she added as an afterthought, "If she's there at all..."

She tended to speak with a lot of ellipses, as if none of her thoughts were complete, open to interpretation.

Carol leaned forward. "Surely your salaries wouldn't stand up to that treatment?"

Irene looked askance at her and then at Pointer. "Dear me, neither of you have done your homework, have you?" she chided. "Fay's father was quite wealthy and left her a large inheritance shortly after she came here. Ever since then, she's thrown the filthy money about."

Carol couldn't resist it: "What about the teamwork, then?"

Irene smiled maliciously. "Oh, she worked well enough, when not fluttering her false eyelashes..." Her gaze wandered into the middle-distance. "If I'd had her money..." She sighed, returning to reality. "I wouldn't squander it, that's certain!"

NOON ALREADY, Pointer noticed as he sat at Fay's workbench beside Carol. She dutifully scribbled character-sketches in her notebook: observations on the various reactions to their direct unorthodox questioning. "No clues," she wrote and underlined it twice.

Pointer's stomach grumbled.

"We need a sandwich, sir," Carol observed.

"Yes. We might as well try their canteen. We'll visit Fay after lunch."

Seven hours to the deadline! Hell, how could Thurston expect him to come up with anything in such a short time? Pointer was surprised he wasn't constantly badgering on his cell-phone; yet it was preternaturally silent. He took it out, to ensure that the damnable thing was working. It was—plenty of charge and the signal was strong.

Stuffing the pad and cartridge pen in her handbag, Carol stood and they both left.

Minutes later, they stepped out into the glaring light, fleetingly blinded by white flagstones. The heat buffeted him as he escaped the cocoon of air-conditioning; Carol seemed just as affected.

The contractors didn't stop for lunch, he noticed, cringing inwardly against the deafening stammer of the industrious riveters.

Pointer shaded his eyes and they sauntered across the gravel parking lot with its half-dozen dust-streaked vehicles soaking up the sun. Scaffolding rattled, stretching higher as spidermen balanced precariously on freshly fixed girders.

A familiar alarming prickling at the nape of his neck forewarned Pointer about two seconds before the desperate shout: "Look out!"

His reactions were pretty slow: maybe he'd never reach his forty-third birthday. The girder's shadow flashed across Carol's suddenly blood-drained face. He rugby-tackled her and they sprawled headlong over the rough gravel. As he landed on top of her, breath wheezed between clenched teeth. A massive nerve-scraping metallic crunch reverberated in his ears as his shoulder bundled harshly against the hubcap of a stationary estate car.

Grime adhered to the sweat streaming down his face. He looked up. The steel girder had fallen directly on the car; its roof had buckled, the deep ugly rent reaching to the windowsills; the girder vibrated about two feet above his head, like a massive tuning-fork.

Momentarily incapable of movement, though conscious of Carol's body beneath his, Pointer croaked, "Are you alright?"

"Yes, sir. Thanks. You've messed up my suit, though."

His stomach squirmed in after-fear and his heart pumped maddeningly.

Whistles shrilled. Discordant shouts penetrated dimly.

Awkwardly rolling off her, he regained his feet. He felt the knees wobble uncontrollably, and then offered a hand to Carol. He hauled her to her feet and they both began brushing dust and gravel chippings off their trousers. He noticed his usually steady hands were trembling. The last time they'd shaken so much was when he tried digging through the rubble to reach Eileen.

Palms and knees were grazed and burned slightly. And he suspected his hip was bruised. I'd been lucky, he thought. He turned to Carol. "You're not hurt, are you?"

"A bruised hip, I think. I'll mend."

Pescod and the Royal Marine were the forerunners of the anxious crowd. As the Director panted for breath, Pointer eyed the young serviceman: "Did you see what happened?"

"Yes, sir." He raised his cap-shaded eyes, pointed to a solitary figure kneeling on a girder twenty feet above. "It looked like that bloke shoved it, sir!"

Suspicions confirmed. "Thanks—you'd better return to the gate now. No-one enters or leaves this establishment till I say so. Clear?"

"Yes, sir!" His features grave, he departed at the double.

"Look here, Inspector, don't you think that's a bit over-the-top?" Pescod's fish-lips quivered: Pointer half-expected frantic bubbles to pop out. "Accidents happen. And, I mean, this is *my* establishment, you know."

Blood rapidly swarming Pointer's cheeks, the shock tremors quickly dispelled. "It's the Government's, actually, Mr. Pescod."

With unwelcome malice in his heart Pointer eyed the lone figure above, fully silhouetted in the midday sun: he seemed to be swaying. If the bastard tries suicide...

Feeling helpless, Pointer turned to Pescod as the others ran up. "That was no accident!" Pointer retorted. "My sergeant and I were supposed to be the filling for that bloody metal sandwich!"

"Oh, dear," Pescod murmured, reddening.

"I see it missed," interposed Fisher.

Carol glared at him. "Yes."

A nerve-cringing yell promptly silenced all of them.

The lone figure fell like a film stunt-man, somer-saulting exquisitely. His landing, without benefit of mattresses, was far from aesthetic, though.

Cursing under his breath, Pointer raced over to the body sprawled in the patchwork scaffolding shadows. He'd entirely forgotten the numerous cuts and abrasions: *delete a vital lead.*

A speedy inspection uncovered the man's name— Olsen—plus ten twenty-pound notes bulging from his torn pseudo-leather billfold: *the payoff.*

All the way in his Citroen Pointer had imagined what Under Secretary Rippon must have looked like as he agonizingly disintegrated. Viewing Olsen, he had a fair idea now and fought back the bile. Whoever instructed him to arrange the "accident" had covered his—or her—tracks well.

Pointer searched the sea of horror-stricken faces and demanded authoritatively: "Who's the foreman here?"

Sheepishly, a diminutive swarthy-skinned man shambled forward. "I am," he croaked in a thick Irish brogue. "Meaney, Dom Meaney."

"Do your men wash here in the establishment?"

"Yes." The foreman's black beady eyes showed he was perplexed.

Hell! "When? After work?"

"Bejesus, there's no use any other time, is there? We'd just get dirty again."

Pointer was puzzled. He forced himself to scrutinize Olsen's face, distorted into the rictus of an anguished death. Around Olsen's neck was secured a bandana; already it was turning to fine dust, leaving a spreading deep fleshy groove in his throat. "Did Olsen have a water-canister—a bottle—something to keep soaking his neckerchief?"

Shrugging helplessly, the foreman spluttered, his look seeming to cast doubt on Pointer's sanity.

Then Carol spotted it, about six yards away. "Over there!"

Pointer ran over. It must have fallen separately. Gingerly he touched the canteen; it was composed of rubber and its stopper was tightly shut.

Pointer was willing to wager that whoever hired Olsen had also given him the canteen. But how could he or she guarantee Olsen would use the water?

The sun beamed; Pointer swabbed beads of sweat from his brow and the question was answered.

Pointer faced the foreman again. "You'd better finish for the day. Mr. Pescod'll call the proper authorities and initiate an inquiry. Meanwhile, we leave Olsen where he is—at least, what's left of him." He eyed Fisher. "Would your team try analyzing this water, please?" He passed the canteen over.

"It'll keep us occupied while this farce proceeds, I suppose. But let's get something to eat first!"

Pointer's appetite had lessened considerably, even if the food was subsidized by taxpayers. Carol and he queued; he purchased a ham-salad and a black coffee, while she opted for a cheese and tomato sandwich and tea. She thrived on tea, she said.

Stomach still rumbling uncomfortably, Pointer chose a Formica-topped table apart from the main body. Here they could eat in peace and have time to think. And there was precious little time left, he realized with a start.

"What was the sense in killing me?" Pointer mused.

Carol shrugged. "Well, it wasn't me he was after, I'm sure."

"It wasn't as though we'd stumbled on any clues yet."

Carol munched into her sandwich.

After he'd forced the first few mouthfuls down, to stave off hunger, Pointer pushed the plate aside and drank the coffee.

The cold fear lingered.

"Maybe there's an accomplice," Carol suggested between mouthfuls, "so that the inside person has immunity even if uncovered."

Absently, Pointer noticed the suspects enter. He whispered, "Strange, how all three seem aloof."

"Not quite the epitome of a team, are they?"

Fisher sat on Irene's left and Erskine opposite them. Each one seemed edgy, temper hovering near the surface, exchanging glances at the other—distrusting, wary, even hateful, contemplative—or maybe Pointer was being too fanciful.

Still, fanciful or not, it was information worth filing way, to mull over soon. Probably after they'd spoken to Fay Lodge, the last of the suspects.

POINTER OPENED the squeaking cottage gate and found the place quite attractive in the hot sun, over-grown garden of wildflowers, rambling roses and all. Carol followed him through and shut the gate.

The salt-encrusted door was ajar. He knocked once and paint flaked off. "Hello! Miss Lodge!"

Silence.

Carol came up beside him, eyes full of concern. "Should I go in first?"

"No. That's my job."

"Okay. But if it's dark inside, switch on the bloody light!"

Very droll. Chuckling at her tone, he entered and headed for the lounge to the right.

"Odd," Carol said in a hoarse whisper. "This untidiness seems at odds with her notably immaculate workbench, don't you think?"

He glanced over his shoulder. "I don't think, I just arrest the villains..."

"Very droll, sir."

"Anybody at home?" he shouted.

No response.

A couple of framed color-photos lay on the sideboard. One featured Fay doting over a red-haired spaniel. The other showed Erskine with her. The neatly fringed blonde hairstyle suited her oval face. She looked happy, cheeks shiny, blue eyes bright. They seemed to be enjoying a day out at the nearby seaside resort.

"Miss Lodge!" Using a handkerchief, he opened the sideboard drawers, rummaged under the starched tablecloths and silver cutlery. He came across her leather purse with a three-days-old bus ticket valid from town to Pethewray Point. Saturday shopping, probably. There wasn't much money inside—about eighty pence.

He couldn't see her handbag anywhere.

Then Carol gestured at a check-book in the clean fire grate, half-burnt.

He called again. Now, he was concerned. The old gut instinct nudged as the stillness quickened his pulse.

His heart jumped, surprised by a dog barking. The spaniel.

The yelping came from the kitchen.

Carol opened the door fully.

Fay's dog was tethered to a table leg.

"Come here, boy," Pointer whispered. He let the animal smell the back of his hand first, to get to know him. Stroking gently, he released the dog. "Where's your mistress? Where is she?" he said, not wanting to know.

He straightened as the dog whined. Sniffing the air, it turned, blunt claws scratching at the back door.

Pointer opened the door, let the dog out and Carol followed.

The earth was fresh behind the wooden shed. A garden fork rested against the wall, the soil on its tines damp. Freshly turned, the surrounding earth bore a faint sign of footprints. Somebody had been careless.

The dog howled with grief.

INSPECTOR PASSMORE of the local constabulary agreed to keep the body's discovery a secret from everybody at Pethewray Point, at least for a while. He was still too concerned about the mysterious demise of Olsen.

Mike Newbolt, an old friend, headed the team of forensic scientists; they hadn't taken long in getting down—literally, in a helicopter. "Looks like a good set of prints on the fork, Alan," Mike said. "I'll compare them with your samples. The footprints aren't so clear—a small foot, I'd say. But I'll let you know."

"Make it soon, Mike, please."

"Nothing's changed there, then, has it? I presume this is something big?"

"And nasty. I'll leave you to it." Pointer strolled to the front of the cottage.

As he gazed seaward, surf savaging the sea-stacks beyond the cliffs, it was as though his mind emptied. It was always like this after a murder: the unreality of everything but the corpse. Carol Basset knew better than to intrude and left him to it while she did her own investigating at the rear of the building.

A short while later Irene Carter sauntered up.

Pointer hoped Mike and his men would adhere to instructions and keep out of sight. "Fay's not in," he said. "Have you finished for the day?"

Feline lips pursed. "I left them working on your water-sample—they don't need me now. You know, it looks like some of the dye-sample *was* dissolved in that water in the canteen."

"That's interesting news, Mrs. Carter."

"Irene, Inspector." She eyed him, warily. "I wonder where Fay is. Gallivanting about, probably!"

"What are you doing here?" It was a slim possibility: it was not unknown for murderers to return to the scene of the crime.

"Oh, the Marine sentry knows I wouldn't abscond—besides, I live beyond that rise behind her cottage. Care to walk me home?"

Away from Mike's team. "My pleasure, Irene."

The breakers crashed noisily below. White spume patiently gouged clefts of rock-face. As they walked along the cliff path, Pointer captured the fanciful notion that it wouldn't take much effort for Irene to thrust him over the edge now. For a dizzy second he glimpsed himself sailing wildly in the air, falling, matchstick limbs flailing, to be battered beyond recognition.

Irene touched his arm.

Involuntarily, he started, all too conscious of the crumbling cliff near his feet. A pebble dislodged itself, tumbling, echoing into oblivion.

"Isn't that Fisher running toward us?" she queried, glancing back. There was alarm in her voice, Pointer was sure: "I wonder what he wants?"

Fisher drew near, breathless. Blood-red splotches marred his white coat. Gasping in air, he said, "It's Erskine! He confessed—he—he's tried to commit suicide!"

Irene's color drained. "Oh, God!" she wailed. "No!"

Wringing his hands, Fisher wailed, "I tried—tried to stop him but—hurry!"

Pointer grabbed Irene's hand and, as they ran toward the establishment with Fisher following at a slow trot, he felt callouses on her finger-pads, the abused skin only now hardening.

When they dashed into the lab, Erskine was lying spread-eagled amidst a jumble of shattered retorts and beakers. Blood covered his wrists. The locked glass cabinet had spewed its myriad-colored potions; an indescribable stench pervaded the place.

Wary of the fumes, Pointer held his breath and, keeping clear of the assorted spilt liquids, he crouched and reached for Erskine's throat. But, no surprise, there wasn't any pulse; indeed, the blood had stopped pumping from the deep arterial gashes.

As his stomach churned sickeningly, Pointer stood and stepped a pace back from the fumes and finally exhaled a breath. He wondered why Erskine chose such a terrible method of self-destruction: surely a chemist had better alternative means.

Behind him he discerned the choking labored sobs of Irene. He glanced round as she shunned Fisher's comforting arm.

"That," Pointer said, ushering them out of the room and away from the potentially toxic fumes, "seems to end the case."

Carol joined them, raising an eyebrow at Pointer. He filled her in hastily and ended, "It's not a very tidy ending: the formula is still missing."

"Superintendent Thurston won't like it," she said. She was adept at stating the obvious.

"No, I suppose not. And doubtless the ever-suspicious security people will maintain that the formula has been handed to a foreign power or a terrorist group and Erskine's suicide merely rigged to provide a suitable scapegoat."

Carol nodded. "I can go along with that, sir. Stranger things happened after the WMD fiasco concerning the invasion of Iraq, as I recall."

"I know," Pointer said. "I'm not wholly satisfied, either. It was a close thing."

"Only four hours to the deadline," Carol answered. "Whichever township was earmarked, it's safe now."

As Pointer went over to the lab phone to ring Mike at the cottage, he noticed the receiver's smoothness. And a number of stray threads wound together. Without dialing, he replaced the phone in its cradle and turned to Fisher and Irene. "Could you leave us alone, please?" he asked.

The pair stared at him curiously then reluctantly agreed.

"Humor me," he told Carol, and he soon found the scalpel that severed Erskine's wrists. Using his handkerchief again, he slipped the weapon into a polythene bag from his pocket.

Returning to the phone, he recalled how Irene's hands were calloused—with recent digging? He dialed the cottage number and Mike answered after the third ring.

"Alan here. We've a suspected suicide in the lab, I'm afraid."

"Christ, Alan, you're piling them up!"

"Yes, aren't I? Any luck with the prints?"

"Dead ringer. Irene Carter's."

"Fine. And thanks." He hung up.

"I take it Mike's confirmed it?" Carol said.

"Yes. Irene wouldn't have premeditated Fay's murder, nor the need to conceal her fingerprints."

"And Fay was buried instead of her dead weight being dragged to the cliff edge because Irene wouldn't have managed the distance on her own?"

"Highly likely. I'm almost sure that hers was a crime of passion. The photographs in Fay's cottage tend to confirm it. Erskine had obviously dated Fay frequently."

"So Fay wasn't killed to divert suspicion to her absence. She was murdered through jealousy."

"So," Fisher said, "you're returning to London?" He sat opposite Pointer in his snug cottage, fondling a glass of brandy.

Pointer had declined a drink twice. "As soon as I trace the formula, yes."

"But—Erskine—I thought he—I mean—we'll never know, will we?"

"Oh, it's not impossible," Pointer said noncommittally, looking around the cottage.

"Anything wrong?"

"Oh, nothing—it's just—when you invited me I had the impression that Mrs. Carter would be here, too."

"Couldn't make it at the last moment. Wouldn't give a reason, though." Fisher seemed rather annoyed about her refusal.

The telephone on the nearby desk trilled. "I trust you won't mind?" Pointer said. "I took the liberty of telling Inspector Passmore I'd be here." He went over to the desk.

"No, not at all."

He lifted the phone, answered with his name and then confirmed Fisher was present: "Yes, Inspector," Pointer said. "And they've confirmed the footprints?"

"And a strand of hair, sir."

"A strand of hair? Good. I'll buy you a pint when I get back! Oh, Inspector..."

"Yes?"

"Formally charge Irene Carter with the murder of Fay Lodge. I won't be long in joining you. 'Bye."

As Pointer hung up, he turned to Fisher and said, "I hope that didn't shock you?"

"Fay—dead? I can hardly credit it." There was something wrong with the emotion in his voice.

"You're quite fond of Mrs. Carter, aren't you?"

Fisher sank his drink. "Why?"

"I've noticed the way you've eyed her when she wasn't looking. She's an attractive woman."

"There's no law against looking—yet. She *is* very attractive... I can't believe she could do—commit murder..."

"I believe your work required unusually close contact, and each one of your group reacted on the other in much the same way as your chemicals. And desire was the catalyst."

Fisher bit his lips, then raged, "I've said it before, Pointer: I resent my team being maligned!"

"You no longer have a team, Professor. And you can't deny the truth—you desired Irene and loathed Erskine because she wanted him, not you."

Fisher paled. His eyes wavered. Then he exhaled resignedly: "You're perfectly right. But so what? It isn't a crime to fancy a colleague."

"You murdered Erskine to deflect suspicion from yourself and make it easier for you to seduce Irene."

Fisher burst out laughing. "What a load of nonsense!"

"The blood spatter on your coat—which my sergeant has taken for testing—will confirm you wielded the scalpel, not Erskine."

"That's—that's preposterous! I knelt down to try to stop the bleeding! I was trying to save his life, not take it!"

"We'll see, shall we? I'm arresting you on suspicion of murder, Mr. Fisher."

Fisher backed away. "You've no proof! I'm in the clear." He grinned. "Erskine's death was self-inflicted."

Pointer sighed. "We might prove it was impossible for blood to splash you as it did unless you actually used the scalpel on Erskine. And the absence of even Erskine's fingerprints on the tool seems suspicious, too."

"You've checked...?"

"Of course."

Fisher shook his head. "No—not proof enough." He chuckled and stood up. "So, what if I did steal the formula? I wanted the money—to attract Irene."

"Unfortunately, Erskine guessed the truth this afternoon during the water-analysis?"

Leaning his great bulk against the drinks cabinet, Fisher lowered his glass and absently fingered the soda-siphon. "I had no choice."

"How often have I heard that!" Pointer snarled. "And the 'suicide' conveniently eliminated your rival for Irene's affections?"

"Two birds with one stone, you might say."

"You know, that was pretty desperate of you, hiring that workman, Olsen."

"Was that his name? No, not really." Fisher snorted. "I hoped he'd either kill you or scare you off. A calculated risk, if you like. It nearly worked—only you're more agile than you look."

"I was lucky. By the way, what did you do with the dye?"

Fisher beamed. "Since you're arresting Irene, I've no need for the ransom money," he declared. "Here's your flaming dye!"

And he squirted the soda-siphon at Pointer.

The translucent liquid rushed at his face. He felt the cold wetness trickle over his cheeks and neck. Everything blurred for a nightmarish second and panic nearly surfaced as he feared blindness.

Hazily, he lunged, making body contact.

Grappling together, they fell to the carpet, the siphon soaking them both.

Damned stars flashed as Fisher clubbed his temple with the still-hissing siphon. Dimly he was aware of Fisher breaking free, scrambling to his feet and racing out of the door.

Sunshine streamed harshly through the hallway.

Groggily, Pointer rose and stumbled to the window.

Fisher had vaulted the fence and was scrambling recklessly down a rough cliff-face path. Hesitating in the shade, Pointer wiped his face and swore: like an idiot novice, he'd neglected the most fundamental precaution. He should have obtained immediate authorization to post armed guards on all nearby reservoirs.

True, if Fisher had an accomplice, the stuff could have been emptied into any reservoir in the country after one brief phone-call. But at least he would have done his level best in the immediate area. Damn!

He pulled out his cell-phone, rang Carol.

She answered at once. "Carol, Fisher's the killer—and he's escaped. He's soaked me with the dye-solution."

"Oh, my God, Alan...sir. What can I do?"

"Contact Inspector Passmore, explain and get him to mobilize. I'll get in touch with London."

Fisher was out of sight now. The roar of a high-powered motor-boat carried across the sea. He could be miles away in no time!

Pointer phoned Superintendent Thurston and was put through immediately. He was succinct: "I need Ministerial clearance to approach the local Army Commander."

In a level growl, Thurston said, "You'll have it within the hour."

He closed the call and squinted at the killer sun. It hadn't really hit home—condemned to nightlife, until the antidote for the indelible disintegrating dye could be devised; if there was one. "Roll on the winter nights!" he whispered feelingly to himself.

"How bad is he?" Pointer enquired of the Commander as they hurried through the hospital ward.

Commander Goff cleared his throat. "Shock. The poor fellow's in a bad state."

Considering the short notice, the troops had been mobilized very quickly indeed. The locals, naturally, had wondered at these unscheduled maneuvers, but the few journalists sniffing about kept quiet, the impending D-notices probably having a lot to do with that.

The sun had gone down by the time a private had rushed into the pub. Inspector Passmore was handing Pointer the long-awaited pint and Carol a gin and tonic.

The young soldier had been ashen-faced, trembling, and gave a hasty salute. "Sir, little Andy's found him! At the Tregarth Reservoir!" He gasped. "He's in a bad way."

"Fisher?" Passmore asked, not knowing the full story.

"No—no, Andy...Fisher's—finished, dead..." The soldier had shuddered. "Andy's suffering from shock— seeing Fisher like that, leastways what's left of him..."

Andy was in shock alright.

"Traumatic," the nurse whispered gently.

They got most of it from him in cathartic spurts.

He had been checking the south bank of the Tregarth Reservoir, the sergeant the other. At about 2200 hours his torch had detected something that reflected near the water's edge.

A large carboy, cracked wide open and empty.

In the dark, his feet accidentally scuffed something else close by.

He suddenly felt violently sick as he illuminated it.

There wasn't much left of Fisher at all; in a short time, even these ghastly remains would be dust.

Andy hadn't fired his shot on purpose; the trigger was pulled as he fainted. The sergeant found him about fifteen minutes later and guessed what had happened. He reported on his radio immediately then brought Andy to the hospital for treatment.

"So the reservoir's been treated?" Commander Goff remarked, shutting the bedside curtains.

"Yes, our worst fears realized."

"Well, what are we going to do?"

Pointer didn't know. The whole project had blown up in his face. If only he had been able to restrain Fisher, if only he had guessed. It was no use recriminating himself. Yes, they could drain the reservoir. As soon as the authorization arrived. Of course they had cut off all supplies from the reservoir and announced the reasons through the media. Bowsers and standpipes would be brought in. But that wouldn't be the end of it. Far from it!

That would stop any more contaminated water reaching the townsfolk. But too much had already seeped through in the hours before the discovery. The shift-workers, they would be the first seriously affected.

Perhaps most would only lose a limb or two. It was insidious stuff, though, biting its way right through the flesh, through the bone, drying body-fluids, even marrow. Deadly. Effective.

Commander Goff looked at Pointer. "Christ, it's a mess, isn't it?"

"It is. Avoiding panic as the deaths mount will be a problem."

"We take our water so much for granted."

"Warn the populace, Commander. Not everyone will be listening to the radio or watching TV."

"Yes, if we keep them indoors, out of the sun..."

"You'd better start arranging road-blocks at the reservoir's perimeter—and as far as the water supplies reached..."

"Yes. I'll arrange for some jeeps to be rigged for microphones and loudspeakers. Oh, Christ, what a mess!"

Pointer glanced at Carol and her eyes were moist, for she knew only too well that his prospects were not good. He wouldn't be able to venture outside into naked sunlight; he would be stuck in the action headquarters all day.

And tomorrow promised to be a long, long day.

AFTER A LENGTHY CONVALESCENCE, Pointer was declared fit to return to work.

However, he was advised that he should not expose himself to direct sunlight *ever again*.

Sergeant Basset was reassigned to work with him, and he was glad to see her.

Chapter 1

Cat On a Hot Wet Roof

2015—Nice, France

Despite the drizzle, due to the residual heat of the day the roof sent steam spiraling. A light breeze from the sea spat rain against Cat Vibrissae as she swung over the lip of the roof's guttering. Suspended at full stretch, she landed with both feet on the narrow ledge. Her Nike soles provided sufficient purchase on the marble surface. She turned and straightened; her backpack pressed against the dark window. She was already drenched, her black jeans and cotton T-shirt clinging uncomfortably; tied in a pony-tail, her dyed blonde hair would appear dark.

June was the start of summer here and the forecast had been accurate enough: halfway through the month and this was the second day that it had rained. Now, she looked around. The evenings were not dark. Chuck Marston, her instructor had inculcated into her that when at risk of being in full view, she should scale a building in wet weather if at all possible. Her target apartment block qualified in that regard, as it was on the Promenade des Anglais, overlooking the beach and the sea, so on this occasion the rain, while dispiriting, was welcome. It averted the inquisitive eyes of any passing pedestrians.

Four stories below was the dual carriageway. Almost immediately below the desultory traffic moved to her right, headlights glittering, rear lights like red eyes, occasionally flashing brighter as brakes were applied. In the central reservation, grass and palm trees wafted under subdued lighting. And then on the other side vehicles streamed to the left, alongside the promenade. Beyond was the sea, gray and uninviting. Ornate street lamps shimmered in the drizzle with halos of buttery light; thin streamers of steam meandered from the paving slabs.

The sill she stood on was on the fifth floor, too low to wear a parachute, but high enough to kill her should she fall. Directly beneath were the windows for each story, a sheer drop to the paving and stacked tables and chairs. The sill itself was a marble ornamentation for the top of the window beneath. Down to her right was a balcony accessed by three French windows; on its left, a single balcony and glass door topped with the same sill decoration; light glowed but she knew the apartment was empty. Four more single balconies were beneath that; they would serve as her exit route.

She had considered using a rope to drop onto the balcony, but she knew from experience that dangling from a saturated rope was tricky at the best of times. It would have made her getaway easier, true; but there was also the risk of the rope being spotted as it dangled from the roof for as long as she was inside. She was confident in her ability to descend a balcony at a time without being observed.

Petra Grimalkin's apartment was the one with the single balcony. The distance from this sill to Grimalkin's upper sill was six feet. In dry conditions, she'd be quite sanguine about jumping. But the likelihood of slipping on the wet surface was high. The thought of the rope niggled; she shrugged it off as she was now fully committed. Nothing for it, she'd have to jump onto the single balcony. Many apartment and hotel blocks on this thoroughfare possessed balconies attached all the way along their frontage; but a few, like this one, resisted that temptation to burglars.

Taking a deep breath, she eased her toes to the lip of the sill, leaned out, braced her knees and then sprang out and down. She cleared the black metal railing and landed firmly on the patterned tiles with a resonant thudding sound, her soles arresting forward momentum. She didn't want to bash into the opposite railing or, worse, tumble headlong over it.

She crouched, motionless, and steadied her breathing.

After about thirty seconds, she straightened up.

Nobody had heard her or seen her silhouetted against the French window, which was lit from inside.

Opening her belt pouch, she grabbed a slim lockpick. The apartment door to the corridor was alarmed, she knew from earlier reconnaissance. But the French window wasn't. A welcome oversight; but in reality not many living five stories up would be concerned about cat-burglars.

Within seconds, she opened the door, stepped inside, glad to get out of the rain.

She shut the door behind her as a strong cloying mixture of perfume smells hit her; she shouldn't be surprised, since one of Grimalkin's roles was as head of Ananke's Cosmetics Division.

Hastily, she removed from her pack a large sheet of polythene, unfolded it, spread it on the floor and stood on it, so the drips of rain that dribbled off her would collect there. She unfastened her belt and its pouches, lowered them to the plastic, and these were followed by the backpack. She removed her shoes, stripped to her black underwear, took out a small towel from the pack and dried herself, all the while studying the long lounge-dining room.

Overhead lights were on, as she'd noted from the rooftop; in fact, the whole place was lit up. Petra Grimalkin wasn't cost-conscious or ecologically concerned about wasted electricity.

Immediately in front of her was the apartment door that opened onto the corridor, complete with spyhole. To her left she saw a dining table, six chairs, a wall-mounted TV screen, and two armchairs. Beyond were three open doors, and the lights were on in all of them; apartment plans indicated these led to a bathroom and two bedrooms. On her right was a walnut drinks bar with two matching red leather stools.

A red light flickered on the answerphone on the bar counter, next to a large empty silver ice bucket. Cat resisted the urge to check it. Instead, she hunkered down and from another belt pouch she retrieved her cell-phone, and fitted the earpiece. She selected Rick's number, and when he answered, she whispered, "I'm in."

He gave a sigh in her ear. "Good. I reckon you've

got an hour, that's all. Zabala's supposed to be bringing Petra back then." He'd only been in Petra's apartment once, before he'd met Cathy; on that occasion he had located the safe—behind the bar unit.

"Back from where?" Cat had queried earlier.

"The invitation was for the pair of them to visit an art show, given by one of Loup's protégés. Then they have to return, collect their bags and fly on to Tangier."

"Gadabouts."

Rick had chuckled.

Now, Cat noticed a couple of red Samsonite suitcases standing at the nearest bedroom door.

She heard a shower dripping, as if in counterpoint to the rain that pattered against the windows.

Tucking her phone in her briefs, she tugged on a pair of latex gloves and then padded across the thick pile carpet, the sensation quite pleasurable for her bare slightly damp feet. She lowered to one knee and swung open a cupboard door. Inside she recognized the type of safe, with its distinctive handle and combination wheel. She took out her phone and spoke: "Found it."

"Glad it's still there!"

"Me, too. I'll be in touch." She closed the call and again tucked the phone in her briefs.

Now, for the first time, she would test her safe-cracking skill in earnest. Compared to her other pursuits, this had taken what seemed like an inordinate time to master. At least Chuck was a patient instructor, and his training had been intensive.

***

HER PREVIOUS ENCOUNTERS with Ananke Corporation had convinced her that if she was serious about continuing her crusade, she needed to learn safe-cracking. Five months ago, Rick had said rather sheepishly, "I might know the man who can help you." Chuck Marston was one of the useful contacts in Rick's little green book. "My father says Chuck has proven useful from time to time. He's an American, a retired jewel thief."

"Can we afford to pay him?" she'd asked.

"He's retired—on his ill-gotten gains, I imagine. He doesn't need money."

"Will he help me?"

"Let's try him and see."

"Sure, your proposition sounds intriguing, son," Chuck replied on the phone. "Let's do dinner. You pay." He named a medium priced restaurant off the beaten track: "So we can maintain a low profile, huh?"

They met outside.

Chuck was five-foot nothing, thin and wiry with a pot belly. He was in his early sixties, she reckoned, and he was balding, with tufts of unruly white hair over his ears. Fine white hair sprouted from his ears and nostrils. He had long drawn features, with drooping eyebrows and a lined forehead. His hazel eyes flashed mischievously as he spoke; she liked him immediately.

As she shook his hand she felt his skin was dry, leathery. "Never mind these hands, honey," he said, speaking round an unlit cigar. "They've got like that due to fondling a thousand metal mistresses." The pads at his fingertips seemed unusually smooth. "I managed to unlock the mystery of every one of them." He winked. "If you pay attention, you can do the same."

"Then I will pay attention, Mr. Marston," she responded.

He chuckled. "Good. I like your no-nonsense attitude, Cathy. We'll get along fine. Oh, and call me Chuck. That's the drill."

"Was that a joke, Chuck?"

"No, honey, I don't joke about my name. I have a reputation, you know. Fortunately, it's all based on scores that have passed the statute of limitations." He winked again.

He shoved the cigar in his top pocket, led the way into the restaurant.

The maître d' clearly knew him and showed all of them to a secluded table. A bottle of champagne was chilling in its bucket on a stand.

The sommelier popped the cork, charged their flutes and then they were left alone to decide on their order.

Chuck opened the menu, leaned back in his chair. "The deal's off, by the way."

Cat eyed him. "We haven't arrived at a deal yet."

He grinned at both of them. "I like the pair of you. The meal's on me."

"That's generous of you," Rick said, "but—"

"No, Rick," Cat interrupted, "let Chuck pay. If we're going to learn from him, we need to do as he says."

Chuck chortled. "Hot damn, you're on the ball, Cathy. That's precisely it!"

"As I said, Chuck, I pay attention." She opened her menu.

AFTER SHE OPENED THE SAFE, she pulled the phone from her briefs and photographed where everything inside lay. She whistled softly. On the shelf were several thick bundles of pristine €50 notes amounting to €500,000. At the back, behind the money, was a black velvet bag. She opened it, poured into her palm a diamond necklace and an exquisite gold filigree brooch with a diamond at its center. It was tempting to take some of this loot, if not all, but she didn't want anyone to know that the safe's contents had been compromised. On the floor of the safe were five folders. Fortunately, Petra Grimalkin was Dante's bag-lady as well as one of his heads of division, so carried important documents when accompanying her boss; that fact had prompted this latest break-in.

Cat grabbed all of the folders and stood at the bar, checking the titles.

- *Tangier*
- *Marrakesh*
- *Tenerife*
- *Rome*
- *Durban*
- *Shanghai*
- *Izmir*

Rick had mentioned Tangier; she wondered if he'd heard of any Ananke operations in these other places. She shrugged; no matter. A quick flick through them revealed that every folder contained a half-dozen sheets; they might prove useful in her ongoing war of attrition against Loup Dante and his organization.

Cat diligently photographed each document from

the folders, then replaced them as she'd found them, checking with the photo on her phone. She shut the safe door, twirled the combination wheel. Petra Grimalkin wouldn't be aware that anyone had tampered with the contents of her safe.

"I've got the full details," she informed Rick.

"Good. Now, please get out." She loved him for that, the measure of concern in his tone. Not strident, but firm.

She returned to the bundle of clothing and her shoes on the polythene sheet. They were still wet, understandably, and a small puddle surrounded them. She dabbed the towel in the puddle, absorbing most of the rainwater, glanced around and spotted the ice bucket and bundled her jeans, T-shirt and towel in there, then carried it to the bathroom. She'd squeeze the surplus water into the bidet. The clothing would be marginally easier to put on then.

She passed the two suitcases at the bedroom doorway and peered in.

The bedding was in disarray. She stopped, puzzled. Perfume bottles lay scattered across the top of the dressing table, a few of them broken. The mixture of scents was pungent, even from here. That's what she'd smelled on entering the apartment, and then her nose had become accustomed to it.

Maybe Petra and Zabala had argued.

She stepped into the bathroom and instantly dropped the ice bucket. Luckily, it missed her toes by inches; it emitted a ringing sound as it rolled over the tiles.

Cat gagged, felt the bile rising, kicked aside her wet clothes and the ice bucket and rushed to the bidet on her right. She was just in time. Her lunch erupted, her stomach suddenly cramping. She turned on the faucet, careful not to send the water-stream full force, and washed away her weakness. She clutched the porcelain rim; her heart pounded against her chest as she leaned over. Gradually, she sensed her pulse slow, returning almost to normal. She switched off the water. The strong perfume smell throughout the apartment couldn't alleviate the powerful stench of vomit in her nostrils.

Snagging a toilet roll from the rack next to the bidet, she tore sections and wiped her mouth and nose and then discarded it in the toilet bowl, and flushed it away.

She got to her feet, stood on wobbly legs.

Trembling, she stared, her heart fluttering. She'd never seen anything like this. Ever. She fumbled at her briefs, gripped the phone. Selected Rick, shakily punched the dial icon.

"Are you out yet?" Rick asked.

She shook her head, tears blurring her vision. "Did you see them both leave?" she demanded, her throat raw, dry, her voice croaking.

"What, Zabala and Petra?"

"Yes, dammit!"

"What's the matter, Cathy? You sound—"

"Well, *did you?*"

"No, I'm going on what I overheard in the lobby... Why, what's wrong?"

"Petra never went to the art show." Cat stared at Petra Grimalkin, her naked body eviscerated, lying in the open shower cubicle. A small trickle of blood dribbled from her soaked corpse and snaked toward the plughole. "She's dead—murdered."

Chapter 2

Marmalade Cat

Cat's mind reeled as she stood, unmoving, her cell-phone again tucked in her briefs.

Rick's words echoed in her mind, "Get out, Cathy. Now!" That was her first instinct, too. But she couldn't. Not yet. Adrenaline pumped through her veins; she could barely keep her hands steady. Violent death was not something she'd ever encountered. This was only the third dead person she'd seen in her life; her mother's death had been natural, if premature. Her father was killed in a car crash—murdered, she reminded herself; but he hadn't looked like this: he had appeared to be asleep, serene.

Dark red swam before her eyes and she felt as if the whole building vibrated through her bare feet. She struggled to think rationally, to take it all in, to observe.

Hunched in the corner of the shower unit, her legs splayed out, Petra stared sightlessly at her. That stare gave Cat a jolt. A sheet was bundled at Petra's feet, soaked with blood and water. The tiled floor all around the base of the shower was wet but mercifully there was no blood outside the cubicle. The shower head dripped droplets of water onto Petra's head; her brunette hair hung lank and glistened blackly.

Think! Difficult. She'd known Petra, briefly, and hadn't liked her. That dislike had intensified when Petra and Zabala held her prisoner in Dante's office in Barcelona. She shuddered, remembering their catfight on the jetty. There was still the faint scar on Petra's cheek from the whiplash Cat had inflicted on her. They'd struggled, Petra's vibrant warm flesh against hers, inflicting hurt and pain. It was hard to grasp that this still, pale form, its innards exposed, had been a living, breathing vital person.

Petra stared. Cat wanted to close those eyes, but didn't dare go near. She told herself she had no intention of contaminating the murder scene, but she suspected her reason was more primal than that; probably plain fear of violent death.

The dead can't hurt you? If she left traces of her presence, maybe Petra's death could harm her, Cat thought.

She screwed shut her eyes and remembered seeing her father in his coffin. Petra's boss had engineered Papa's death. Hold onto that. She gritted her teeth, opened her eyes and looked away.

Think!

Her heart fluttered and her stomach scrunched up, as if she'd been punched. Trying to ignore these symptoms, she stooped, picked up her fallen clothing and the towel and hurriedly squeezed tightly each item over the bidet, getting rid of as much rainwater as possible. Would the crime scene people notice the different type of water here? She doubted it. She left the ice-bucket where it was, a mystery for the investigators, and turned, padded into the lounge dining-room.

A little awkwardly, she tugged on her wet clothing; it was cold to her flesh. She put the cell-phone in her back pocket and left the towel on the polythene sheet.

She'd come to a decision.

Cat returned to the safe. Having remembered the combination, she opened it again and lifted out the bundle of money. Now, there was no sense in not taking this. If Dante was aware of it, then its loss could be blamed on the murderer. She left the safe door open.

Her heart still pounding, she wrapped the money in the towel and tucked it in her backpack. She fastened her belt and the pouches, removed the latex gloves and bagged them, then slipped on her shoes.

One last glance. Nothing left behind. The carpet was damp near the French door. She opened the door, and then carefully carried the polythene to the door, tipped the little pools of water onto the balcony floor, then folded the sheet, dumped it in the backpack. She stepped onto the balcony. The wind's direction had altered by some twenty degrees, and it was light drizzle now. She was so grateful to feel the rain on her face, to taste the fresh air, to get away from the cloying smell of perfume and death. Grateful to be alive. But now she must get away.

She left the door slightly ajar; that would explain the damp patch near the door. She leaned over the rail, checked the balcony below.

No light on.

She scanned the paths and road.

No pedestrians, and the vehicles passed at a speed close to the limit, their tires sending up a susurration that would conceal any noise she might inadvertently make.

She swung her leg over the rail and slowly lowered herself till she was hanging at arms' length from the base of the balcony. The rain would wash off any fingerprints here. Then she dropped and swung inwards, feet hitting the balcony tiles firmly. She immediately hunched down in shadow and held her breath. Nobody was around to notice her.

She employed the same method again, dropping to the next lower balcony, until she landed on the paving flagstones, beside a small tower of plastic chairs stacked to the right of the apartment block entrance. The lobby was brightly lit but nobody was in view.

Slowly, she breathed out, relieved, and strolled away on shaky legs, a bag full of thousands of Euros slung on her back.

Once she rounded the block, she stopped, flipped open her cell-phone and whispered, "I'm out."

Rick replied with a heavy sigh, "Thank God."

She closed the phone and a horrible chill ran through her frame as the brutal murder of Petra Grimalkin hit her anew.

"I STILL CAN'T BELIEVE it, love," Rick said, handing her a glass of Napoleon brandy.

She looked up from the sofa and, with shaking hands, cupped the glass. Even after several weeks, she found it strange to see him with brown hair, instead of black. She'd dyed her auburn locks strawberry blonde. "Maybe—maybe I should have photographed her?"

"No—that would put you at the scene."

She nodded and gulped the fiery yet smooth liquid. Despite the warm evening, even after the rain, she trembled in her black La Perla short silk satin nightgown. Her hair was still damp after a shower that couldn't wash away the sight of Petra's grisly corpse. Her lips quivered as she sipped again.

He sat beside her, hands on her upper arms. "This is nasty. Sabotaging Dante is one thing, but this..." His misty blue eyes held concern. He seemed stuck for words.

"Do you think it could have been Zabala?" Her voice rasped; her mouth was dry no matter how much brandy she'd swallowed.

"I honestly don't know." He dragged a hand down his face, clearly distraught. "We know he's capable of ordering a death—in fact, he was going to do me in, wasn't he?"

"Yes... but the way she was cut...open..."

"I know—monstrous."

She lowered the glass to the nearby coffee table. "I should have telephoned the police before I left."

He hugged her tenderly. "No, you did the right thing. There's no telling how quickly they'd have been on the scene. You couldn't guarantee getting away."

"I wanted to shut her eyes but—"

"I think you should go to bed, darling, shut *your* eyes. This has been a terrible shock for you." He stood and glanced at the pile of money on the sideboard, together with her belt, pouches, backpack and cell-phone. "*If* you can get to sleep." He offered his hand and she got to her feet and let him lead her to their bedroom. "And meanwhile I'll spend the time printing your photos."

As she slipped under the sheets, she didn't think she would be able to fall asleep, yet no sooner had her head touched the pillow than blessed oblivion swamped her.

Tangier, Morocco

The passport checks were done on the ferry, Zabala's passport stamped with an entry number. He debarked from the ferry at Tanger Med, where a policeman smiled and said, "Welcome to Morocco."

A shuttle bus took him for a short ride to the terminal building and then he joined a queue to pass through customs and immigration. The official's scrutiny was thorough. He was eventually waved through. His training ensured he was vigilant and noted the security and cameras. For years Morocco had been terrorist-free; until 2011 when a bomb exploded in a Marrakesh café, killing seventeen people; and recently eight Moroccan IS members were shown posturing on video, stating they "intend to bring jihad to Moroccan soil". Maybe Algeria was a buffer between Morocco and strife-torn Libya, but they weren't taking chances. As a retired terrorist himself, he couldn't blame the authorities.

He opted for a taxi to Tangier city; it was 40km from the terminal but the route was so circuitous that it took almost forty minutes. During the journey, he thought again about the death of Petra. He was shaken by it. None of his other victims had affected him this way. Perhaps because she was a kindred spirit. He hadn't meant to lose control. It had been too long since the last victim; and it was lousy timing.

They passed many locals in all kinds of dress, from western through to traditional. There was amusement and laughter, and the occasional raised voice, probably on a cell-phone. He didn't feel comfortable among these people. They were proud of their country and their king, it seemed, and he felt those sentiments were misplaced. He still yearned for a republic in Spain. On balance, he'd rather deal with the likes of Kamal Saleem; that man knew his place, even if he was a director of Ananke's health foods company.

The taxi driver dropped him at the Hotel Continental. He was familiar with its white edifice, red flags fluttering from its rooftop. The nineteenth-century building seemed to mirror the town itself, being on several levels and featuring balconies, sun terraces and flights of exterior stairs.

He mounted the steps, passed through the entrance arch and approached the receptionist, an attractive young Moroccan woman dressed smartly in white silk blouse, broad black belt and tight red skirt. He addressed her in French and she responded with a throaty accent and offered the register. He gave her his passport, which she photocopied and returned, and he signed in; then she gave him his room key and directed him to his room on the first floor.

The passageways were decorated in colorful tiles, the arched windows draped with red curtains.

Once in his room, he flung the suitcase on the settee. The view through the window was panoramic, taking in the port, but all he could see was Petra, dead Petra.

He emptied his pockets onto the small round ornate brass coffee table at the foot of the bed. He needed a shower and a stiff drink. Forget Petra, he told himself. You have a job to do. Head of Security. And overseeing the Moulay Project, too. His pleasures came expensive and this little jaunt was the ideal means to acquire enough wealth from the Moulay find to indulge himself. Petra's demise was unfortunate, a mistake. Best forgotten tonight with another woman.

Then, tomorrow, refreshed, he'd visit the Ananke health foods plant in the new town, Ville Nouvelle.

———

Nice

Cat woke refreshed and was surprised to find she'd slept well. If she'd had any nightmares, she couldn't recall them. Still in her nightgown, she stepped onto the balcony that overlooked the marina. The sky was cloudless, last night's rain a distant memory; the sun shone brightly on dry paving. Casting its shade, their awning billowed slightly with the faint sea breeze. She sniffed the ozone, invigorated.

Rick sat reading a newspaper at the small round table cluttered with a teapot, cups, saucers, plates, toast, and marmalade.

"Lovely morning," she said.

He turned, lowered the *Telegraph* to the floor, stood, and grinned. "It is. Toast and marmalade or jam?"

"I'm a marmalade cat."

They sat and he buttered two slices of toast and passed the plate and the dish of marmalade. He appraised her, eyes appreciative. "You look refreshed. Sleep well?"

She nodded, pouring herself a cup of Earl Gray from the china pot.

"What do you want to do with all that money?" he asked. "Put it in one of your bank deposit boxes?"

She bit into the toast, chewed, and then said, "No."

A few months ago she had finally revealed to him details about her six bank deposit keys, which she had hidden at her father's grave site. Each key was for a different bank in Rome, London, Paris, Valletta, Madrid, and Amsterdam. In each deposit box: several personal items plus the keys to an apartment that she had stocked with the paraphernalia she believed essential to combat Dante and his corporation. "After my father's death," she'd explained, "I had enough to purchase the Paris place. I had to save for the rest, putting aside a fair portion of my modelling earnings, biding my time over the years."

"Why so many places?"

"Eggs in baskets, an English phrase, springs to mind. In case I was discovered, identified... We've had difficulty already with our homes in England."

Rick grimaced. "I know. I mean to do something about that."

"I got Len to sell my car. He picked it up at the airport." She'd been sorry to abandon it, but its sale had helped finance her Toyota Land Cruiser.

"A pity about your house in Alverstoke," he said.

"Yes. NCA had no trouble finding my address, it

seems. Len asked a contact or two in the area. They got a court order, searched the place—"

"And found your private room?"

"Yes. But I have others—I tend to think of them as Narnia cupboards. I guessed I might have to go on the run from any of my addresses."

Rick whistled. "If you consider the value of all the properties you've bought as bases of operation that must be a tidy sum."

"The financial crash meant I got a lot of quite small properties at good rates."

"Even so. Did you ever think about jettisoning your crusade and living again?"

She rubbed the back of her neck. "Every time I hit Ananke, I tell myself it will be the last. I've cost him money and grief. That was until I learned he arranged for my father's death. Now, I have no doubts. I intend to ruin him. Completely."

Now, she possessed €500,000 that belonged to Ananke. In some manner she wanted to use that to hurt Loup Dante.

She swallowed more toast, sipped at the tea. "No, I think we'll keep the money with us for the time being. It might come in useful." She licked marmalade off her fingers. "What did you make of the documents I photographed?"

"There's a financial link between the Tangier health foods plant and a notary in Marrakesh."

"Don't they have notaries in Tangier?"

"Yes, they do. But, if my interpretation is accurate, the Marrakesh one seems to be funneling money through the Tangier plant."

"Laundering?"

"I don't know, but it could be. I'm still amazed that I haven't heard of these business connections. Yes, I knew about Barcelona's perfume concern, but not the sordid details of the Catananche project. I was aware of his offices in Shanghai, and yes, I'd heard of the Tangier food processing plant—it was acquired before I joined, and I'd read up on it. Morocco's a good investment—the Big Four auditors say so. But these other links—Rome, Durban, Tenerife, and Izmir—I've never seen any of them on the books."

"Isn't Izmir in Turkey?"

"Yes. Why?"

She studied him over the rim of her cup. "I've always wanted to go to Turkey."

"I don't think you should be going anywhere that's crucial to Ananke. It's getting too dangerous."

"I understand, Rick, I really do. But I can't stop now."

"Even after what you saw last night?"

"We don't know why Petra was killed—or even who the murderer was, do we? It might not have had anything to do with Zabala or Ananke."

"You're going to Tangier, aren't you?" His tone was full of resignation.

"Yes." She stood. Spontaneously, at mention of Petra's grisly death, she wanted to grasp at life—every glorious aspect of it. She ran a hand provocatively over the curves within her nightgown. "Are you coming with me, dear 'husband'?"

"Are you going to be this manipulative when we're properly wed?"

"Manipulative, *moi*?" she purred and pulled at his hand, led him toward the bedroom.

Chapter 3

Caterpillar

Tangier

Next morning, Zabala cleared the last vestiges of his indulgent evening in the hotel's *hammam*. He paid a *kias* to soap and massage him. After he had sweated for a while, Zabala let the professional scrape his flesh to remove the outermost layer of dead soiled skin; it peeled off in small spaghetti-like threads and the *kias* rinsed it away with water from a bucket. It was moments like this when he wondered if he'd been born in the wrong time. He could imagine himself in the ancient Roman baths, with slaves using a metal strigil to scrape him clean.

After a breakfast of *baghrir*, the pancakes layered with honey, and cinnamon flavored black coffee, and feeling thoroughly refreshed, Zabala left the hotel with his briefcase and accosted a taxi. The driver regretted his meter was broken—which Zabala doubted; he haggled for a fair rate before getting in. The driver was an annoyingly cheerful fellow and Zabala had to snap at him to be quiet. He'd rather have a modicum of silence, as much as could be found in these busy streets. Despite his irritability, his thoughts wandered as he idly noted the Jewish cemetery on his left along Rue de Portugal. Seemingly, those interred were now the only Jewish occupants of the city where in days past there'd been thousands, many living here since they were thrown out of Spain hundreds of years ago. They'd emigrated en masse when Israel was created. Fortunes can change in an instant, he reflected. Catherine Vibrissae seemed to believe in that dictum, too, and was hell-bent on radically altering the fortune of Loup Dante. For a fleeting instant, Zabala sensed a chill trace his spine and wondered if the woman would succeed. No. Impossible. She was one woman. He was more than a match for her and her lawyer accomplice!

The taxi dropped him at Boulevard Pasteur and he paid the exact amount; the driver scowled and drove off with a screech of tires. He strolled a short distance to the Ananke health foods plant.

It was a modern building, with big windows, and appeared out of place alongside the 1950s edifices. Above the entrance was a blue sign, *Ananke Health Food Processing, S.A.* There was a plainclothes security man at the door, tall, muscles bulging under his unkempt suit, and he asked for identification. Zabala was impressed. He was cleared to go in and the female receptionist welcomed him—more gracious smiling!— and then rang through to alert the CEO.

She escorted him to the elevator and accompanied him to the second floor. They walked along a tiled corridor toward the rear of the building, turned left at the end and crossed an echoing gantry with glass walls.

Below, he noticed several sections of the processing plant—here, the goods were moved on conveyors and packed into boxes. Men steered forklift trucks to transfer the boxes on palettes to a doorway in the rear.

Doors led from the room, each labelled:

- *Amino acids*
- *Botanical extracts,*
- *CLA*
- *Enzymes*
- *MCT oil*
- *Omega 3 products*
- *EPA/DHA*
- *Propolis*
- *Dairy and whey products*

Zabala was ushered into the office of the Ananke CEO, Kamal Saleem. They'd met before and Saleem's corpulent frame hadn't altered; indeed, he'd gained weight, not the best advertisement for their products. Almost a caricature of an old Hollywood Arabic businessman, Saleem stood behind his desk, stroking his thick black mustache, and held out a chubby be-ringed hand. Beneath a hooked nose, his thick fleshy lips curved, though there was no mirth or greeting in his dark glinting eyes. His skin was swarthy. Rather than shake hands, Zabala bowed and wished him well.

He noted the wall behind Saleem; two warning posters showing Catherine Vibrissae and Rick Barnes were faded from exposure to the sunlight through the window. He withdrew from the briefcase a fresh set and flung them across the desk. "Have you disseminated these to your people?"

"Yes, of course. Months ago. Neither has been near."

"Well, be vigilant. They're really dangerous."

"Can't you alert the port and the airport?"

"No. They've left no incriminating evidence. It has to be unofficial."

"Then how do you know they are the dangerous ones?"

"I've met them. I know them."

"I see." Saleem shrugged.

"Just remember, Saleem. If either of them enters this plant, I'm to be informed immediately on my cell-phone." He tossed a business card on top of the posters.

Before leaving the building, however, he asked the receptionist to contact Abdi Ahmed, a buyer for the company.

Ahmed's office was nearby and he soon joined him in the foyer. "How may I be of service, Sidi Zabala?" He had a light complexion and was short but muscular. His eyes were a surprising blueberry color. His head of black hair was close-shaved, and he had a straggly mustache.

Zabala gave Ahmed a business card and copies of the two posters of Barnes and Vibrissae. "Contact me on this number if either of these two visits Kamal Saleem."

Ahmed rubbed a hand over his stubbly chin. "I will do this for you."

"Very good."

Zabala left the building. During earlier visits he had plied Ahmed with gifts so that the man was greatly beholden. It might prove useful. He didn't trust Kamal

Saleem, not at all; that weight gain meant he wasn't working hard enough for Ananke.

London

Carrying a slim buff folder, Sergeant Basset entered DI Pointer's office. "I've just been informed about another murder connected to Ananke, sir."

He leaned forward, elbows on his desk, suddenly alert. This might be the break they were seeking, and it was well overdue. "Where this time?"

"Nice, France, as the Americans would say." She grinned, sat opposite him and passed him the folder marked *Interpol*. "It's Petra Grimalkin, the head of their cosmetics division. Murdered and left very clean and very dead in her apartment's shower cubicle. The balcony door was the access, they say, since the alarm was set on the front door."

"Thank you." He leafed through the pages, studying the crime scene photographs, and the typed report. Apparently, Loup Dante, the head of Ananke, had been attempting to get in touch with Petra on a business matter. Getting no response, he contacted the building concierge who observed that she had not left the building for over a day. He was instructed by Dante to enter the apartment. Carrying his cell-phone, the man complied and set off the alarm; fortunately, Dante then gave him the code to silence it. The body was found minutes later.

Pointer ran a hand across his forehead. "This type of murder rings a bell, Carol. Last year..." He clicked his fingers at remembering. "Southampton! Yes, that was it. Can you get me DI Jardine? He talked about a similar case—"

"But it had nothing to do with Ananke, sir."

"True, but the coincidence still seems bizarre."

"One of your hunches?"

"Could be."

Nice-Almeria-Melilla

While Rick was out buying sandwiches for the journey, Cat made a few phone-calls. She was a great believer in preparing her route and making plans ahead of time. She wasn't a fan of Mr. Micawber's belief, "in case anything turned up." Chuck seemed to confirm her approach, too.

Using their Spanish aliases of Catalina and Ricardo Moreno, she'd booked the *Acciona Transmediterranea* ferry; it ran daily but, allowing for their travel time, she'd opted for the sailing two days' hence from Almeria to Melilla. There were others sailing from Selé in France, but that was a thirty-six-hour crossing, and from Algeciras to Ceuta or to Tangier direct. Ceuta was closer to Tangier than Melilla, true, but she needed to be in Melilla, anyway, and in addition her guide Abdel was going to be there when the ferry arrived.

The journey from Nice to Almeria was a good 1,100km, Rick had reckoned. Even if they shared the driving, and allowed for comfort breaks and stops to eat, they were unlikely to make it in less than fifteen hours.

Before they set out, she made sure they carried their

Spanish passports and had hidden the genuine British ones. "It's prudent always to carry ID with you," she said.

Shortly after eight in the morning, Cat drove the Toyota Land Cruiser out of the apartment basement garage and through Nice. She was happy to take the first stint at the wheel, since she was familiar with the French road system and signage. She skirted Marseille via Aix-en-Provence, passed Montpellier and pretty much stuck to the E15 south, going round Perpignan.

Once they crossed the border into Spain, they stopped for a snack and Rick took over the driving. He commented that he preferred driving on the continent as kilometers clocked up faster than miles. "A psychological thing, I know, but it's great to note the number reduce..." She agreed.

The roads were mostly open, certainly not crowded, and the mountain scenery and the route along the coast were spectacular. "Maybe we should stop over," he suggested, "enjoy the many sights."

"I'm tempted—but I've already made arrangements in Melilla now. Another time, perhaps. Besides, you'll get spectacular views in the Rif Mountains."

"That's a definite promise," he said firmly.

A short distance outside Almeria, they called in at a wayside restaurant, and the meal was only accompanied with still water, as neither had any wish to impair concentration or fail a breathalyzer.

They made it in time to board the ferry and it sailed at 11:30pm. Fortunately, Cat had booked an air-conditioned cabin. Replete with good food, they were too shattered even to make love.

The early morning call was not welcome, as both

complained of stiff backs due to the relentless driving. Sitting in a vehicle for in excess of a dozen hours had taken its toll. Still, they had no choice but to get up. Cat decided upon a white linen shirt, beige cotton slacks and Josef Seibel desert boots.

"You seem over-dressed," Rick remarked as they ate a hasty breakfast.

"I want to be comfortable and practical," she said. "There's no telling where we'll end up."

"Yes, of course." He pursed his lips. "You're sounding mysterious again!"

"Did you take my advice? Have you got some sensible footwear?"

"Yes—Caterpillar." He tugged the bottom of a trouser leg to reveal a nubuck mid-boot. "Will they do?"

"Seem a bit like a fashion statement, rather than practical."

"Well, you should know, I suppose."

She grinned. "They'll serve."

A few minutes short of 8am, the ferry approached the harbor. Cat recalled that Franco launched the Spanish Civil War from here in 1936. So much bloodshed and horror inflicted, a Communist and Nazi testing ground for the bigger conflagration to come. Somberly, she stood at the rail with Rick and pointed to the medieval fortress that dominated the city, with its massive defensive walls. She never ceased to be awed by the view of ancient cities from the sea—there were so many in the Mediterranean, the ochre-colored stone contrasting with the differing and enchanting blues of sea and sky.

When the ferry drew alongside the jetty, she scanned the dominating fortress wall with her binoculars. There, on the bastion, next to the Boca de Leon—mouth of the lion—the lighthouse beyond, a man waved; he wore a smart tan-colored suit, a brown tie and, despite the heat, a black astrakhan hat. She waved in return. That had to be Abdelfettah Malik, a journalist she'd met a couple of times when she toured Morocco for a fashion shoot.

Earlier, Rick had asked, "Since Abdelfettah works in Tangier most of the time, wouldn't it have made more sense to meet him there—and we ferried across from Algeciras? Enter Tangier and Morocco direct?"

"When I phoned him it was short notice. He was honor-bound to come to his home town—that's Beni Ansar, next to Melilla. Don't worry. He has agreed to be our guide."

"Right, I see. Yes, as you said. Him knowing the set-up in Tangier helps, too."

Melilla

Their Spanish passports cleared them for the enclave. They descended to the car deck and Rick got behind the wheel of the Toyota Land Cruiser and drove ashore. They soon joined the flow of vehicles on the broad Avenue General Macias until he came to a bend and braked briefly, ignoring the honk of horns from behind. Abdelfettah Malik stood at the curb, waving.

Abdel hadn't changed much in the intervening year or so, she realized. He still had a neatly trimmed black beard and his dark eyes sparkled, darting, taking in his surroundings, observing like the good journalist he was.

"Hop in," Cat called and Abdel opened the rear door and slid in onto the back seat. "Take off, Rick, and keep to this road till you come to the Plaza de España."

"Okay."

She made the introductions.

"Cathy," said Abdelfettah, "it is good to see you again."

"It's been too long," she said. "By the way, it's now Mrs. Moreno."

"Ah, then congratulations are in order!"

She flushed. She didn't like lying to him; he was a good honest man. Fleetingly, she wondered if her vendetta was changing her—and not necessarily for the better. "Thank you."

"Call me Abdel, Mr. Moreno," Rick was told. "Everybody does."

"And it's Rick, I insist."

"Here we are," Cat said as Rick entered a wide roundabout. In the center, a massive splash of green, palm trees, and stone passing in a blur as he maintained speed with the traffic flow, vehicles darting on both sides. "Turn off next right, here."

He turned, accompanied by horns blaring, and they entered the Calle de General Marina.

"Find a space anywhere you can," she told Rick.

Abdel laughed at that. Then he barked, "Here, here!"

Without indicating, Rick smartly slid into a parking space that was just vacated by a pickup truck.

"Rick, you drive like a local already," Abdel commented.

"Thanks, Abdel. I'll take that as a compliment."

Cat opened her door and jumped out. "Won't be a

minute!" She slammed the door shut and ran past two entrances and entered a building with the sign *Hostal Parque*.

Twelve minutes later by her watch, she returned, carrying a khaki holdall. Rick popped the trunk for her. Cars hooted behind them.

"What are you doing?" Rick called. "I'm getting tooted here!"

"Get used to it," she shouted and slammed the trunk shut. She came round, opened the door and sat in the passenger seat. "Abdel will direct you from here," she said.

"Very well," Abdel said. "I will *direct* you to where I have parked my car, first. Then you will follow me. I have to make a small diversion and then we will go on to my home for a meal."

"We are honored, Abdel," she said.

This was the old Melilla, Spanish in appearance, if a little careworn. Within the fortress walls, the town had a Castilian flavor, with its narrow twisting streets offering welcome shade, and colonial-style squares and ornate gates.

As they were about to pass a petrol station, Abdel advised, "Fill the tank with fuel here, it's duty-free."

Once they'd refueled, they set off for a short distance along dusty roads and deposited Abdel at the car park next to a black grime-covered Dacia Sandero.

Abdel then drove with them tailing him, the wheels churning dust.

It was barely twenty minutes to the Moroccan border post, which was on a hill. Cat noticed people swarming toward them on either side.

Before they got there, Abdel stopped his car, got out.

Dust collected all around as men and women moved up and down the hill, laden with bundles as large as washing machines.

Rick pulled in behind the Dacia and he and Cat got out and joined Abdel.

"What's going on?" Rick asked.

"I've written about this a number of times," Abdel said. "These are our mule women." His tone seemed filled with exasperation. "You will find more at the border of the other Spanish enclave, Ceuta."

"What," Rick said, "carrying drugs so openly, surely not?"

"No, they are not drug mules." Abdel pointed to the chain link and barbed wire that served as the border barrier; white signs bearing black silhouettes of men and women porters hung high on the iron railings of the narrow passage in Barrio Chino to indicate the entrance. "Mule ladies don't need a visa to cross the border. For the last twenty years they have hauled toilet paper, used clothing and small electrical goods from Spain into Morocco. They earn as little as three Euros each trip, or perhaps as much as ten. Humiliating treatment is meted out to the women by some police on both sides of the border. Not so long ago a young woman porter from Tetouan was so tired of so much humiliation that she set herself alight at the border post, after the authorities confiscated the goods she was carrying."

Cat wondered guiltily about the €500,000 concealed in their vehicle. "But why?"

"Before the 1990s there was no serious border

between Morocco and Melilla. Then, membership of the EU meant that Spain was expected to strengthen its border controls. So now a few hundred million Euros' worth of goods arrive in Melilla's port each year," Abdel explained. "And the women are used to avoid import taxes because any package that is hand-carried in to Morocco is considered as luggage and therefore duty-free."

A narrow corridor led to the border turnstile, the overburdened men and women jostling to squeeze through. "Those packages they carry can weigh up to 220 pounds, though most are about 150."

"My God, look over there!" Rick pointed.

A couple of men hustled a woman, knocking her into the dust, while two more blocked a woman from climbing the hill.

"Massive unemployment has driven men to hustle for these mule jobs now," Abdel said, "so they are not so nice about blocking the women and pushing them aside."

Guardia Civil officers stood by, but she could see that the numbers were too great for them to do much, besides remonstrate. "This is no way to treat people," Cat seethed.

Abdel shrugged. "The mayor of Melilla has asked the Moroccan government to increase the size of the crossing, but they will not." He pointed to the Guardia Civil ambulance parked near. "That is used about four times a month."

"I wish we could help them," Cat whispered.

"They don't want charity, only better conditions of work. They are single mothers, widows, abused women, wives with disabled husbands, women excluded by society, who turn to contraband in order to make ends meet.

They are willing to work, oh yes, even though it is not an easy life." Abdel gestured at three young girls bowed under enormous bales. "No prospects for a better life, either."

"You write a lot of human interest stories, Abdel?" Rick queried.

"Oh, yes. I must be careful, Rick. But I know people who you might regard as 'shady customers' who can obtain almost anything on the market. They provide me with contacts and stories." He pursed his lips, slapped a hand on the roof of his car, raising dust. "Let's go."

Chapter 4

Cat's Mint Tea

At the border post, Abdel showed his documentation and drove through.

Rick and Cat proffered their Spanish passports and were allowed to pass without any search of their vehicle. She breathed freely; she was glad the hidden €500,000 were new currency bills; there'd always been the chance that dogs might have sniffed out drug-covered banknotes—apparently most paper money in circulation was tarnished nowadays. Oblivious, Rick steered behind Abdel into the township of Beni Ansar.

There was a mixture of old and new buildings; some still had scaffolding but no work ensued on them. A few dwellings comprised cinder-block bricks with no windows. Others were smart with high walls, either white-washed or rose pink. A number of roofs were made with corrugated iron and held down with large stones, not unlike places seen in Spain.

Following Abdel through a warren of narrow streets, past several dented parked cars, one or two without side-mirrors, Rick finally braked outside a half-finished building behind the Dacia. The windows had iron grilles and the door was solid metal, patterned with scroll-work. A potted red geranium thrived to one side.

An elderly woman, her back bent, emerged through the doorway. The lower half of her face was covered; her robes were smart and colorful, albeit frayed at the edges.

Abdel got out. Cat and Rick followed him.

"This is Nora," Abdel said. "She used to be a cross-border mule, but now her husband works in the Tangier Ananke factory. She sees him every fortnight or so. He sends her money when he can, though it isn't much." He briefly introduced Cat and Rick.

"*Merhaban,*" Nora said, her dark eyes wary. *Welcome.*

Cat saw the gorgeous wide eyes of children behind Nora. At least four, all girls, all not quite teenagers, she guessed. Not strong enough to haul bales of goods yet. "*As salam aleykum,*" she said.

Nora bowed politely and turned her attention to Abdel.

He handed her several banknotes. "Her husband gives me his money when I visit Tangier. I bring it here. Sadly, they trust me more than other means."

Nora stepped back, ushered her children away but before she could say anything Abdel forestalled her and spoke rapidly. Cat glimpsed the floor within, covered with thin reed rugs.

They said goodbye and as they walked back to their cars, Abdel said, "Nora would have invited us inside, but we're expected home, so I gave our apologies before she made the offer. I promised to return in two weeks with more money from her husband."

Rick's face reflected puzzlement.

"It would have been rude not to accept her invitation to take tea," Cat said.

"Oh, I see. I think I've got a lot to learn."

Abdel grinned and nodded. "Nora used to be a maid for a Spanish family in Melilla. She worked long days and earned the princely sum of €300 per month. That was before the crisis, of course. At that time many families got rid of their maids."

They set off again and drove on through the streets in the dusty wake of the Dacia.

Arabic writing was everywhere, and Rick remarked that he found it worrying; "I'd soon get lost!"

"Just keep an eye on Abdel's car," she berated.

Children played, grinned, and shouted and shrieked; boys hammered and forged copper and brass plates over fires; men in burnooses studied Abdel's car in open curiosity. Many young men roamed the streets, doubtless the visible jobless. Rick had the distinct impression that the Spaniards and Muslims were wary of each other. Yet they seemed to cope, co-exist, regardless. "Most men seem Islamic," he said.

"Islam's a religion, Rick, not a fashion statement," Cat said.

"That's me, love. Their clothing, I meant." And then he laughed as a bunch of men and women crossed the street ahead, all wearing western clothes.

"Their clothing is designed for the climate," she added, "and has nothing to do with politics or religion."

"There speaks an ex-fashion model! I stand corrected."

Rick noticed that the ubiquitous cell-phones appeared to be attached to many ears here, too; he'd seen it in Spanish streets, the seemingly constant chatter on phones, often loudly. Here, though, more groups of men sat at curbside cafés and just talked to each other.

Finally, after negotiating a sequence of bends, Abdel pulled up at a two-story white building. He got out, rapped on the thick wooden door. On the wall to the right was a hand-print in green paint, to avert misfortune from befalling the inhabitants, Cat whispered in explanation.

"I'll get the bags," she said and got out first. By the time Rick was beside her, the cases and her holdall were out. He lifted the cases; she carried the khaki holdall.

When the door opened, they were met by a woman about Abdel's age, and behind her was a young girl. Abdel made the introductions, "Mr. and Mrs. Moreno." As far as he was aware, they were married and guiltily Cat wasn't going to disabuse Abdel of that belief. "Amina, my wife, and Sheera, my daughter." He affectionately squeezed the shoulder of the little girl, who was about eight; she had beautiful golden eyes.

"Pleased to meet you both," Amina said.

Abdel removed his shoes. Cat and Rick slipped off theirs, leaving them at the side of the doorway with Abdel's.

Then Abdel and his wife led them inside, along a shadowy passage.

A maidservant hovered in the background, then darted forward and relieved them of their baggage, and then disappeared into an arched doorway.

For a fleeting and uncharitable moment, Rick whispered, "Will we ever see the bags again?"

"Don't be crass. We're honored guests. Leave your prejudices at the door with your shoes."

"Ouch. Well, that's me reprimanded again. Still, I'm really curious about what's in your mysterious holdall."

"I'll tell you when I'm ready. But not here."

———

THEY WERE SHOWN into the large guest-room. Abutting one wall was an assortment of expensive inlaid wooden furniture and gold ornaments; the other walls were lined with long narrow chintz-covered couches with no backs, only cushions, and in one corner was a low round brass table.

She was prepared for the greetings, which were usually lengthy. She shook hands with Amina and her daughter Sheera, lightly touching her hand to her heart to show respect, and asked after their health and the girl's studies. Following her lead, Rick did the same.

Then, finally, Amina and Sheera excused themselves.

Abdel gestured at the couch and Cat and Rick sat in the corner in front of the table.

Then the maid came in with a basin and a kettle. Cat held out her hands over the basin and the maid poured water on them. She used the soap provided, offered her hands ready for a rinse, then she took a towel to dry. "Shukran," she said—*thanks*.

The maid moved to Rick who performed the ritual flawlessly and finally to Abdel.

She noted there was just the one tablecloth, and commented.

Abdel smiled. "There will be three courses, but we now only use one tablecloth—instead of three, as it is more eco-friendly." Rick looked puzzled, so Abdel explained, "Tradition has it that a tablecloth was laid for each course for the repast and removed after each course."

"Oh, I see," Rick said, politely. "Seems eminently sensible, anyway."

She had already primed Rick about eating etiquette and now he used the fingers only of his right hand to scoop up olives and pickles, as well as freshly baked bread.

During this salad course, Cat asked Abdel what he knew about the Ananke plant in Tangier.

Abdel frowned. "They bring work, which is welcome."

"Yes," she said, "you mentioned that you have high unemployment here. So, why the frown?"

"The CEO, Kamal Saleem, he is a harsh taskmaster. If a worker does not dance to his tune, he is sacked. He wields the day-to-day power; the other three directors rarely show themselves."

"Don't you have unions and laws about that kind of thing?" Rick queried.

"Yes, we have unions," he replied, chest inflating with pride. "Our labor laws safeguard our workers, and we have a minimum wage. Ours is not a backward country, Rick."

"Sorry, Abdel. I didn't mean to imply it was."

"Truth is," Cat said, "only about five percent of the fulltime workforce is in a union."

"How'd you find that out?" Rick demanded with a smile.

"Before my father's death, I'd studied a few countries with a view to starting a business in one of them. I did some research." She bit into a pickle, swallowed; it was strong, brought tears to her eyes. "About twenty years ago, new laws were introduced to coax foreign capital into Morocco, investment incentives and exemption from taxes or import duties for a fixed period. Red tape cut to encourage businesses. So, the financial inducements tempted me, but I didn't go ahead. I imagine Loup Dante has taken advantage of all that when he established his health food plant."

"Yes, I read about the start-up. He registered the public limited company with four others. I think the share capital was £200,000."

"I know two of those shareholders," Cat said, nodding.

"Really?"

"We'll be meeting them in Tangier." She turned to Abdel. "Sorry, we got side-tracked a little. You were telling Rick about the labor force in Morocco?"

Abdel said with a hint of pride, "We also have paid holidays and a statutory working week."

"Good to hear," Rick said, his face slightly clouded, doubtless pondering on how much Cat knew about his old firm.

The maid returned and served the main course, tagine—meat and vegetable stew in an earthenware dish.

"Eat, eat!" Abdel urged. The bread was necessary now to avoid too much mess.

Abdel shrugged as the maid retreated. "Still, the main power is in the hands of the men with money. They say 'jump' and we jump. It has always been so. Money is power. It is the same in your country, and others, too."

"Do you write about these wrongs?" Cat asked.

"Oh, yes. But not all that I write gets published. My editor has to watch how the land lies and often falls back on self-censorship. Yes, most press restrictions were lifted years ago, when our king ascended the throne. But much of that is mere lip service." He broke some bread, gestured wildly, dropping crumbs across the table. "We do not have a free press. Our newspapers and editors can suffer crippling fines or even imprisonment for the slightest thing. Opposition dailies have tackled social and political issues that have been traditionally out of bounds, and I've written articles on those subjects. But where government corruption, human rights, American and European industry are concerned, we must tread as if on egg-shells."

"Really? What are the taboo subjects?" Rick asked.

"Anything to do with the health of the king or the royal family. Criticizing a government minister for drinking alcohol can earn you a fine and a suspended prison sentence. For the slightest pretext, editors may be charged with promoting terrorism by simply publishing details about terrorist groups."

"I can understand them getting jittery about terrorism right now," Rick said.

Abdel smiled wanly. "Earlier I bemoaned the lack of a truly free press. Yet, look at the so-called 'freedom' the west has spawned in the Middle East, a scourge that has laid waste much of Libya and northern Iraq." He shuddered graphically.

Cat leaned forward. "And don't discuss the Western Sahara situation?"

"Precisely." Abdel folded his hands. "Even so, we try to push our envelope of constriction. With care."

"The Internet isn't as constrained, is it?" Rick asked.

"The same selective censorship applies, though the authorities may find it harder to prosecute. An engineer posted a fake profile of the king's brother on Facebook and ended up in prison; he was pardoned by the king after forty-three days in jail..."

The maid returned with a course of fresh fruit, which marked the end of the meal.

Cat said, "I'm really full, Abdel. That was wonderful."

Beaming at this, Abdel addressed them both, "To your health."

She responded, "God give you health."

Shortly after the mint tea, Amina entered and bowed. "Sheera is ready to retire."

"I will see her later," Abdel said.

His wife nodded and left.

"Is your wife comfortable about you coming with us?" Cat asked.

"A woman without a man is like a nest without a bird," he said. "The Koran says that men are in charge of women, because Allah has made the one of them to excel the other, and because we men support our women. Good women are obedient. Thus my wife accepts that I make the decisions. I am freelance, a free agent." He tapped a loose fist against his chest. "Well, as free as I'm ever likely to be where the woman of the house is concerned." He grinned and squinted over his shoulder guiltily, and winked. "Amina knows you will pay me well."

"Good to hear it," Rick added.

Cat wondered if she was right to involve Abdel, after all. The sudden thought of Petra's death left an unpleasant aftertaste in her mouth. Yet they needed a Moroccan to guide them.

Pouring a second cup of tea, Abdel said, "It might put a few things in perspective for you, if I show you around Tangier before we approach the Ananke CEO, Kamal Saleem. Then you will understand how Ananke can so easily flout international law here."

Intrigued, Cat and Rick agreed, since they were not working to any tight schedule. Really, this was a fishing expedition. "Prospecting," as Chuck called it.

"I really appreciate you doing this, Abdel," she said. "You will be a great help when I tackle the CEO—as well as other VIPs, I'm sure."

He glanced at the tablecloth, clearly embarrassed.

"What is it?" she asked.

He didn't look up. "I regret to tell you, Cathy, but you will not be able to 'tackle' the CEO—or anyone else in authority."

Her heart sank. "Why, what's happened."

His eyes met hers, regret in them. "I am sorry, but you are a woman. They will only speak with a man."

She gave a slight moan. "Is that all?" She turned to Rick. "How's your French?"

"Blimey, it's not that good. I never thought—I mean, you're fluent, naturally!" He swung round. "Surely in this day and age, Abdel, Cathy can—?"

"Some businessmen won't appear to mind, I agree," Abdel said, "but I can assure you that the people you wish to speak to are not that enlightened."

"Will you back us up in the interviews?" Cat asked.

Abdel puffed out his chest. "I will stand at your shoulder, Mr. Moreno, er, Rick, as must Cathy."

Marrakesh

Clutching his black leather briefcase, Zabala alighted from the Tangier train. After the ten-hour journey, he felt as crumpled as his suit appeared. He'd left the Tanger Ville station at 8:15am and though he'd eaten a snack, he was now famished. His stomach rumbled as he stepped out onto Avenue Hassan II and he was immediately deafened by the clamor of traffic noise and people shouting. A taxi driver tried helpfully to grab his flight bag but retreated when Zabala growled, "Touch my belongings, and you'll regret it!"

He chose to walk the avenue and found the street easily enough, which was not surprising since he'd been here twice before. He turned left into Avenue Mohammed V.

A few buildings along, on the corner of an adjoining alley, a quiet section of the town, the brass plaque at the side of the front door stated: *Mohammed Hassan— Notary*. There was no shortage of Mohammeds in Morocco, he mused caustically.

Zabala was shown in at once and when the door closed he salaamed to the notary.

Hassan stood behind his broad desk and returned

the gesture of greeting. He was in his mid-forties. He wore a white djellaba and his bare feet were tucked into a pair of babouches, backless yellow slippers. "What is the purpose of your visit, Monsieur Zabala?" He pointed to a seat and sank into his plush leather chair, its arms darkened with sweat stains.

Sitting down, Zabala kept his features stern. Hassan was never one for niceties; straight to the point. "You know it's that time of year. I check on all our establishments. That's the job of Head of Security, after all."

"And you are most assiduous in that regard, monsieur."

Lifting his briefcase onto his knees, Zabala unzipped it, flicked through a sheaf of papers and removed two A4-size posters. He handed them over. "Ananke is being targeted by a small terrorist group headed by these two. Their names are Catherine Vibrissae and Rick Barnes." He paused, and then added, "I suspect they will be using aliases now."

Hassan's dark eyebrows arched. "And you think they will come here?"

"I'm covering all bases, Mohammed."

"You could have sent these posters to my computer. There is no need for a personal visit."

Zabala grinned. "You know I like to indulge myself when in Marrakesh."

Hassan paled. "I would rather not learn the details."

Zipping up his briefcase, Zabala stood, a leg easing back his chair. "As they say, Mohammed, the devil is in the details." Chuckling, he pivoted on his heel and made for the door.

Once outside the building, he moved further along the avenue and entered the Avis office. He was accosted by an attractive woman in the Avis uniform, her black hair swept into a bun. She wore light make-up and her thick sensual lips curved as she greeted him. He felt he could sink in her dark sultry eyes. Her name-tag told him she was named Aisha. Zabala turned on the charm.

That evening, he dodged motorbikes, mopeds, vans and mules and edged past the musicians who beat drums and played lutes, and the acrobats and story-tellers who performed to crowds on the edge of the square, Jemaa el Fna.

The square had been transformed into perhaps the largest outdoor café in the world and all the familiar sights and smells greeted him. Snake charmers, men with monkeys, vendors hawking carpets, henna artists, herbalists and hustlers worked alongside the open-air kitchen booths. Beneath the flickering light of kerosene lamps, fires were built in charcoal grills and fresh meat and vegetables were laid out. Young boys negotiated the crowds while holding aloft big wooden trays crammed with glistening sweetmeats, shouting "Balec, balec!" *Make way, make way.*

The red sun sank behind the snow-capped Atlas Mountains to the accompaniment of the Koran being sung a cappella through a tinny loudspeaker.

He would have to check on the Moulay find, perhaps tomorrow. But tonight, he would indulge himself, as he told Hassan.

Smells from food beckoned from the stalls: sizzling fat, tantalizing scents, ginger, cumin, cinnamon, garlic; he was spoilt for choice: succulent grilled lamb and chicken, couscous, tagines, fried fish, tiny beef sausages, almond-filled pastries, boiled snails, vegetables, salads,

soups, honey-soaked desserts, and of course the ubiquitous mint tea.

And then he would pay a visit to Aisha. Must be
controlled, though, he warned himself, still annoyed at
killing Petra.

Chapter 5

Russian Blue Cat

London

"Petra Grimalkin's grisly fate is uncannily similar to the woman's death in Southampton last year." Basset handed the report and glossy photographs to Pointer. "Same MO. It isn't pretty, sir." A shiver scurried over her flesh.

Pointer studied the images. "We have a serial killer, it seems."

"We, sir?"

"The killer crosses borders with impunity. We Europeans must stick together if we're going to catch people who can do this." He flung the report and photographs onto his desk. "Send a round robin to European police forces, describing the main points, see if we can detect a pattern."

"Right, sir. And if we do?"

"Then, we visit the most recent place where he is known to have committed murder."

"Well, sir, I believe we know the answer to that, don't we? Nice is nice this time of year."

He groaned at her word-play. "And hot—don't forget that sun..."

Shanghai

The insistent bleeping of the phone disturbed Dante's dreams and he opened his eyes. Still groggy from too little sleep, he rolled off the attractive blonde. He'd never known that she snored. He shrugged and padded to the adjoining room in his apartment.

He reached his desk and lifted the receiver. The Caller ID told him it was his Chinese secretary, Zoo Peizhi.

"Yes?" he said irritably.

"So sorry to disturb you, sir!"

He realized he'd been too abrupt. "No, Peizhi, it is I who should apologize." Her name meant "respectful", which suited her demeanor perfectly. He'd long since accepted that her people did things differently, and Zoo was her surname. "I spoke too rudely—I have just woken up."

"Oh, sir," she continued in impeccable English, "there was an urgent call from head office."

"What did they say?"

"It is terrible news, sir. They regret to inform you that Miss Petra Grimalkin was found murdered in Nice."

"Petra...?" *Murdered?*

"Yes, sir. They want your authorization to repatriate her body for the funeral—when the authorities release it."

His mouth was exceedingly dry. "Get them to email me the paperwork and I will sign it."

"I will do, sir. May I offer my condolences, sir, Miss Grimalkin will be missed greatly."

"Yes. Of course. Thank you."

Marrakesh

Zabala's cell-phone rang while he was packing his bag for his expedition. He went over to the hotel room's sideboard and picked it up. I was Mr. Dante. What did he want?

"Hello, sir. What can I do for you?"

"You can begin by explaining why Petra isn't with you in Tangier." There was a pause which Zabala was not sure how to fill. "I assume you are in Tangier?"

"I was, sir, but now I'm in Marrakesh. I've been to see the notary and I'm now packing so I can get on my way to the Project."

"I see. So you're still on schedule?"

"I believe so."

"Good man. But why isn't Petra with you?"

"Oh, she met somebody, decided to stay in Nice for a couple of days. I reckon I can manage without her. We agreed to meet in Tangier on my return, once I've arranged the latest transshipment."

"You should have informed me of this change in your schedule." *A mild rebuke, nothing more.*

"The schedule hasn't suffered from her absence, sir."

"Alright, I'm pleased to hear that. But who is this 'somebody'?"

"I wouldn't know, sir. It is her private life, after all."
He'd almost used the past tense for her then! *Stay alert.*

"I thought you and she—"

"No, no, sir, nothing like that. I'm fond of her as a colleague, but our relationship is always kept on a business level."

"Then since you're fond of her you'll be upset to hear she has been murdered."

By God, that was blunt!

Zabala inhaled deeply. Her body had been discovered. Already? His delay in any response was credible, he guessed. Put it down to shock. "Yes, sir... I—I am shocked to hear that. Murdered, you say?"

"I haven't got the details, but her death is regrettable. She was a useful and dedicated employee."

What an epitaph! "It is very sad, sir. Have the police caught the culprit?"

"No, I don't think so."

Nor are they likely to!

"Well, sorry to give you bad news. I've taken up enough of your time, Zabala. You'd better get on with your packing."

"Yes, sir. Thank you, sir."

Dante hung up.

Zabala went to the sideboard and poured a double shot of brandy with a trembling hand and then gulped it down.

He exhaled, thankful that he'd only enjoyed rough sex with the delectable Aisha last night. She had been

Nik Morton

ambivalent to begin with but then enjoyed the experience. It would have been the height of recklessness to leave a corpse here.

―――――

Melilla

Next day, Cat bid goodbye to Amina. Abdel's leave-taking was brisk, perfunctory, with no outward show of affection.

Rick drove with her beside him and Abdel in the back. He negotiated the clogged roads through Nador, sticking to the national highway. Throughout the journey, Abdel either dozed or keyed into his iPhone.

It was a good four hundred kilometers to Tangier, and would take at least five, maybe six hours to drive without stops. As they weren't expected in Tangier until tomorrow, Cat said they should stay somewhere overnight.

Once they started to climb into the Rif mountain range, Cat took the wheel so that Rick could enjoy the view from the mountain crests. "I appreciate it," he whispered, while Abdel slept, unaware of the change. "It's much better when you share the sights."

Feeling a surge of strong affection, she reached over and squeezed his thigh.

The views were breathtakingly beautiful—a duck-egg blue sky, a rich cobalt sea with stretches of aquamarine, the white foam of surf crashing on ochre rocks, and the gold and white ribbon of the coast line. It was the kind of place she could imagine riding a white horse in the surf! This road she took was one of the rare places along the coast where the Rif dropped away and debouched into a bay with several small beaches.

Later, shortly after Abdel woke, Rick glimpsed an attractive small islet off the coast, with buildings, a church and a wall seeming to emerge from the rock.

"Ah," Cat said, "that's Peñon de Alhucemas—it's controlled by Spain; prison and military fort, not a resort."

"Spanish rule dates back to 1559, when several territories belonged to the Moroccan dynasty of the time," Abdel added. "It was given to Spain in exchange for helping to defend them against Ottoman armies. In 1673, Spain sent a garrison to the island, and it is still occupied. Morocco has sought sovereignty since independence in 1956."

"Don't mention Gibraltar," Cat whispered under her breath.

Rick grinned. "Thanks, Abdel. There's a lot of history here, I can see."

"And it is still being made, I assure you," Abdel said, his tone light.

Presently, they drove into Al-Hoceima, with its attractive cluster of white buildings. "They seem mostly Spanish in style," Rick commented.

Already the streets were crammed with parked vehicles.

"Holiday-makers," Abdel explained. "It is a popular spot for Moroccans."

She found a parking space in front of the Hotel Marrakech, a short way from the chaos of the main square, on Calle Mohammed V. Unlike the cheaper hotels, this at least had hot water showers and en suite bathrooms. Their room offered a sea glimpse; Abdel bedded next door. They ate at the Restaurant Al-Maghreb Al-Kabir on the same street: brochettes on a bed of rice with French fries sufficed, washed down with chilled freshly squeezed orange juice. Bed beckoned.

The following morning, they breakfasted at the patisserie next to the restaurant and then were on their way again.

Following Abdel's directions, Rick drove inland, the road skirting the "immense national park", as he termed it, and then at Ait-Kamara he joined the N16, the road smooth and fairly deserted.

Eventually, they hit the coastline again at El Jebha, a welcome contrast from the ochre and green, now the gold and white coast and glittering sea. Then he turned on to the N2 at Tetouan, inland once more.

While Cat was driving, they met with a roadblock, but the police didn't keep them more than fifteen minutes, during that time mainly chatting to Abdel.

On the way, Cat explained that she'd made arrangements to stay with Howard Greenleaf, a retired millionaire who still dabbled in business affairs. "He got to know me quite well when we did a fashion shoot. Before I left Nice, I phoned that I was going to be here and he invited us all to stay."

"That was good of him," Rick said noncommittally.

"I know of Monsieur Greenleaf, naturally," Abdel said. "I will find alternative accom—"

"No, Abdel, he knows you're our guide and insisted you stay, too."

Abdel fidgeted with his tie. "I cannot refuse a generous invitation."

Rick eyed her, puzzlement written on his face.

She refrained from commenting further and concentrated on the road.

Tangier

Cat was lucky to find a parking gap in the old city, outside the gate to the kasbah, which was on the highest point of the city and isolated from the rest of the medina by its walls.

Abdel stayed with the vehicle while Cat led Rick through Bab el-Assa, one of four gates. They stepped onto a large open courtyard; to the left were a number of houses, with balconies, some of which were in various stages of disrepair, while others seemed refurbished and sported hotel signs. "Quite a number of these houses are owned by wealthy foreigners; though not all of them live here all the time," Cat said, then pointed directly ahead. "This is Bab al-Raha, the Gate of Rest." They passed through and climbed to a walkway along the wall that presented a splendid view across to Spain.

A few moments later, ahead of them, a man in his late forties approached. He held his slight frame upright, his smile belying the permanent frown of his furrowed brow. "You made good time, I see."

Cat grinned. "Gerard, it's good to see you again!" He moved into her embrace, and they briefly exchanged kisses on their cheeks. He still used verbena scent, a light concoction of citrus and lemon.

Gerard let go and took a pace back, his dull brown eyes glinting behind wire spectacles. He whispered coquettishly, "And who is this handsome man with you, my dear?"

She made introductions. "Gerard Kominsky is the companion of Howard Greenleaf."

"Charmed to meet you, Rick." He shook hands then turned to Cat. "Howard sends his apologies, but he is busy with a phone conference to the States."

"I thought he was retired?"

Gerard's thin lips twisted. "Semi-retired. He'll never retire, I fear. He loves wheeling and dealing too much to give it all up! His cats and my painting are not enough to occupy him, it seems." He lightened and offered a smile. "Even so, we get to go sailing most Sundays."

HOWARD MET her at the arched doorway, a Russian blue cat winding itself round his left leg. "It's good to see you again, my dear. Do come in—and we'll do the introductions in the courtyard." He was tall, with a slight stoop to the shoulders. He had prominent jowls, and a complexion mottled with liver spots, unusually early for someone in his mid-fifties, she thought. Salt and pepper hair was long and covered his ears, falling to his open-necked shirt collar. His eyes glinted blue-green.

He led them along a warren of passageways hemmed in by high walls and shortly afterwards emerged onto a much narrower passage, dimly lit; then through an arch they stepped into a covered courtyard, its walls decorated with intricate arabesques and glazed zellij tiles. The floor tiles were a mixture of blue and ochre patterns, representing the sky and the land. A little way along the edge of the wall, earthenware pots stood crammed full with gum and false pepper trees, jacaranda and creepers and assorted thick shrubs.

A large empty bird cage stood next to six metal chairs that surrounded a big table; on it lay a huge brass tray, a steaming kettle, a pewter basin, three bowls for sugar, mint and tea leaves, three brass tea-pots and five glass cups. One chair was occupied by a tortoiseshell cat, dozing.

The introductions were over quickly.

"Time for mint tea." Howard gently lifted the cat, put it on the floor; it pranced away. "Please sit! Gerard will do the honors, won't you, old fellow?"

"I always do, Howard dear," Gerard responded. Cat noticed he was familiar with the tea ritual. If offered a glass of tea from a prepared pot, you're welcome. If the tea was made in front of you, you were very welcome.

Gerard poured a little hot water into the three teapots, rinsed them and discarded the water in the basin; then he added the tea leaves and hot water. "I let it steep for about two minutes," he explained.

"It is worth the wait," Howard told Rick.

Then Gerard swirled the teapots and discarded only the water. Finally, he added sugar and mint leaves to each teapot and then boiling water, and closed the lids.

Rick licked his lips. "I can almost taste it already," he said.

"Soon," Gerard said, smiling. "Five minutes."

"I think we've lost something in the modern world with all this instant coffee and teabags, don't you think?" Howard said.

"Yes," Rick said.

"Too busy to savor life," Gerard added.

"Quite so, my friend," Howard replied.

Finally, Gerard poured the golden liquid into the glass cups, letting the stream fall from a reasonable height to cause slight froth.

"Delicious!" Rick enthused, sipping his drink.

Cat noticed that Abdel seemed at ease. Howard had that effect on people; or maybe it was the tea?

"What happened to your parrot?" Cat asked.

At that moment, two black cats rushed up to Howard and jumped onto his lap. Automatically stroking them, he wrinkled his nose. "One of our feline companions ate it—I don't know which one was the culprit, though."

She eyed Rick. "My point exactly," she purred. "Cats make ideal predators."

THAT EVENING, they all sat at a long table, Gerard on her right, Rick on her left. Opposite were Howard and Abdel. The walls of the dining room were adorned with oil paintings, landscapes, views of Tangier, and seascapes, all executed by Gerard.

"You've captured the light perfectly," Cat said. "Your style reminds me of the Orientalists."

"Why, thank you, my dear. I simply adore Delacroix." Gerard wore a cravat, a red silk shirt and loose flannel trousers with turn-ups and open-toed sandals. Quite the Bohemian, she thought.

Glad to be free of pants and shirt this evening, she'd chosen a simple black dress. But out of respect for

Abdel, she'd draped her shoulders with a wispy black lace shawl that covered the enticing generous 'v.'

Howard nursed his Volubilia Gris, a white wine he recommended, and stared away into memory. "I remember you wearing that black ensemble, it was more like mourning clothes—except for the revealing décolletage, I might add."

"And no visible panty line, as I recall," chimed in Gerard with glee.

"Because," Cat replied, "I wasn't wearing any."

Howard guffawed.

"I've been to some of Cathy's fashion shows," Rick said. "I'm sure she'd appear elegant even in a bin-liner!"

She closed her hand over his and squeezed it. "Thank you, kind sir."

Gerard chuckled. "I agree. Elegant even in glitzy tat!"

Howard whooped loudly. "Sheer dress, sheer wantonness!"

"Remember that wedding dress with the see-through top?" Gerard chortled. "A few eyes popped at that!"

"I can imagine," Rick said.

Shaking his head, Howard moaned. "The new trend seems to be to expose what is usually covered and to cover what used to be exposed. I can't say I like it much. It loses the allure."

Cat smiled at Abdel, who appeared uncomfortable, his face slightly flushed, as if unsure where to rest his gaze. "The pendulum will swing, as it always does. Ignore these critics, Abdel, they're only baiting me."

"I know, Cathy. But it is—"

"Unseemly," chimed in Howard. "You're right. We

should behave better with our guests." He winked at Gerard.

"Consider us both chastised." Gerard coyly lowered his lids.

"Now, tell us," Howard said, leaning close to her, "why are you *really* here?"

"Am I that transparent?"

"Utterly see-through, my dear."

Keeping to only minor details, she explained about Loup Dante's machinations and her discovery that he'd had her father killed.

This time, Abdel's face didn't flush but his eyes stared in disbelief. Even though clearly shocked, he did not comment.

"My God, if only I'd known any of this before," Howard said.

Rick leaned forward, "Why, Howard? What difference would it make to you?"

Howard and Cat exchanged glances, and then he beamed with secret amusement. "You haven't told him?"

Cat shook her head and smiled at Rick. "Howard and Gerard are directors of Ananke Health Foods."

Rick's mouth dropped open, slowly closed. He eyed Abdel, nodded, said, "I should have guessed."

"The other directors are Ayad El Foukai, the company secretary, Kamal Saleem, the CEO and Dante, of course."

"Of course." He studied his empty plate.

"Moroccan company law requires that two ordinary residents of the country must be directors—and they have to have at least three on the board. Dante had no choice but to find suitable shareholders."

"I see." Rick lifted his eyes. "Couldn't you have explained this earlier?"

"What, and spoil the surprise?" chortled Gerard.

Abdel said, "I was not aware you didn't know, Rick, since you said you had read up on the company. Sorry."

Smiling at Abdel, Rick said, "Don't worry about it, my friend. I should have remembered Howard's name at least. It was a while ago..."

"Now, Cat, tell me," Howard said, "tomorrow you're going to visit the Ananke health food production plant here?"

"Yes."

"What do you hope to achieve?"

"I won't know for sure until I've been there."

Howard made a steeple with his fingers. "It seems a rather loose strategy, my dear."

"I'll be the model of reticence."

"I know you're a model, my dear," Howard said, "but it's the other bit I'm worried about..."

Rick bobbed his head in agreement and raised his eyes to the ceiling.

AFTER A NIGHTCAP OF BRANDY, they all retired to their rooms. Cat lay on the bed in her dark blue silk satin short nightgown with georgette frills, basking in the cool draught of air from the efficient air-con.

Rick exited the bathroom wearing red boxer shorts. The dark hair on his body and limbs didn't match the hair on his head, but he didn't seem to care. He grinned, showing clean teeth, and jutted his chin at her holdall lying against the escritoire by the balcony curtains. "Are you finally going to tell me what's so important in there?"

"Among other things, there's a gun. An Astra A50 automatic. It's lightweight, but even so it has stopping power."

Arms akimbo, he stared. *"What?"*

"The seven .765 caliber rounds can stop—"

"What the hell are you doing with a gun?"

She sat up, her cheeks burning. "I felt it might be necessary."

"My God, you crossed the border with *that* in the car!"

"So? I hid it in the tool box in the trunk."

"That's what kept you, is it? Doesn't seem well hidden to me."

"Unless they were doing a deep search on a tip-off, they'd miss it—well, so says Chuck, anyway."

"Chuck again! I'm almost sorry I introduced you!"

"Well, I'm not. Besides, he's a lovely man."

"He's a crook!"

"Ex-crook. Reformed."

"Alright, alright!" He held up his hands, stared accusingly. "Is the gun even legal? I bet it isn't!"

"You should be on one of those TV quizzes, Rick. You've answered your own question. Does that make it rhetorical?"

Scowling, he knelt at the holdall, started unzipping it.

Her stomach churning, she swung her legs off the bed, raced over to him, and snatched the bag from his grasp. Taking a step back, she took out the weapon, brandished it. "This is mine!"

He raised a hand, mollifying. "Cathy, please, I'm worried for your safety, that's all."

"If I have a gun, won't I be safer?" She took care to point it at the floor.

"Yes, no... I really doubt it. The people who deal in guns, they're like the drug-traffickers—they're not nice people."

Trembling, she snapped, "Neither is Zabala, is he?" Tears trickled at the corners of her eyes. Falling like those drops from Petra's shower-head. "After I saw Petra, I contacted someone I'd met here on our fashion shoot."

He flung his arms in the air. "My God, your fashion shoots throw you into the company of some odd people!"

"There's nothing wrong with Howard and Gerard, they're—"

"I know, I know—they're great hosts, a lovely couple. But—"

"*But* nothing! What about the revolver in your office safe? What did you do with that when you left Ananke in a hurry?"

His features went blank for an eye-blink or two, and then he said, "Oh, of course, your safe-cracking escapade...after the seduction... You saw it."

"Seduction! Nothing happened then, and you know it!"

"I only have your word, Cathy!"

"I'm telling you the truth!"

He shrugged, as if doubting her statement. "When it suits you! I've seen you lie glibly at the drop of a fashionista's hat!"

"You're—you're changing the subject. What about the revolver? A Ruger GP 100."

"My God, you've got a good memory!"

"Chemists are known for that. Well?"

Rick gestured with his arms, spread his hands out: body-language telling her he meant no harm? "It was my father's. He got it from a client. He couldn't hand it in to the police, as it would incriminate the client. He confessed to me that he honestly didn't know what to do with it. I agreed to take it off his hands."

Did she believe that? "The Thames is big enough, surely?"

He pursed his lips, eyes shifting momentarily from hers, and then said, "Alright, I admit, it crossed my mind that I might have to use it if I got in deep with my Ananke investigation. So I kept it in the safe. But if I ever used it then it would only be to threaten…"

That sounded so lame! "Oh, so it's alright for you to consider using a gun to threaten the bad guys, but because I'm a woman it's not alright?"

"No, of course not!" He glared. "I didn't get a chance to empty my safe, as you know. It's probably still there."

"With your father's or your fingerprints on it, perhaps?"

He flushed, eyes darting; clearly, he hadn't considered that. "Perhaps…yes…"

"If Dante has used a locksmith to open your office safe, he'll have that gun. He could use it and even plant it as evidence against you."

"My God, Cathy, sometimes I think you really are paranoid!"

"Me, paranoid? Who got you out of that mine?

Who saved you from the clutches of Zabala? They're thoroughly nasty people who work for Dante, and you know it! They won't hesitate to shoot either of us."

"That may be so, Cathy, but I've never so much as fired a weapon before—what about you?"

"France isn't so anal about firearms. I mean in England, villains carry them, but the police don't? What kind of sense does that make? I spent a few weeks on a firing range in Paris before I went to Uni. I kept at it whenever I visited Papa. His gun was in the glove compartment—and quite legal... But it was damaged in the crash." She ended with a sob, an unwanted image of her dead father invading her consciousness.

He seemed to intercept her sudden mood-change. "I'm sorry I shouted." He crossed the floor and embraced her.

Fleetingly, she wondered if he wanted to get close as a ruse to snatch the weapon off her. No. She hated herself for thinking that. She felt his warmth and sensed sincerity in his words. They'd been through a great deal already. She trusted him. Christ, what was she thinking? She loved him.

His hands stroked her hair, sent tingles running over her flesh. "I know you're angry about your father's death, but I don't believe that anger and firearms mix."

"If we come across Zabala again," she mumbled against his chest, "I want to be ready."

He broke the embrace, held her at arms' length, and gazed into her eyes with concern. "Shooting at a static target on a firing range is a lot different to shooting at a person, I imagine."

"If that person's going to be shooting at me, or intent

on doing me or a loved one harm, I'll have no qualms, I assure you."

"Loved one..." He smiled fleetingly and his eyes shone with love. "Alright, I concede. Does it have a safety lever or something?"

"Of course." She showed him the catch at the rear, presently in the UP position.

"You know, I think we've almost had our first falling-out." He kissed her forehead. "Am I forgiven?"

She looked at him, grinned. "I'll sleep with this under the pillow, I think."

"As long as the safety's on."

"Puts a new meaning on 'safe sex', doesn't it?" she purred.

Chapter 6

Paraphrasing Mark Twain

On their way down to breakfast next morning, Rick held her upper arm, waylaid her. "I find it a bit odd, Howard and Gerard living here so openly, since I've read that homosexuality in Morocco is illegal."

"That's true, my love." She stopped on the stair, clasped his hand. "Tangier has been a mecca for gay artists long before they were called 'gay'—Truman Capote, Tennessee Williams, Joe Orton... Providing they don't exhibit in public, they're safe enough."

"Seems harsh, putting them in prison. I'm thinking of Oscar Wilde. That was bad then; I thought the twenty-first century was more enlightened."

"Fundamentalist religion can be harsh; some countries are far worse, barbaric even in their attitude. I think the authorities here turn a blind eye, paying lip-service only when they have to."

Rick shook his head. "I can't imagine either Gerard or Howard accepting a prison term."

"Who welcomes jail, Rick? We're potential candidates, since we're 'bending' the law. Oh, and it's also illegal for an unmarried couple to have sex."

His mouth dropped open. "Now she tells me!" Then he shuddered. "Let's go down."

Abdel, Gerard and Howard were already in the courtyard, seated at the table, the detritus of continental breakfast littering the white cloth. They were speaking but ceased in order to welcome the couple. Then Gerard poured their coffee.

"Sorry we were late," Cat said.

"Young wedded life is like that, I believe," Gerard said.

Rick flushed. "We interrupted your conversation," he observed, sipping his drink.

"Oh," Howard said, "we were talking about the health food plant. Abdel's enlightening the two of us, the sleeping directors."

"The wages are cheap." Abdel wiped his mouth with a napkin and hunched his shoulders dismissively. "But it is work."

"Well, Cat, what do you plan to do?" Howard asked, buttering a croissant.

Gerard moved his chair slightly apart from them and gripped a white pad. His pencil darting across the pristine surface as he sketched a side-view of Cat.

"I can't destroy the plant," she said. "That would be taking the jobs away from the workforce; there is so little available employment anyway—we've seen the desperate men snatching work from the mule women."

His mouth full of croissant, Howard nodded, licking a flake of pastry from his lips.

Lowering his pencil, Gerard said, "Ah, yes, but it's obscene, is it not? People of the west pay top dollar for health food produced right here where women go hungry to feed their kids?"

"It boosts your share price, though," Rick said, buttering toast.

"Yes, it does, young man," Howard riposted, "and Cathy's recent escapades have done the opposite for the entire Ananke global empire, I might add. The shares have tumbled almost continuously, worsening after each upset or revelation."

"Shouldn't the shares be localized to the affected plant?" Cat asked.

"You'd think so, wouldn't you? But share dealing isn't particularly logical, my dear. It is usually motivated by animal spirits."

"That's right," Rick said. "Keynes' view of economics—emotion, not logic, essentially. Logic says 'sit tight, it'll blow over' while animal spirits say 'sell, sell!'"

"Just so," Howard said. "Gerard, discussing the morality of modern manufacturing isn't going to help Cathy with her crusade."

"No, I didn't say it would help. But we owners should be more...more receptive to our workers' needs!"

Howard chuckled. "I never knew you had communist leanings, my dear!"

Abruptly, Rick snapped his fingers. "Ownership—that could be it!" Cat turned to him, puzzled. He grinned at her. "I have an idea. I was their company lawyer, after all!"

"You've lost me, I'm afraid," she said.

"Me, too," added Gerard, and resumed his sketching.

Rick stood up. He glanced at his watch. "The office

will be open now; London's in our time zone. Howard, can I use your phone?"

———

RICK TELEPHONED HIS SECRETARY, Mandy, hoping that she was still employed at the Ananke head office in London.

When she answered, he breathed a sigh of relief. "Hi, Mandy, it's Rick Barnes."

She let out a gasp. "My God, it's like speaking to someone from the dead! Where've you been? Rumors even spread about your death!"

"Rumors of my demise have been greatly exaggerated."

"Paraphrasing Mark Twain?"

"Oh, I thought I'd just said that."

"Enough of the joking around, Rick. You left very suddenly and we had no word. I had a visit from an odd couple, Pointer and Basset, asking about your address. I hope that was alright?"

Pointer! "You had no option but to give them the details, love."

"Good. You know, a few here have even suggested you were wanted by Interpol!"

No rumors, dear Mandy, but true! Still, he wouldn't alarm her concerning that. He had more important work to do. "Who's taken my job?"

"Lysander Stevens."

That little shit? Who authorized that, for God's sake? Stevens was malleable, though; he'd do anything he was told, and would agree that the world was flat if it meant getting a bonus. "Ah, I know him, competent enough," he lied.

"I wouldn't know. He won't trust me to do even the simplest thing. I'm his gopher without a brain, it seems to me!"

"I'm appalled to hear that, Mandy. And I'm sorry I couldn't explain my departure—it was rather sudden and traumatic."

"Oh?"

"I got married." One more lie wouldn't matter. He had the grace to blush, recalling his shouting bout with Cathy last night.

"She's a lucky woman, then." She paused, and he could picture her twirling the phone cable round her little finger, a habit she'd developed. "You didn't phone me to give me that good news, though, did you?"

"You know me too well! Do you still retain access to the files?"

"Yes, Lysander hasn't worked out that bit yet. What do you want to know?"

"You're comfortable with this, considering I'm no longer working for Mr. Dante?"

"Yes, of course. I don't think I'll be staying here much longer, unless Lysander has a brain transplant. So, shoot."

"Can you e-mail me the files on the Tangier plant? It was set up before I joined, I think."

"Yes, it was signed and sealed in October, 2007, not long before the crash."

"What a memory!" Again, he recalled with shame his argument with Cathy.

"Yeah, except Lysander doesn't acknowledge that I

have one, so long as I remember he wants two sugars in his coffee and one in his tea."

He spluttered at that. "The chauvinist swine!"

"Tell me about it." He heard her tapping on her keyboard.

"So, can you send me the details about the plant?"

"Yes, it'll be a pleasure. Anything else? I've just this minute flicked through the folder, and see Morocco shows two pdf files—Tangier and the other's Marrakesh. Do you want that as well?"

"Thanks. Appreciated. Marrakesh would be good, too."

Marrakesh

Zabala was scheduled to check on the latest secret discovery that would put the Welsh gold mine in the shade. He hoped also to come away with sufficient items to finance early retirement. And for that he hired a 4x4, a Mitsubishi Montero. He recalled that it was originally named Pajero, but since the vulgar meaning of the word "pajero" in Spanish means "wanker," it was altered for other markets. Even allowing for the space taken by two full 20-liter petrol cans, there was plenty of room for the contraband.

Dressed in camo pants and a khaki bush jacket, he drove out of the city, the climate control cold air at full blast, motoring in comfort along the P31 road.

Some fifty kilometers further on, the road crossed the bridge over the Oued Zat.

Then, soon, the road began to climb—passing a

profusion of oak trees. He drove through a small village and gradually the landscape on either side lost its green mantle.

He headed for the Tizi n' Tichka Pass.

Tangier

Howard, Gerard and Cat sat round the courtyard table. Rick had accessed his email account on Howard's computer and now tapped the two files Mandy had sent, which he'd printed from Howard's Epson machine. He felt free to reveal his plan since Abdel was away visiting relatives in the town.

He faced Howard and Gerard. "Although this is Dante's company, he had to take you both onboard plus Saleem Kamal and Ayad El Foukai, the company secretary."

"Yes..."

"Can you get in touch with the company secretary urgently, arrange an extraordinary meeting?"

"Why?"

"Vote Dante off the board of directors. It's been done before—the director who built the company is thrown out on his ear. Usually because of a vote of 'no confidence'." He eyed Cathy. "It's what Howard said about the share situation. It makes sense." He pointed to Howard. "The shares are on the Casablanca stock exchange, right?"

"Yes."

"And from what you're saying, they're falling, right?"

"Yes. Plummeting, actually."

"Buy up as many as you can—using Cat's purloined Ananke money. Added leverage."

"But this will take time to arrange," Gerard said.

"That's the legal way to go. And it'll hurt Dante when he finds out—and it'll be even worse for him in the business world when it's announced."

"Just out of interest," Gerard prompted, "what is the illegal way you were thinking of?"

"I can prepare documents to change ownership of the plant, a buy-out by the workforce, financed by you, Howard."

Howard slapped his hands together. "It's audacious, but I can't see that working. The paperwork couldn't be easily altered; it's filed in the registry office." His eyes sparkled as he rubbed his hands together. "It's a pity, because I love a good scam if the crook gets burned!"

Rick flicked the pages of the Tangier file. "I think we can hustle the CEO, Saleem, get him to vote off Dante."

"And you want me to buy these shares using the €500,000 cash you just happen to carry?"

Cat leaned forward. "You have the contacts and means, Howard. Neither of us could do it."

Chuckling, Howard slapped Gerard's back. "Isn't it simply beautiful, old friend?"

"Less of the 'old' Howard, if you please!" Gerard remonstrated good-humoredly.

"Apologies, dear chap. But it is so appealing, isn't it, to think Dante is being ousted in no small part by using his own money!"

"It is," Gerard replied soberly. "But I do wonder about the repercussions."

"Don't be a wet blanket, Gerard, I *want* to be involved!" Howard said. "I don't get this kind of rush often enough these days!"

"Oh, forgive me, I must try harder," Gerard simpered and glanced away.

Rick added, "Dante might not even notice he's being deposed—he has so many irons in the fire."

"Oh, he'll notice," warned Gerard. "You wait and see." His eyes brimmed with incipient tears. He stood. "Excuse me. I have to be somewhere else right now."

HOWARD ARRANGED a meeting with the company secretary and then led Cat and Rick to the Ananke health food production plant. His director status opened doors and within a few minutes they all stepped into the CEO's office and were greeted cordially.

Cat and Rick were introduced as Señor and Señora Moreno, "business associates." Saleem eyed them both, squinting. "Have we met before?" he asked in French.

"I don't think so, no," Cat said, smiling, glad that they'd both dyed their hair.

Saleem showed his teeth in an approximation of a smile and waved a hand. "No matter. I am honored to meet you both. Any friend of Monsieur Greenleaf is a friend of mine. What can I do for you, Monsieur Greenleaf?"

Howard delved into his battered leather briefcase. "Ayed El Foukai has drawn up a memorandum to convene an extraordinary meeting in twenty-eight days' time."

"An EGM?"

"Yes. I'm seeking to impeach Loup Dante and remove him from the board."

Saleem licked his lips. "Indeed?"

Howard placed the sheets on the CEO's desk. "I have the backing of Monsieurs Kominsky and El Foukai."

"Don't we need a replacement for Monsieur Dante?"

"No. As long as we have at least three directors, including the company secretary, we are within the law here."

When the deal was struck with Saleem, they returned to Howard's house.

Gerard was nowhere to be found.

Howard lifted his shoulders despondently. "He sometimes goes off in a sulk. He'll come round, I'm sure."

London

Basset rushed into Pointer's office. "Boss, one of our flags hit gold at GCHQ. There's been communication between Rick Barnes and his secretary in Ananke, London."

"Has there now? What's the gist of it?"

She sat opposite him. "Intercept report's on its way. They were talking business, surprisingly, mostly about Ananke operations in Tangier and Marrakesh."

"And where is Barnes now?"

"Tangier."

"What the hell does he want there? A sex-change op?"

"Sir, keep up, it's gender reassignment surgery. But no, it seems Ananke has a health food production plant there."

"By God, Dante certainly diversifies!"

"I think he goes where the money is—and there's money in health foods. And of course the government offers incentives."

"Yes and the labor's cheap." He ran a hand down his face; he was drawn, yet wearing his pain without complaint. "Have we alerted Interpol yet?"

"Yes, sir. A blue notice was raised on Barnes and Vibrissae."

"Good, good; let's hope they come back on that. Where's Dante right now?"

"In Shanghai."

"Doesn't he have any factories in cool, dark Scandinavian places?" he asked feelingly.

Basset shrugged sympathetically. "He seems to build business connections faster than my godson builds a house with Lego."

"Well, we can't go gallivanting halfway round the world chasing Dante, even though I suspect he's a bigger fish than Barnes. So, in the meantime, let's look closer to home—Barnes in Morocco. Is there an NCA agent close by?"

"No. We'd have to liaise direct with the Moroccan police."

"How's your Arabic?"

"Non-existent, sir, as you very well know. I can manage with Get-by French, I imagine."

He grinned. "Me, too, probably. Alright, book

flights to Morocco. I'll get authorization. I'd very much like to interview Mr. Barnes in Tangier."

"I'll start a conversation with the Interpol agent there; he's in Rabat, their capital; he'll have a direct line to the Moroccan police."

"Good. Tell him we'll fly direct to Tangier. Visas?"

"I'll make all the arrangements online, sir."

"Thanks, Sergeant. I don't know how I could cope without you."

"That's alright, sir. Remember to pack your sun-block, and plenty of it."

"It's always ready," he growled, "believe me."

High Atlas

Driving round the last bends of the Tizi-n-Tichka Pass, Zabala took in the scene ahead: every time he drove here, he was impressed by this view. The lunar land-scape of the Anti-Atlas stretched before him, and beyond was the desert, in stark contrast to the greenery he'd passed.

At that moment he was startled by the ring tone of his cell-phone. He braked, answered, while feasting his eyes on the stark vista.

'It's Abdi Ahmed, monsieur. You asked me to contact you."

His pulse raced. Could this be it? "You have news on Barnes and Vibrissae?"

"Yes. Two foreigners visited our CEO, Saleem. Their description is similar to the photographs, but their hair is different; she is blonde and his is no longer black, but more dark brown."

"That is good. Thank you, Abdi."

"And...there was a man with them..."

"Oh, do you know who?"

"I made enquiries, monsieur. He is one of our directors, a millionaire. His name is Howard Greenleaf."

At mention of Greenleaf's name, Zabala felt his skin crawl. He despised men like Greenleaf. Why the country tolerated people like that queer was beyond him; Islam was quite clear on the subject: Greenleaf was an abomination!

"Monsieur?"

"Ah, yes, I know Greenleaf. I must admit I am intrigued by his involvement with Barnes and Vibrissae." He shrugged. It could wait. The contraband beckoned. "Leave Greenleaf to me—at a later date I shall deal with him."

"As you wish. Shall I continue to keep an eye on Saleem, see what he does, learn where he goes, and who he sees?"

"Yes, do that. I can't come back to Tangier just now."

"What about the foreigners, Monsieur?"

"Put another man on them, give him my number."

"I know the ideal man—thorough and ruthless—his name is Jabra al-Rashid."

Zabala repeated the name, committed it to memory. "You have been invaluable so far, Abdi. Thank you." He quickly closed the call so he wouldn't have to hear the man's profuse thanks.

Chapter 7

Dirt of the World

Morocco

The driving distance from Tangier to Marrakesh was about six hundred kilometers. The route took them along the coast road for much of the way. Alternating driving chores, both Cat and Rick stuck to the speed limit; she'd told him about friends who had been stopped a number of times on a single road and given on-the-spot fines—anything from one hundred to three hundred Dirhams.

On two occasions they were halted at roadblocks and had to show their papers, but otherwise the journey was uneventful.

They pulled in at Rabat for a couple of hours to rest. Abdel was grateful to stretch his legs, though Cat was keen to get a move on.

Over lunch at Le Restaurant de la Plage that fittingly overlooked the beach, they discussed the Marrakesh file Mandy had sent.

"It isn't very helpful," Cat said.

"The notary Mohammed Hassan handles the money that comes in and goes out, according to these records. The Moulay Project, whatever that is."

"Moulay means ruler," Cat said. "You'll find that Moulay Ismail for example was one of Morocco's most successful—and blood-thirsty—sultans. He was a pal of Louis XIV, the Sun King."

"You never cease to amaze me." Rick grinned.

"I did some research last visit." She scrutinized the pages, running a finger down the financial columns. "Maybe the project relates to an ancient ruler?"

"It might have been a chieftain, perhaps?" Abdel suggested.

Cat jabbed her finger at the page. "Whatever the project's name, the money shown here seems to come from several sources. Miscellaneous machinery parts, mostly. Seafood, as well."

"Ghost companies, I guess, ghost individuals," Rick mused.

"This worries me greatly," Abdel said. "If they are doing something illegal, and if they are discovered, then the plant will be shut and all our workers will be laid off."

Cat shook her head. "Howard won't let that happen, Abdel. He'll make sure it becomes a legitimate company, doing what it says on the label."

Rick frowned. "But where's the money really coming from?"

Cat smiled at Rick. "That's why we need to talk to this notary employed by Ananke when we get there."

Marrakesh

Cat booked them into a small yet delightful hotel with wooden doors that soared high. A fountain murmured in the middle of a tiled courtyard; two galleries snaked above. She sensed the cool air from the water effect immediately. Roses twined out of huge silver vases, next to palm trees. They were escorted to the elevator and exited on the third floor, along a landing that overlooked the courtyard. Abdel was allocated the room next to theirs.

All three of them were weary after the long drive and, following a light meal, retired to bed early. Tomorrow, they'd tackle the notary.

Rick wasn't looking forward to that. He skimmed through his compact French language book for accountancy words and phrases; not that there were many in the slim volume. "Won't he get suspicious?" he asked Cat.

"I shouldn't think so. He's a notary, not an accountant." She grinned. "He's more like you, I suppose—deals in law, not flous."

"Flous?" He rubbed his eyes with the back of his hand.

"Moroccan for money. They call money 'dirt of the world, *wusakh d-dunya*.'"

"Oh, great, that's bound to come in really useful, I'm sure!" He yawned.

"Well, it's not far off the old English saying, 'Where there's muck, there's brass,' isn't it?"

He lowered the phrasebook. "My head's spinning like a coin. Can we pack in now?"

"Alright. Sleep tight." But he didn't answer, he was

already fast asleep, the phrasebook on his chest. She put the book on the bedside table and pulled the single sheet over him, and then switched out the light.

Tangier

Pointer and Basset flew with Royal Air Maroc from London Gatwick at 8pm. There was a layover of about ninety minutes at Casablanca, where Basset voiced her regret that she couldn't stay to tour the city. They finally arrived at Tangier's Ibn Battouta airport at 1:50am. It resembled most modern airport buildings, an architect's dream wrought in steel and glass. Quickly cleared through customs, they were not met by anyone as Pointer had emphasized that their visit was low-key. Basset led him straight to the Avis desk. The Interpol man had arranged for a car.

The night air was warm and clammy. Imposing dark shapes of palm trees cast shadows in the brightly lit area. They entered the parking lot and Basset opened a white Hyundai i10.

"At least the sun isn't out yet!" Pointer enthused.

"Make the most of it, sir."

Basset drove; nothing new there, she nearly always drove him. The car's air-con was most welcome. "If you can, grab some sleep, sir, though it's only about thirty minutes to the hotel."

Leaving the airport, she turned onto the N1, the Boulevard des Forces Armées, a dual carriageway that went in for roundabouts in a big way. Even this late, a few army trucks were in evidence, but none in force.

Eventually, the road became the Avenue Moulay Ismail as they hit the main city of Tangier, ville nouvelle.

Basset listened to her GPS and drove them to Boulevard Pasteur then pulled in at Hotel de Paris.

The reception foyer was quiet at this early hour, and their footsteps tended to echo. The receptionist spoke English which made registering much easier. They saw no need to trouble a bellhop and carried their own luggage.

As they let themselves into their separate rooms, Basset said, "The Ananke health food processing plant is close by. We'll pay them a visit first thing tomorrow, sir. Interpol has forewarned them we're coming."

"I'll look forward to it."

Pointer felt drained as he undressed and then cleaned his teeth. He should be used to being awake at these early hours—when the sun wasn't up. The surrounding silence was welcome. He didn't think he would get to sleep now. But he was wrong. As soon as he switched off the bedside light, he fell into a deep sleep.

Carol knocked on his door and he jerked awake. I was 7:30am and he was so groggy it was as if he'd only just fallen asleep. Shaking his head he got up and answered the door.

"I'll see you at breakfast in half an hour, sir," she said, smiling. She looked fresh and relaxed. Maybe he'd feel better after a shower.

"Right. See you then."

After a breakfast of croissants and honey, Pointer donned his white fedora, made sure his white shirt's sleeves were pulled down and fastened at his wrists, and it was buttoned to the throat. He also wore an old school tie. Sunscreen factor 50 liberally covered his hands and neck, the only exposed parts of flesh.

Basset wore a fawn lightweight flannel suit and black leather pumps.

They strolled the short distance to the modern glass building with its blue sign above the entrance: *Ananke Health Food Processing, S.A.*

The tall muscular plainclothes security man at the door asked for identification; in his left ear lodged a communications earpiece.

Pointer showed his ID and explained they were expected. The man spoke into his lapel microphone, bobbed his head a couple of times and then cleared them to go in.

At the desk the female receptionist welcomed him but seemed to ignore Basset and then escorted them both to the elevator and accompanied them to the second floor. They walked along a tiled corridor toward the rear of the building, turned left at the end and crossed an echoing gantry with glass walls. Below, the processing plant was a hive of industry as various boxes of products were transported to a doorway in the rear.

They were shown into the office of the Ananke CEO.

Kamal Saleem stood behind his desk, his bulging belly resting on the blotter, and stroked his thick black mustache, appraising them. Then he held out a hand. Beneath a hooked nose, his thick fleshy lips held amusement, while his dark glinting eyes remained cold.

Pointer shook his hand, which was slightly clammy, and introduced Basset. "Thank you for seeing us, Monsieur Saleem," he said in faltering French.

He noted the wall behind Saleem; two glossy

warning posters showing Catherine Vibrissae and Rick Barnes. Interesting.

As they all sat, Saleem said, "My pleasure, Detective Inspector, but I don't know how I can help you."

"We're interested in the whereabouts of a Mr. Barnes."

"I don't think I know him."

Basset pointed to the posters behind Saleem. "Mr. Rick Barnes."

Abruptly flustered, Saleem said, "Oh, that Barnes..."

"Yes." Pointer waited.

"Our head of security recently gave me those posters. He held the belief they were saboteurs."

"Really? Have you alerted the police?"

Saleem shrugged. "That is the province of our security head. I am sure he is in touch with the appropriate authorities."

"So you haven't seen Barnes and Vibrissae, then?"

Saleem's eyes shifted to his desk blotter, and then he said, "No." He got to his feet and turned, ripped the posters from the wall. "Our security head was mistaken. I simply forgot to remove these." He crumpled the sheets into a single ball and tossed it into his wastebasket.

Confusing messages. Basset glanced at her boss.

Pointer stood. "Sorry to have taken so much of your time, Monsieur Saleem. I'm sure you are a busy man."

Saleem grunted as he got to his feet, and then offered a placating smile. "I regret that I cannot be of any assistance."

On their way out, Basset said, "What do you make of Saleem, sir?"

"He may have seen and perhaps even talked to Barnes and Vibrissae. I can't fathom why he's being evasive."

"I thought I'd plug in my laptop when we get back to the hotel and check on e-mails."

"Yes, good idea, Carol. As for me, I'm curious about the Ananke head of security. Saleem was quick to discredit him, don't you think?"

"Yes, I do. Security people make me twitchy, too." She added, anxiety in her tone, "Your sun-block's holding up?"

"Yes. We're nearly there. Thank God it isn't far." Although they kept to the shaded side of the street, the heat of the day was mounting, and with it the intensity of the sun. He needed to be indoors before the UV rays penetrated his clothing and the sun-block.

As they entered the hotel foyer, Pointer removed his hat. "I'll stay in the bar and have a coffee. Then I'll retire for a few hours. Alright, Sergeant?"

"Yes, sir. I'll give you a knock for lunch." She collected her key and stepped into the elevator.

Pointer wondered how she always managed to catch an elevator; he usually missed it and had to wait. He went into the bar, put his hat on the counter and ordered a cortado. When it came, it wasn't as good as the Spanish coffees he'd enjoyed, but it hit the spot.

He was seriously concerned that they were wasting tax payers' money on this little jaunt. What threat did Barnes and Vibrissae pose to the UK? The fire in Wales was circumstantial, though Ananke and their lawyers tried to make a case out of it. The witness was suspect— particularly when that body was found in the sea.

Another Ananke employee who had met an untimely end.

He retrieved his hat and made for the elevator. He had to wait but eventually the doors opened for him and he was carried to his floor and exited. He used his key and opened the door and stared, dumbfounded.

A dark-haired man draped in a loose-fitting charcoal-gray cotton shirt and pants, his feet in sneakers, was rummaging in Pointer's suitcase. The man looked up and snarled. He swiveled round and raced to the balcony door, which was open.

Pointer launched himself across the room and his outstretched right hand grabbed hold of the man's shirt. The sleeve tore and came away in Pointer's hand. They both tumbled through the doorway and fell to the hard tiled balcony floor. Into blazing sunlight.

Searing heat burned Pointer's left hand—as his right was wrapped in the shirt sleeve. Pointer recoiled in agony, bashing his shoulder against the open balcony door. A pane shattered.

Sergeant Basset came out on the adjacent balcony. "Sir, what's the noise?"

As she saw the intruder, the man swung onto the balcony rail and swiftly dropped to the balcony below. He moved from balcony to balcony like a free runner. Within seconds, he was gone from sight.

Stumbling inside, Pointer nursed his burned hand. He reached the bed, riffled through his suitcase and found a plastic bottle containing golden liquid. Hastily, he opened the cap and dabbed some of the concoction on his hand. The pain instantly receded. The burn mark remained, but with that instant relief he was at peace.

Basset was banging on his door.

He forced himself off the bed and opened the door.

Anxiety lined her face. "The sun, sir, are you alright?"

"Yes, it's only a small burn. I'll have a few blisters—but at least the medicine has allayed the effects and stopped it spreading. I'll keep my hand, I think."

"Thank God." She thumbed at the balcony. "I got a good look at him. Maybe Interpol will know him?"

"I doubt it. He was probably just a common thief, saw his chance. I imagine he didn't expect me back so soon. Holiday-makers tend to leave their hotel rooms during the day and go about the town."

"Some holiday-makers we make!"

He forced a grin. "Let's give it a try, anyway, combine our memories and provide Interpol with a description. We might get lucky."

Basset sent to Interpol via Internet their description of the intruder.

Impressively, she received a response after only ten minutes: there was a positive ID: *Abdi Ahmed. Employee of Ananke Health Food Products, S.A.*

When Basset telephoned the plant, she learned that Ahmed hadn't come in for work today.

She hung up. "Now, why doesn't that surprise me?"

Marrakesh

Mohammed Hassan rose from behind his desk and offered a smile that appeared fake to Cat. He was immaculate in his white djellaba, his dark brows in stark contrast. "Mr. Barnes, why does Ananke send to me the company lawyer?" he enquired in French.

Direct, to the point, unlike most Moroccan men, Cat mused. She noticed that Hassan squinted at the telephone, as if expecting a call. Unless he was suddenly anxious to make one?

Rick had introduced her as his wife and acting secretary, Cathy, and Abdel as his local interpreter. It was a calculated risk, but he had to use his real name to gain access to Hassan.

"Your latest money transfer has come to my notice," Rick said. They'd agreed there'd be no niceties from him, since he was supposed to be speaking from a position of authority.

As soon as all three of them had entered the notary's office, Cat detected bad vibes. Whether free climbing, fighting a taekwondo opponent, or even walking the fashion runway, at times she sensed something amiss, and she was rarely wrong; an insecure hold on the rock, an ill-judged blow, a badly designed hem that caused a misstep.

Although wary, she stayed in the background as agreed and let Rick do the talking, backed-up by Abdel if necessary. Apparently, his French was up to par, at least. The more he spoke, the more his confidence with the language increased. Abdel hardly had to intercede with any explanation.

Hassan stared. "You know about...? I mean, what money transfer?"

Abdel said, "Monsieur Moreno will ask the questions."

"Of course. Please sit." He cast a glance at Cat, his gaze running from her face down her body, the eyes narrowing as he noted her elegant cotton pants. "All of you." His tone contained a tremor that betrayed anxiety. He fleetingly eyed the telephone again.

Two chairs were already in front of Hassan's desk; Rick and Abdel took them; Cat sat on a spare by the door, attempting to appear as the dutiful but silent secretary.

"An audit is due at headquarters," Rick explained. "Naturally, I must ensure that nothing untoward will be found in the accounts."

"I thought you were the company lawyer," Hassan countered.

"If we're in line for any fiscal fine, I'd be derelict in my duty if I hadn't prepared a brief, Monsieur Hassan. It is my concern that nobody has in fact been derelict in their duty here. Do I make myself clear?"

"Yes...of—of course."

"I have the authority to hire or fire staff."

"That...this is a great responsibility, Monsieur Barnes."

"Quite." Rick glanced over his shoulder at Cat, raised an eyebrow.

She nodded encouragingly. Come on, Rick! He must dig for information about the money transfers.

Hassan's face seemed pale now, yet his brow appeared moist with sweat.

She'd known a few notaries in her time, and this one was unlike any of them. They were calm, confident people, almost staid, and never exhibited distress or concern. They knew their business. Yet Hassan was chary of speaking, and stumbled over his words, which was odd, since notaries used words every day to seal deals and confirm bargains.

She noted the windows, the door and, following Chuck's dictum, studied the office with care. Behind Hassan and his desk was a beaded curtain; as it was an outside wall, she guessed it covered a door onto the balcony she'd scoped on arrival; she'd noted opaque glass set in the metal door frame which was in need of paint.

Behind them, on the right of the entrance door were two filing cabinets. On the left was a table with a photocopier, an inkjet printer, and a coffee percolator. She kept coming back to Hassan and that telephone, which continued to hold his attention rather more than Rick.

Worse, Rick was floundering, and now gestured vaguely. "The money transfer I'm alluding to has to do with the—"

"Sir," Cat interrupted, "I'm sorry, but you're running late. I suggest you continue this discussion tomorrow, perhaps. Cazador is waiting."

Rick turned to her, squinted, unsure. "Cazador?"

"He has a pre-arranged appointment, sir." She checked her watch. "We have ten minutes to get there."

Her use of Leon Cazador's name must have rung alarm bells, because Rick played it just right, apologizing for taking up Hassan's time. "I'm sure it is a minor accounting issue," he stated, "nothing to be worried about."

Seemingly bemused, Hassan stood and they shook hands. He bobbed his head politely to Abdel, and bowed to Cat. "Perhaps next time you will allow more time for your visit?"

He was so forthright he bordered on rudeness, Cat thought.

"Yes," Rick said, standing. "It's my fault entirely. Sorry."

"There is nothing to apologize for, Mr. Barnes."

As they opened the door to leave, Cat glanced back. The notary reached for his phone.

"Let's go," she whispered. "He suspects us."

Chapter 8

Catsuit

Moulay Project, High Atlas Mountains

Zabala idly watched three Berber women sitting at an adjacent table, busily wrapping silver ornaments in bubble-wrap and placing them carefully in wooden crates at their feet. Then his cellphone rang. It was Jabra al-Rashid. "Yes?"

"I spotted Barnes and Vibrissae visiting Hassan at his office."

"I know," Zabala replied. "Hassan phoned to let me know. They left in a hurry for another appointment."

"Well, they didn't keep any appointment. They went straight to their hotel. What do you want me to do?"

"Good. Find out what you can about them. If possible, learn their plans."

"I will do that without difficulty, I am sure. I presume they are expendable?"

"No! For now, keep them alive."

"That is disappointing."

"They might be valuable to me. I might ask you to abduct them soon."

"I would like that. In the meantime, I will see what I can discover about them." Jabra al-Rashid closed the call.

Zabala smirked. The fools! They shouldn't have blithely walked into Hassan's office like that. When the time was right, he wanted to capture them and offer them as a present to Loup Dante. Or at least the Vibrissae woman. He wasn't too sure Mr. Dante had any interest in Barnes; that suited just fine, as he had a score to settle with the interfering lawyer.

Marrakesh

On their way to their hotel, Cat, Rick and Abdel passed several shadowy alleys: in one a barber worked, his customer ensconced in a plastic chair in front of an old fly-blown mirror suspended from a hook in the stone wall. They strolled past an open doorway where a man squatted on the step, a pile of detritus from the modern world displayed on a thin linen sheet. Cat abruptly stopped and studied the items: a pair of Jimmy Choos, but only one with a heel; a variety of rusty metal springs; a wall clock with its numbers faded; brass monkeys and plates; and a tarnished bicycle bell. With a mixture of French and hand gestures, Cat enquired about the bell. The man hedged, shrugged, set a price, they quibbled, and finally settled on a figure. She paid him the coins and he wrapped the bell in a few glossy pages of an old Spanish magazine.

As they moved on, Abdel said, "Is the bell a special gift, Cathy?"

"No."

"Then why'd you buy it?" Rick said.

"I've seen men and women like him at so many flea markets. I wonder if they ever sell any of their stuff."

"Probably not," Rick said. "It's rubbish, most of it unusable."

"Those items of rubbish signify hope in the seller. One day, somebody will find something they want—and he will supply it."

"I suppose."

"I think he would rather sell something than accept charity. That way, he saves face and we both close the transaction satisfied."

"That is probably so, Cathy," Abdel said. "Though beggars are everywhere."

"Indeed they are, even in England."

"Less inclined to hustle, I think," Rick said.

"Depends where you go." Cat halted in front of a clothing shop. "Just what I need!" She asked Abdel to go into the shop and buy her a black djellaba. "Do you have one?" she enquired.

"Yes, Cathy, though I only wear it when visiting family and friends—never while on business. I am proud of my country's dress, but must appear western-ized as a journalist."

Cat smiled agreement. Abdel always seemed anxious to present himself in a good light, she noticed. His honor was at stake, after all. For himself and his family. She'd learned on her earlier visit that a Moroccan's most cherished possession was his personal honor and dignity, and that of his family. The concept of *hshuma* or shame was very destructive.

While Abdel conducted his purchase—she was as tall as him, so the measurements were not a difficulty—Rick stood impatiently outside with her, pacing. "Why do you want to wear one of those?"

"It's merely an idea—considering we had to leave the notary in such a hurry." A convoy of tuk-tuks motored by, half motorbike, half-mini-cum-pickups with big grilles, and deafened them both. "I'll explain in our room."

"You're doing that again, talking in riddles!"

"Life is one big puzzle, don't you find?"

Abdel joined them, carrying a brown paper parcel, tied with string.

"Let's get back to the hotel," Rick said. "It seems the day's been a total loss!"

He sounded quite exasperated. Doubtless she had caused that, Cat mused. Maybe she could make it up to him—afterwards.

THAT NIGHT, after their meal and against Rick's arguments, Cat insisted she must break into the notary's office. She had dressed in a black tight-fitting catsuit and now fastened a belt with four pouches, and then strapped on a black backpack over her shoulders.

"This is madness, Cathy. If you're caught breaking in, you could be shot. The Moroccan police are armed."

She patted her backpack. "That's a specious argument and you know it. They're armed in France and

Spain, too, but you made no objection in Nice and Barcelona. Anyway, I'm armed as well."

"Oh, for God's sake, this is plain stupid. If you're caught with an illegal firearm they'll shove you in jail and throw away the key!"

"I won't get caught. I studied the building while we were there. It's straight-forward, I assure you."

"What about alarms?"

"Hassan didn't have any."

"Unless they're hidden!"

"Alarms are a deterrent, Rick. If they had them, they'd let potential burglars know."

"But you can't go alone!"

"I'll take Abdel—he can speak for me if we're accosted." She donned the black djellaba, pulled up the hood.

A triple knock on their door sounded. "That's Abdel. Let him in, will you?"

Morosely, Rick strode to the door and opened it.

Abdel stood in the corridor dressed in his dark gray djellaba.

"Abdel," Rick demanded, "are you happy to accompany Cathy?"

Abdel grinned. "I'm honored, Rick. This is an adventure, is it not?"

Rick flung out his hands in despair. "I give up!"

Cat pocketed her cell-phone. "I'll call you when I'm inside. And again when I get out."

"Alright. And don't go finding any more dead bodies!"

"Dead bodies?" Abdel queried, his eyes showing concern.

"It's a long story, Abdel," Rick said.

"There was only one," Cat added, "and it was another time, another continent."

___

Tangier

A folder under her arm, Basset knocked on Pointer's hotel room door. He opened it and she stepped in. "Sir, the *Sûreté nationale* have been in touch. They have Abdi Ahmed in custody."

Sûreté nationale—Moroccan police. He beamed. "Take a seat."

She sat on the bed and he took a chair opposite her.

"That's good news, Carol."

She rested the folder on her lap. "He is unwilling to talk."

"That's not surprising. But you have more to tell me," he goaded.

"You know me too well, sir. However, Abdi Ahmed was in possession of a cell-phone and from this they've discovered that one of his most recent calls was to someone named Zabala."

"And can they get a fix on Zabala's whereabouts?"

"Yes. They're working on it now. It won't take them long."

"Zabala. You know, that name rings a bell."

"It does, indeed." She rooted in her file and dug out a sheaf of Ananke staff documents, which she handed to him. "He's their head of security."

"Is he now? It gets more interesting."

Basset's cell-phone rang. She answered it, listened and then said "*Merci*" and closed the call.

"That was the police again. They confirm that Zabala is in the High Atlas Mountains."

"Good work on their part. Can we fly there?"

She produced the *Guide to Morocco* from the folder, flipped its pages. "There's an airport at Ouarzazate, which is near to the spot they've pinpointed." She nodded. "A flight can be arranged."

Pointer rubbed his hands together. "Good. Thank you, Carol. Please make it so."

Marrakesh

Cat and Abdel strolled down the dark street. Earlier she'd noticed an abundance of stray cats, and now there seemed even more. To left and right alleys and side-streets loomed, poorly lit. From a window, a radio blared with the song "Maghlouba" by Samira Said. From several houses came the trill of canaries or the raucous noise of parakeets. As they passed the occasional empty premises, guard dogs barked; dogs were kept for security, not as pets.

The lighting on rooftops and at corners tended to reflect the red of the stonework. People milled around, murmured voices rising into a persistent hubbub. As they both wore robes and were therefore not tourists, nobody pestered them with goods or services to sell.

Soon, the noise drifted away and they came upon the building that housed the notary Hassan's office. It was on the corner of an adjoining alley, a quiet section of the town.

No lights showed in any window of the structure;

which wasn't surprising. On her way up the access staircase, she'd noted that every door on the landings was accompanied by a brass business plaque. Unlike European and North American office blocks, here they switched off lights when the workers went home.

Cat removed her cell-phone from her djellaba, then divested herself of the garment and gave it to Abdel. "Stay here. I won't be long." She pocketed the phone, studied a wooden pole where thin black wires and thick cables snaked upwards—phone and electricity lines, no doubt. Above her head were metal foot-holds. She backed away, ran at the pole and jumped, gripping hold of the rough surface. She clasped the next foot-rest and soon her soles were on the lowest metal rung and after that it was easy climbing.

Below and behind her, Abdel exclaimed something. It sounded like he called upon Allah.

She climbed the pole, careful to avoid snagging her clothing on protruding nails and clips.

When she was level with the second floor, she glanced to her left. She smiled, pleased it was as she remembered from earlier: a small balcony beckoned, a little wider than the door that opened onto it. She leaped the short distance and grabbed the metal safety rails. Rough and rusty, but they were solid—thank God! She hadn't considered the state of them, she realized belatedly. So much for planning ahead.

Briefly suspended, she hauled herself up and over the rail and landed soundlessly on the tiled floor of the balcony. She brushed her hands together to dislodge gritty rust.

From a pouch on her left hip she extracted a special penknife recommended by Chuck. It didn't take much wiggling to crack the lock of the door with the opaque glass. Gingerly, she opened it and swept aside the bead curtain. It was a little strange, being offered a different perspective of the office she'd been in. A mixture of tobacco and spice lingered in the room; she hadn't noticed that before, probably too intent on the anxious Hassan. She closed the door, let the beads fall back into place with a clacking sound.

She fished out the cell-phone from her pocket, activated its torch and gave the room a quick once-over. Then she speed-dialed Rick.

He answered at once.

"I'm in," she told him. "No problems." She was tempted to say "And no bodies" but refrained.

"Alright," he replied. "Take care."

"I will." She switched off the light and closed the phone, pocketed it and then scanned the shadowy office. She could remember where everything was and edged round the desk and negotiated the floor area with ease.

When she reached the filing cabinets next to the door, she took a pen-torch from a right-hand pouch. The locks were basic, quite familiar after Chuck's intensive sessions, and soon clicked. Sliding the top drawer open, she clamped the torch between her teeth and searched the files.

Sod's law: it was the second filing cabinet that held what she was seeking. Two files, labeled *Moulay* offered some information, though not a great deal. At least there was a map leading to the site of the project. She removed the files and crossed over to the photocopier.

She switched on the machine, waited for it to warm up, and copied the relevant sheets.

Once she'd replaced the files, restocked the printer's paper-tray, and locked the cabinets, she checked Hassan's desk drawers. Among a sheaf of legal papers were two posters, photographs of her and Rick, with their real names, not their aliases.

THE HOTEL ELEVATOR doors opened on their floor. Both still wearing djellabas, Cat and Abdel stepped out. Suddenly, they were pushed aside as the doors began closing. The man squeezed into the elevator car and the doors shut.

"He dropped something," Abdel said, pointing.

On the floor was a British passport. She knelt, opened it. Her stomach churned. It was hers, in the name of Vibrissae. Her Spanish passport in the name of Moreno was in her belt pouch. She glanced at the elevator indicator but it had already stopped at the ground floor. Whoever the man was, he'd be long gone before she could get down there.

Rick!

Her mouth dry, she raced to their room, knocked but there was no answer. Stupid! She delved in the voluminous folds of her djellaba and got the key from her pouch, opened the door.

Clothes were strewn all about the room. Rick lay on the floor, groaning. Thank God he was alive!

Abdel helped Rick rise and sit on the armchair by the bed.

The room had been searched, the drawers tipped out, their clothing in disarray. The wall safe had been forced; she knelt and checked inside. The thief had stolen their British passports, but in his haste had dropped hers. Oh, hell, the files Mandy had sent were gone, too. Most of the cash in Dirhams was missing, as well, but not the credit cards.

"Rick, where do you keep your Spanish passport?"

He tapped the back pocket of his pants, grinned. "It's here, with my wallet."

She released a sigh. "Our intruder wasn't a normal thief, then. He was here for a reason, and it wasn't financial gain."

"I don't like the sound of that." Rick gingerly rubbed a hand over his head and nursed his jaw and the base of his skull. Blood trickled between his fingers.

She got up and moved toward her, but he waved her away. "It'll be alright. I think I'm getting used to this." He managed a grin and her heart went out to him.

"We shouldn't have left you alone."

"Hey, I'm a grown-up, you know. He knocked on the door, said he was room service. I opened the door and before I knew it, he'd shoved me back, and clobbered me with something hard and painful." He pursed his lips, rueful, and gestured at the chaos of the room. "I was out cold while he made all this mess."

Moulay Project, High Atlas Mountains

In the shade of an awning on the right of the cave mouth, Zabala brushed dust from his bush jacket. He answered his cell-phone immediately as the caller was Jabra al-Rashid. "You have news for me?"

"I have, Sidi Zabala. I have obtained papers and a

passport from the pair you are interested in. I do not know what the papers say, but printed on them is an Ananke logo and the lettering of 'Moulay', the same as on the site sign. And the passport is for the Englishman."

"That's good, Jabra al-Rashid. You have done well. Join me at the Moulay Project site."

"You no longer wish me to follow them?"

"No. I have a strong suspicion that they will come here."

"Very well. I will leave immediately."

Zabala closed his phone and chuckled. The redoubtable Catherine Vibrissae would be unable to resist coming here. Stupid woman!

Chapter 9

Crusading Cat

Marrakesh

Abdel sat quietly eyeing them as they both sipped orange juice from the fridge. She told Rick about the posters in Hassan's desk drawer, and added, "You can't use your company lawyer pitch anymore."

"Well, without my passport, that's a no-brainer, I guess. I'm just glad you insisted we carry our Spanish passports at all times."

"Prudence pays."

"She must be rich, no?"

"Not funny, Rick. What it means is that in future I'll have to break into any Ananke office if we need to learn anything."

"In future? I don't think so. Morocco is going to be our last try to get even with Dante. After this, I think we should both retire from the crusading business..."

Crusading cat? She liked that. "Dante still has a lot of businesses worldwide."

"So? They can't all be shady. Some have to be legit. You said yourself, we want to hurt him, not innocent workers."

"The finance is suspect, at least. And, besides, the bastard had my father killed—probably employing Zabala! And don't forget your brother-in-law David's death..."

"Okay, okay. I know there's a saying that revenge is best served cold—after contemplation, perhaps. But there's another saying, you know—Chinese, I think—Be careful what you wish for."

"I wish for the death of Zabala and Dante. Is that clear?"

She glanced at Abdel. His face had turned pale. She remembered his daughter Sheera, her trusting eyes. "Abdel, tomorrow, we'll go to the bank and withdraw the money we owe you. You should then make your way to Tangier—or home."

"No, no, I promised to be your translator. I made a promise."

"I no longer hold you to it." She held his hand. "This is too dangerous. You have a family to think about."

"Shouldn't we go home, too?" Rick asked, rubbing his head. "It's dangerous for us as well, you know."

She eyed him and he winked. "Very well," she said. By pretending to give up on their vendetta, they would save face for Abdel. That *hshuma* concept again. What was that Moroccan proverb? "Praise your friend in public but reprimand him in private." Once they had parted, she and Rick would continue as before, hoping they could rely on his command of French when addressing Moroccan men.

JABRA AL-RASHID SOFTENED a small piece of hash over the flame, crumbled it and carefully rolled it into a cigarette with a mixture of black tobacco. He had earned this. He lit the end and smoked the jwan with great pleasure. One would suffice, for he believed that the intoxicant endowed him with cunning. Too much at one time, he knew, and he became a fool.

Yes, before he set out for the High Atlas, he must obtain photocopies of all the documents he'd stolen. Those copies might be valuable to other men, so he would keep them safe, together with the details he'd gleaned from the hotel.

He had no intention of informing Sidi Zabala what he discovered from the hotel register, either. The names didn't tally with those that Sidi Zabala mentioned: Catarina Moreno, Ricardo Moreno, and Abdelfettah Malik. That information was a bargaining chip to be saved for a later transaction. Never keep all snakes in one basket, eh?

He chuckled.

As he smoked the last of the jwan, he prepared to visit his cousin Jamal and obtain those photocopies. Then he must be on his way to the Moulay Project site.

He estimated the journey would take about four hours, maybe longer, since he was driving at night. Still, the effort was worth it, as Zabala promised to pay well.

IN THE EARLY HOURS, Cat was awoken by her cellphone ringing. Sleepily, she answered it. First light percolated through the window jalousies. And with it the muezzin announced the dawn prayer, *Soobh Fegr*: *"God is good..."*

It was Leon Cazador. "Sorry to phone so late. Sounds like it's dawn there."

"Yes, it is. The call to prayer. What is it, Leon?"

"I've discovered something you both really need to know."

"God is good..."

"Oh?" she said, sitting up straight. She could detect seriousness in his tone.

Drowsily, Rick turned toward her, blinked and rubbed his eyes.

"It's Leon," she whispered." She said into the phone, "What do we need to know?"

"One of my contacts tells me that Interpol has a blue notice issued on you and Rick."

"Blue notice? What the hell is that? Nothing saucy, I imagine. Just so you know, I don't download my nude images to the cloud..."

Leon chuckled. "No, I never took you for a foolish celebrity. Interpol has different colors depending on the seriousness of the request. Blue is raised when it's necessary to locate, identify or obtain information on a person of interest in a criminal investigation."

Person of interest. That sounded ominous.

Rick sat up, very curious now.

"Come to prayer..."

"Sleep's out of the question now anyway," she said and switched the phone to speaker. "I'm on speaker. Rick's listening now."

"Good morning, Rick."

Rick groaned. "Hi, Leon."

"Come to prayer..."

She asked, "Are we of interest in a criminal investigation, then?"

"You know you are. I told you about DI Pointer already. That Welsh mine fire, remember?"

"But it was a stitch-up!"

"I know that. But Pointer doesn't. He's spreading his net, hoping to catch you and Rick in it. I don't know; he may have another agenda entirely. Whatever, take care, Cathy. You're not trained for this kind of thing. Being a fugitive from justice isn't fun. I really think you should call it a day."

Rick gave a crisp nod and mouthed, *I told you so.*

"Prayer is better than sleep..."

"Thanks for the advice, Leon. But no, I can't. My father—"

"Your father's dead, Cathy," Leon said firmly. "Don't go on some hopeless crusade and end up joining him."

"That's blunt, Leon," she said. "Very."

"Put bluntly, I like you. And I don't want to have to avenge your death. I assure you, I've seen enough death to last me two lifetimes."

She shuddered. "You don't pull any punches, do you?"

"Only on the dojo mat, Cathy—nowhere else."

"Prayer is better than sleep..."

"Thanks for the warning, anyway. Rick's nodding away. He tends to agree with you."

"Sensible of him." Leon sighed. "You're obviously going to ignore me, so all I can do is say *tread carefully*."

"Thanks. I will. I promise."

"I'll hold you to that." The call went dead.

But the muezzin continued unabated: *"Allah is greatest..."*

OUTSIDE THE CITY WALLS, they drove bleary-eyed past the scrubby patch of waste-ground where taxis, donkeys and minibuses congregated. The High Atlas Mountains were visible, a dim blue-gray a couple of hours away. Through the rear-view mirror Cat glimpsed the red stone city walls and the dominating minaret of the Koutoubia mosque, all receding. It felt odd, not to see Abdel in the back. She hoped he got off alright. After stopping by the ATM for money, they'd left him on the station platform waiting for the 9:30 train.

Rick offered directions when necessary using the photocopy of the map Cat had taken from the notary's papers. He didn't have much to do for the most part, as their route was along the N9.

This road crossed the river Ourika, and later the Zatt, both wadis at this time of year, and climbed from the semi-arid plains that surround Marrakesh through the zig-zag bends, with the foothills of the mountains on their horizon. The car's suspension complained occasionally.

Rick expressed surprise at seeing so much greenery amidst the rugged red, russet and brown fissures and crags, many slopes covered in thousands of oleander trees.

They passed through hamlets of one-story flat-roofed houses constructed of mud and stone, plastered with dull pink or adobe or white paint, dominated by minarets. She glimpsed the occasional shepherdess in scarlet hat, white top and red knickerbocker leggings, tending her flock.

Often, on either side of Tizi-n-Tichka pass were the steep walls of a deep canyon, and the road climbed and climbed, with enough hairpin bends to turn hair white. The road tended to double back at times, and each bend seemed to offer more spectacular views of rugged peaks.

They stopped briefly at the Tichka café, "altitude 2260 meters," sign said, complete with crumbling walls and delicious strong coffee and bread smeared with honey.

For a while they followed in the suffocating blue exhaust vapor of a local bus crammed with passengers, assorted luggage and a couple of sheep; happily, they passed it at a wide section, horns honking from both vehicles.

They'd been driving four hours, with stops.

As they passed the small town of Tadoula Zenifi, she gestured to their left. "A few kilometers over the hills is Ait-Benhaddou, an ancient fortified city. We did a fashion shoot there—using it as a backdrop for many of the shots."

"A long drive for not many photos!"

She grinned. "We flew into Ouarzazate, which isn't so far from the fortress, and then flew by helicopter to the site of the shoot. It's a huge tourist spot—you'll probably recognize it from a number of movies—even *Gladiator*; I think it was meant to be Zucchabar."

"Oh, I remember. I should have realized about the

airport. You've certainly led an exciting—dare I say, exotic—life."

"It has had its moments. A lot of the time it isn't glamorous, merely tedious, with long hours of boredom."

"And fine clothes?"

"Sometimes. At other times, very outlandish garments I wouldn't be seen dead in!"

Moulay Project, High Atlas Mountains

In the shade of the awning Zabala impaled a date with his knife; he always thought they resembled dead cockroaches. He lifted it to his mouth. The table was laden with jugs of iced water, dishes of lamb with artichoke hearts, and *pain au chocolat* that tended to turn gooey.

Opposite him, on the other side of the table, stood Jabra al-Rashid, nervously fidgeting with the envelope that contained his payment. Clearly, he wanted to leave, no doubt to count his money.

"You did well to get to me so quickly," Zabala said in French. These Moroccans thrived on praise. And it did no harm, especially if he wanted to use the man again. He wafted the papers and British passport in front of his face, causing a slight cooling draft.

"I know the road, fortunately, even in the dark, Sidi Zabala. I don't think the pair will be far behind me, though."

"I agree." He gestured at the table. "Before you go, have some food and water. You've earned it."

"You are most generous. Thank you."

Zabala eyed three Berber women sitting at an adjacent table, busily cleaning silver and gold ornaments and marble plaques. "Eat, you must eat also," he told them, gesturing at the table.

The women understood his French, he knew, but they only nodded and went back to work.

They'd eat and drink if Allah wills or when they felt the need, he supposed.

God, he despised these people. They were so laid back, willing to let God provide. They couldn't escape what they called *maktoub*, what was written for you. As far as he was concerned it was an excuse to be lazy, to stifle curiosity and impede innovation. Their future, from a fatalistic point of view, was highly conditional; unknown. *In sha' Allah*—if Allah wills. And that also encompassed superstition. Before he could get the drivers and these women to work here, they had to fight off the djinns. He had to hire an expensive exorcist to read verses from the Koran. As extra insurance, the djinns were dismissed with expensive Moroccan incense.

Jabra grabbed a chunk of bread but didn't linger, rushed to his car and drove off.

Zabala strode out into the oppressive heat and hollered to two men at the side of the cave entrance. "Barrou, Oundir, come with me—and bring your weapons!"

Obediently, the two men grabbed their rifles and hurried over to Zabala. "Is there a problem?" Barrou asked. His complexion was leathery and he had a black patch covering his left eye; he'd said it helped him aim his rifle better. His single eye shone bright ebony. He had a bullet-shaped bald head and a bull neck, a square-cut beard and no mustache.

"Not quite." Zabala sheathed his knife. "I need your expertise. I'm expecting two foreigners—intruders."

"What do they look like?" Oundir asked. His complexion was teakwood, the eyes a raisin color. He was ruggedly handsome, clean-shaven, with a square jaw; he gripped a narrow pipe between big teeth, puffing on kif. Zabala hated the smell of cannabis of any kind. Of the two, Oundir seemed the fighter, wiry and lean, with a bent nose and long black stringy hair, while Barrou was perhaps the thinker of the team.

"They are intruders, strangers, we don't need to know more than that," Barrou countered.

"No," Zabala interceded. "Oundir has a point. We don't want to upset an unsuspecting tourist who has become lost." Zabala chuckled and then dug inside his jacket and withdrew two folded sheets, and gave them the posters. "They may have changed their appearance a little, but you should be able to identify them from these."

Barrou tapped a finger at the side of his eye. "We will target them easily with these IDs."

"I want them taken alive."

Oundir twisted his face in disappointment.

"Alive?" Barrou hefted his rifle. "That will be difficult."

"I didn't say they had to be unharmed—just alive."

Oundir grinned, and eyed Barrou. "If our aim is misplaced, effendi?"

"Then you won't get the bonus I'm about to offer."

"Bonus?" Oundir said.

"Five thousand Dirham."

"Each?"

"Of course."

"We will make sure we don't kill them."

"I'm glad to hear it. Bring them straight to me when you have them. Alright?"

Chapter 10

Fuller's Earth

High Atlas Mountains

Cat stuck to the modern road that led to Ouarzazate, which wasn't difficult; it was the only road of note, while Rick attempted to read the map.

Finally, when they came to a turn on the right, Rick exclaimed, "That's it, take this road!"

She slewed the vehicle onto a rough track rutted hard with the passage of trucks. They bounced along a little but she didn't decelerate, kept right on.

A sign in Arabic and English stated, *Moulay Project for Ananke. No admission without a pass.*

"Didn't you see that sign?" Rick asked as she drove past it.

"What sign?"

The vehicle jounced on the hard uneven surface.

"Oh, I don't like this!" Rick shouted. "It's Wales all over again!"

"No, it isn't. The sun's shining." Cat found a turn-off on the right and motored through a cleft that offered concealment for their vehicle.

She braked and while the engine cooled, the metal making odd clinking noises as it contracted, she said, "Nearby is the town of Taliouine, famous for saffron and almonds."

"I don't think I'm in the mood for a tourist talk right now, Cathy." He half-turned in his seat, thumbed out the back window. "This is private property—and it belongs to Ananke!"

"I doubt it. Probably belongs to the king. It may be leased." Her stomach rumbled. "Let's have a bite to eat, and then we can go and learn what they're doing here."

"You're so single-minded!"

She grinned. "I think that's a compliment." She opened the door and they were hit by a wall of suffocating heat.

She bit into a Mars bar before it melted; it would provide energy.

Then she took a swig from the small still water bottle and licked her lips. She could still go back. Call it a day. She'd hurt Dante financially. That was enough, surely? No, it wasn't. He must pay.

She glanced at Rick. Was it fair to involve him, though? Maybe she should have sent him back with Abdel.

She popped the rear of the vehicle and lifted her backpack, and then took the Astra A50 automatic from her trouser pocket and checked the rounds; seven loaded; she then placed it in the pack's net webbing, where it was reasonably easy to grab. Water bottles. Hat. All set.

It was so silent here, their footsteps on stone sounded unnaturally loud.

Rick took out his backpack. "We can't just walk in, you know."

She pointed at the rugged rock face on their right. "We're going up there. I'd hope to see what's going on from a good height."

"Yes, I can see that. You don't mind heights. I'm no rock-climber and I'm not keen on heights either."

"You can always stay with the car."

"What, and miss all the fun?" He gave her a lop-sided smile. "No, I'll try to keep up."

Ouarzazate

As they were escorted through the air terminal, Basset listened to her cell-phone, nodding. She closed the call when they were met by a plainclothes man in his thirties who introduced himself as Lieutenant Aziz Basri, Special Administrative Force of the Royal Gendarmerie. "I have a GPS fix for your suspect's cell-phone," he said as he shook Pointer's hand. He was medium height, slightly shorter than Pointer, with a lightly tanned complexion, an aquiline nose and a thin black mustache and slicked back hair that covered the tops of his ears. His fawn-colored suit was lightweight and tailored; even so, Pointer believed he detected a small bulge on the left.

"Thank you for coming to help us at such short notice," Pointer said.

"We are only too happy to oblige London," Basri

said, smiling, his dark eyes dancing. "I have a vehicle waiting."

"I'm pleased you speak English," Pointer said. "My sergeant and I could have mangled some French, but it would have been difficult!"

"I was fortunate enough to live and work in England for eighteen months—mainly Newcastle on the river Tyne."

"You liked it?" Basset enquired.

"Very much—save for the rain and the cold. The people were good, full of humor. Much like Moroccans, really. Ah, here we are."

They boarded the waiting unmarked gray 4x4, a five-door Range Rover Evoque. The driver was in civvies, too. Basri explained, "Plain clothing attracts less attention. I thought you would want to keep your visit here, how you say, under wraps."

"That's considerate of you," Pointer said, sitting in the rear with the Lieutenant. Basset loaded their bags in the spacious trunk then sat in the front next to the driver. As they moved away from the curb, she shifted in her seat and said over her shoulder, "That call was London, sir. Interpol's found a link for the shower murders."

Pointer felt blood surge with the excitement of the chase. "Don't keep me in suspense, Sergeant."

"Though he tried to remove all evidence by using the shower in Nice, our killer failed and left a trace. What's more, there's a match on file. He's called Ganix Elizondo, a Basque killer who used to work for ETA. He was arrested in 2005 but escaped and suddenly went off the grid at the time of the so-called permanent truce."

"I know it's stating the obvious, but clearly he's using another name."

"Yes, sir. And we haven't a clue what that is."

Basri cleared his throat. "Excuse me, Inspector, but is this killer the man who owns the cell-phone we have located for you?"

Pointer shrugged. "We don't know, Lieutenant. Whoever owns that phone may have been involved in an attack on me in Tangier."

"This is most disturbing. I was not aware of any attack. It reflects badly on our country. Naturally, we were contacted to afford you any assistance in locating the cell-phone and its user. But that is all we know."

"Don't worry, I came to no harm." Pointer absently massaged his left hand. "Did you say you have a fix on that phone?"

Basri fingered his thin mustache. "It is a place not too far—about thirty kilometers. An Ananke Project, according to our documentation."

"That figures," Basset said.

"Is it private property?" Pointer asked. "I mean, are we able to enter?"

"The land in question does not belong to Ananke Corporation. We can enter without a problem."

"Are you confident that just the two of you will be sufficient force, though?"

"I have the authority of the Royal Gendarmerie behind me, Inspector." He withdrew from his jacket a Heckler & Koch Mk 23 automatic. "And I have this, should I need it." He smiled and replaced it in a shoulder holster under his left armpit.

High Atlas Mountains

Despite the heat of the sun, Cat felt in her element. After hours in the Land Cruiser, her body needed to get rid of the kinks that had settled in her muscles.

She took the first slope gradually, her boots gripping the dusty scree. After a short climb, she was lathered in sweat, and was grateful for the hat. She glanced behind her. True to his word, Rick was keeping up; well, almost. He was on all fours, scrambling slowly, dislodging the odd rock. Sweat glistened on his forehead; she pursed her lips in annoyance: he was bareheaded. He wiped the sweat with his palm and looked at her with trusting yet tired eyes. She gave him the thumbs up and he grinned, and then pluckily started climbing again.

Finally reaching the top of the slope, she removed her hat and hunkered, not wishing to provide a silhouette on the crest for anyone nearby. She was on a massive slab of rock that stretched a good five hundred yards to her right, where it collapsed into a jumble of boulders and tumbled away. Tentatively, she crawled to the lip and peered out.

She was about thirty feet above a roughly circular area of dusty ground; in the center of this natural amphitheater stood a small domed structure; surrounding it was a walled courtyard. Both the dome and the walls were in abject disrepair, crumbling in several places. The dust betrayed the hoof prints of an animal, but nothing more.

There appeared to be three separate dark gullies leading away from the amphitheater; one to the east, another south-east, and a third to the west.

Rick collapsed beside her. "What's a stone igloo doing here?"

"Howard told me about that; it's a marabout, a temple devoted to a murabit or saint-like character."

"Saint—as in Biblical?"

"Not strictly. Someone who possesses a lot of spiritual power and good fortune—*baraka*, they call it, and followers hope that some of this baraka will rub off on them. That's why they build these temples and inter the dead murabit, to trap and benefit from the residual power left behind after death."

"Seems to me that the followers of this chap have long-since departed, too."

"Yes. There are many similar structures all over the land, even now hidden for centuries in the sand. Forgotten by time."

"Are there any trinkets left with the saint? You know, gold, jewelry?"

"No, the emphasis is on their spirituality."

"But you mentioned good fortune—that's riches, surely."

"No." She chuckled. "Good fortune means a good life, love and happiness. Not earthly possessions."

"A pity." He scanned around him. "So, where is the Ananke project site? If they're not excavating this tomb, where the hell are they?"

As if in answer to his query, a motor engine revved, somewhere on their right.

In a crouching run, they both covered the ground toward the jumble of boulders. Slipping in among them, Cat whispered, "Follow me—and don't make a sound."

Docilely, Rick nodded.

She stepped down alongside a massive rock, her

boot sole firmly on loose stone shards. Below, the stack of rocks was piled all the way to a clearing cluttered with four trucks and a Jeep, each emblazoned with the Ananke logo. Behind them was a wide cave mouth; the opening appeared to have been enlarged recently, possibly blasted with explosives, judging by the outlying rubble.

Nearby on her right was a large makeshift blue and green awning; in its shade were tables crammed with dusty and soil-covered artefacts, and piled behind them a large number of crates, several of which were empty, stuffed with wood chippings and draped with hessian sacks. Here, too, sat three dowdy women, their heads shrouded, cleaning marble ornaments with a powder from a huge container labeled *Fuller's earth* in English, French and Arabic.

Some distance on the left was another domed structure, this marabout in no better condition than the earlier one; parked near this was a Mitsubishi Montero. Further to the left seemed a dead end, a sheer wall of rock; so this was a closed canyon, another natural auditorium.

SUN GLINTED, caught Cat's eye and she spotted a man among the rocks above the cave mouth, adjusting his rifle sight. She glanced over her shoulder, signed for Rick to be still. Rick gave an "okay" hand-sign and crouched in concealment behind a boulder. Her mouth went dry. She recalled the row she had with Rick about her handgun. She wondered if she really could use the weapon if their lives depended upon it. That rifle made it all too real—and worrying. The sentry had a black patch that covered his left eye; it didn't make him appear piratical, just sinister.

She shouldn't be surprised there was at least one-armed guard here. From what Howard had told her, the land and what came out of it belonged to King Mohammed VI and his government. So there were two possibilities: Ananke was operating under license or illegally. She suspected they had some kind of authorization, though she wondered if what they were up to was actually the same as that described on their documentation. By past experience of the firm, she doubted it. Was the sentry to deter agents of the authorities as well?

Salty sweat streamed into her eyes, and she brushed them clear.

She knew there was gold in these mountain ranges, and a wealth of minerals. Phosphates were big business, too—used in agriculture and computers. Howard reckoned the price of phosphates had multiplied alarmingly the last few years, and the king and his government through the Office of Moroccan Phosphates had taken advantage of that state of affairs. The disputed Western Sahara offered vast phosphate reserves, Howard added, and indeed Algeria had funded the Polisario guerrilla movement to fight for that very prize. Yet, judging by those artefacts under the awning, it was clear Ananke was not mining phosphates; they were grave robbing.

What now? Go back, forget the whole enterprise? Or report them to the authorities? Perhaps that was the sensible thing to do.

At that moment, Emilio Zabala emerged from the cave entrance; he wore a dust-covered khaki bush jacket, camouflage pants, and black leather boots. He walked over to the shaded area and lit a cigarette. Leaning against an upright post, he studied the women working on the marble items. Briefly, he spoke to them, and one woman nodded but didn't look up. Pivoting on his heel, he brushed a hand down his clothes to dislodge small puffs of dust. He flung the cigarette stub to the ground and withdrew an automatic from his webbing holster, checked its magazine and replaced it.

Cat held her breath and a shudder ran through her as she remembered when he'd held Rick and her captive at gun-point. Luck had been with them that time.

Zabala straightened abruptly, peered to his left, toward the road that wound through the rock; it must be the same road she'd driven on earlier, before she turned off. He walked to the cabin of the truck with its motor running, chugging in neutral. He called to the driver's side in French, his words clearly carried to her ears by the natural auditorium, "Have you everything?"

An arm and face leaned out. "Aye, sir. I'll be going now. It's a fair haul for one man to Tangier!"

"Yes, I know, but I can't afford two drivers for each truck."

"Makes for a fairer split, sir," the driver said with a chuckle.

"So it does. Get going then!" Zabala banged his flat palm on the door and the gears engaged, the engine revved and the truck motored toward the gap in the rock.

By her reckoning, that left in the cave *at least* four more drivers, and the eye-patch gunman, plus Zabala.

Moments later a gray Range Rover drove into view.

It pulled up about two yards from the awning and the engine stopped.

The three women raised their heads briefly to look then lowered their eyes and resumed working.

Zabala stood with arms akimbo, one hand close to his holstered pistol.

Dust settled around the vehicle and a man from the nearside back seat and the driver opened their doors and stepped out.

FROM HIS VANTAGE point among the rocks, Barrou watched through his rifle's sight, aiming it first at the disembarking passenger and then at the driver. Were there only two? Difficult to say, the angle of visibility obviously didn't allow him to see under the vehicle's roof, and the windows were opaque to inhibit sun-glare. The way the driver emerged tugged aside his jacket to reveal a belt-holster, the butt of an automatic jutting out. Shit, they're armed!

Barrou didn't hesitate. He fired.

His first bullet slammed into the driver before the man had put his second foot on the ground. The driver jerked against the bodywork and sprawled sideways, blood gushing from his throat, soaking into the dry earth. A fine shot.

The echo of the first shot barely died as Barrou's second bullet hit the rear guy before he could duck behind the door, piercing his head, which splattered like a pumpkin and made a glorious mess.

A woman started screaming from inside the Range Rover. So there *were* others.

The women working under the awning dropped everything and scuttled to shelter behind a pile of crates.

"Stop, for God's sake stop!" a man shouted, the voice echoing. He knew enough to recognize it was in English. Was that from inside the car as well?

Zabala's screaming voice echoed in French around the clearing: "Stop shooting!" He rushed out, waving his arms, swearing. "I said I wanted them *alive*!"

CAT SENSED the blood draining from her face, and strength seemed to leech from her legs. She was transfixed; but even if she'd wanted to stand and run away, she doubted if her legs would respond.

Oh, God. Two brutal deaths in as many seconds. Why?

She swallowed but couldn't relieve the dryness in her throat. She peered over her shoulder at Rick. His face looked very pale; he shook his head, signed for them to move back, away from this place.

She held up a hand. *Wait.*

Her hand groped to her backpack, pulled free the automatic. Her hand trembled. The weapon felt heavy, unwieldy. What the hell was she thinking? The distance was about fifteen yards to the Range Rover. But the rifleman was much further away. Even on a good day, she couldn't have hit a target at that distance. She'd be accurate at about ten yards, she estimated. Though shooting a person called for more than simple target practice skill. She replaced the weapon and, feeling like a voyeur, turned to watch.

Chapter 11

Whiff of Kif

"Barrou!" Zabala snarled, his chest constricted with suppressed ire. The bloody fool, what was he thinking? "Get down here now!" he shouted in French. "And no more shooting!" He walked slowly toward the Range Rover, his automatic pistol drawn. At least the woman in the car had stopped screaming; it didn't seem like Vibrissae to indulge in hysterics like that. "You in the car," he shouted in English, "get out! No harm will come to you!"

"I'm disinclined to believe that, considering we've got blood and brains splattered all over the upholstery!" A tall man emerged from the rear offside and raised gloved hands. Gloves in this climate? He was in his forties, perhaps. He wore a hat and his shirt was buttoned to his throat. Why was he here if he was averse to the sun?

Zabala stared. "Who the hell are you?"

"Before I tell you, I want to know if you're going to shoot us as well."

"No. It was a mistake." Zabala turned as Barrou

approached. He grated his teeth, and then switched his attention to the male passenger with his gloved hands in the air. "Get the woman to come out."

"Very well." His voice sounded very calm, considering the situation, as he talked to the woman in the vehicle. Who was he? What was he doing with Vibrissae? Where was the damnable Barnes?

Tentatively, the woman got out from the front passenger seat and stood up, a hand briefly placed on the roof of the car for support and swiftly removed; she hissed, clearly burnt by the hot bodywork. Her eyes glistened with moisture as she stood, raising her hands in the air. It wasn't Catherine Vibrissae, after all. Had the cunning bitch sent somebody else instead?

Waving his automatic at them both, Zabala said, "Are you going to tell me who you are and what you're doing here?"

"I'm Detective Inspector Alan Pointer and the lady with me is my sergeant, Carol Basset."

"*British* police?"

"Yes."

"But you have no jurisdiction. Why are you with armed men?"

"I might answer your questions if you stop pointing that gun at us."

Out of the corner of his eye, Zabala noticed Barrou, and alongside him, Oundir. He half-turned. "Barrou, Oundir, lower your rifles." Then he aimed his own gun at the ground.

"Thank you," said Pointer. "You're Emilio Zabala, correct?"

Involuntarily, Zabala took a step back in surprise. "How do you know me?"

The woman, Sergeant Basset, seemed to have recovered. She said, "You're the head of security for the Ananke Corporation."

"I am. But why have you brought armed men to this site?"

"Your man with the rifle has just killed an officer of the Royal Gendarmerie and his driver."

Zabala glared at Barrou and he felt his cheeks flush hot with anger. Barrou didn't understand the Englishman and stared with unconcern. Oundir hovered, looking uncomfortable.

Pointer said. "Can we lower our hands?"

Like a flash, Zabala remembered Barnes saying those very words last year at the Welsh mine. He hadn't posed a threat then, and this Pointer was no threat now. "Of course. I have no intention of harming you."

"Unlike our associates." Pointer lowered his hands and gestured in the general direction of the two corpses. He shifted on his feet, added, "Can we go in the shade, please? I'm allergic to sunlight."

Zabala cackled. "Then why come to this land of sun at all?"

"He's not joking, Mr. Zabala," the female said, her voice rising at the end.

"Alright, go into the cave—slowly, no tricks!"

"We're not fucking magicians!" the woman snapped.

"Easy, Sergeant," said Pointer, stepping slowly toward the cave entrance, followed by Barrou. "Let's not antagonize the man with the gun."

WITH A SINKING feeling in her gut, Cat recognized the name. Pointer. Leon's friend from the NCA.

Was Pointer tracking me? Or Zabala?

Pointer, Basset and bull-necked Barrou entered the cave mouth.

Zabala hung back and told the rifleman Oundir, "Stay here and keep alert. The Vibrissae woman and her pal might get here any moment."

Well, he got that right, she thought.

"And I want them alive—understand?"

Thanks, I think.

Oundir nodded. He hefted his rifle, swiveled his head on its scrawny neck and scoured the rocks.

The somber whimpering of the three women under the awning drew Zabala's attention. "And Oundir, drag those bodies away, hide them; they're distressing the women. We still have plenty of work to do!"

"Yes, sir!"

When Zabala had moved from sight into the cave, Cat kept hidden behind boulders and carefully, quietly clambered to Rick's side.

Oundir busied himself hauling the corpses past the blood-smeared Range Rover toward a an area of ground behind a cluster of rocks beyond the awning.

Rick watched, ashen-faced. "Was that some kind of falling out between crooks?" he croaked in a whisper.

"You couldn't hear what was being said?"

"No, the echoing seems worse up here. Actually, I don't know if I want to hear."

"The two Zabala's taken into the cave are British police—Leon's friend Pointer and his sergeant."

Rick's mouth gaped open. "What—what're they doing here?"

"I don't know."

"They can't be following us."

"No, I agree. Whatever their reason, they're in trouble now."

Rick swallowed, ran a hand over his mouth. "Yes, and to think that could have been us if we'd driven in..."

Reluctantly, she came to a decision. "Rick, we've got to rescue Pointer and his sergeant."

He stared, disbelief in his eyes. "This isn't a climbing escapade, Cathy. Those men have guns—and they're not reluctant to use them."

"Not so loud. I heard Zabala tell the rifleman he doesn't want us killed."

"Oh, that's really comforting." He released a grunt. "Only so he can deal with us personally. I'm not too keen on that, you know."

"I don't think you'll be keen on what I'm going to ask you next, either."

CAT SLIPPED BEHIND the crates with ease. Her pulse pounded in her temple and her mouth was very dry. So far, her movement had gone unheard by Oundir. She had told Rick to wait until she was in position. At first, he'd refused outright, and she didn't blame him one bit. She argued that Zabala had definitely instructed Oundir not to shoot. "It's Pointer's only chance," she pleaded. Then she scrambled from one big rock to another, moving in a wide arc, round to the section of rock where the road led.

While Oundir was preoccupied with the cave entrance, she crossed the open space in a crouching run.

The women resumed their work and didn't detect her either.

She came upon the two corpses behind the rocks and stopped suddenly. Her stomach was tied in knots and she tasted that Mars bar at the back of her throat. Willing herself to be calm, she swallowed. Her breathing felt restricted. *More dead bodies.*

Steeling herself, she knelt beside the dead passenger and flicked aside his jacket opening. His bill-fold informed her he was Lieutenant Aziz Basri of the Royal Gendarmerie; just what Pointer told Zabala. He wore a shoulder holster and it contained his gun, a Heckler & Koch automatic. She'd used one at the firing range—it was effective up to fifty yards. She dropped the billfold and carefully unfastened the shoulder holster and slid it free from under the dead man. She unslung her backpack. The shoulder holster needed some adjustment but soon fitted under her left arm-pit. She checked the dead driver; his pistol was in his belt holster. It would be foolish to leave it. She put it inside her backpack, and then she slipped her arms through the straps.

Silently, she moved round the boulders, climbing with care, negotiating crevices and clefts. By now she guessed that Rick would be very anxious, for her and for his imminent ordeal.

At last, she slunk to the area behind the crates. One of the women glanced up, perhaps hearing her footfall. The woman's eyes widened but she said nothing and returned to her work.

Cat peered round the crate, tilted her compact mirror to the sun, let it glint in the direction where Rick hid. He must have seen it, for a few seconds later he stepped out from the base of the tumble of boulders, his hands held high.

Although the three women who had resumed work on the marble curios spotted Rick, the rifleman Oundir didn't notice straight away. He stood next to the pile of crates, so close to her, gazing at the cave mouth.

"Hey!" Rick called, and added in stumbling French, "I heard your boss is looking for me!" He wiggled his hands, added, "I have no gun!"

Oundir looked up and snarled in French, "Step forward slowly." He raised his rifle to waist height and patiently waited for Rick to approach. He didn't speak again. Cat noticed he didn't have his finger in the trigger guard either. The man was confident—over-confident.

Now or never.

She rushed from the concealment of the crates, leaped at Oundir's back and wrapped her left arm round the man's scrawny neck. He grunted, dropped the rifle and clawed at her forearms to no avail. Her weight and training thrust the man to his knees and he gasped loudly, emitting a brief whiff of kif. Ignoring the strong stench of body odor, she held on tight, applying more pressure to her forearm that pressed into his neck. Her Taekwondo lessons also included self-defense —*hosinsul*—in the event of an attack or attempted rape. "With *chil sik sul* you apply enough pressure to temporarily arrest the flow of blood to the brain and oxygen to the lungs," her instructor had said. The alternative, killing the man by applying the pressure longer, or the choke hold crushing the trachea, didn't bear thinking about. After only a few seconds, Oundir slumped in her grip and she relaxed, and warily let go.

Oundir lay still, crumpled in a crouch on his haunches, eyes shut, his breathing shallow.

"You did it!" Rick whispered hoarsely as he hurried toward her.

"Yes. Tie him up, somewhere hidden. Then take his rifle and watch the cave mouth."

"What if someone comes out?"

"I don't care about the others, but if it's Zabala, scare him back inside with a shot or two." She looked askance at him. "Have you used a rifle before?"

He shook his head.

She hefted the weapon, put it in his hands and showed him as she explained. "Wedge the stock tight into your shoulder. That will absorb the recoil—the kick."

He gulped but said nothing.

"Whatever happens," she went on, "do not go into the cave. Understand?"

He gulped again. "Yes," he replied and then glanced at the three women; they averted their eyes, busied themselves with the marble cleaning. "What about them?"

"They're workers, nothing more. I doubt if they want anything to do with Zabala's criminal activities."

"What are you going to do?" he asked.

"I'm going inside to get Pointer and Basset out."

"Yes, of course you are. Stupid of me to ask."

RICK DRAGGED the unconscious form of Oundir along the ground, and behind the crates. By the time he got there, he was sweating profusely. The heat sapped his strength, too. Casting about, he found several lengths of rope and tied the man's feet and hands together. He hesitated to use a gag as he didn't want him choking on vomit if he recovered and reacted by being sick. Then he noticed a pile of hessian sacks the women used to put their cleaned items in. He took one, pulled it over Oundir's head. If he made any sound when he regained consciousness, it would be muffled at least.

He straightened and eyed the women. One of them was watching him. He nodded without smiling and she returned the gesture and continued to work on an ornate gold necklace. He'd have to trust them. He doubted if he could tie up all three.

He returned and grabbed the fallen rifle, headed for the rocks that faced the cave mouth. Here, he crouched down to wait, cursing himself for neglecting to bring a water bottle from their vehicle.

His insides roiled as he worried about Cathy. He shouldn't have let her go in there. Hah, as if he could have stopped her! His mouth was dry, his head pounded with dehydration and his legs trembled. I'm not cut out for this, he thought.

Chapter 12

Catacomb

C at found the shade inside the cave most welcome. The cave widened into a broad down-sloping gulley and she immediately felt exposed. It was well-lit from regularly spaced battery-powered lights placed on the ground along the walls. Traces of mineral and metal glinted in the rock. The cave floor was rutted with narrow wheel marks. Voices echoed. She might be discovered any minute! The thought of confronting Zabala face-to-face again sent her stomach gyrating. The last time they'd faced each other there'd been an expanse of water between them.

The effect of the lights didn't reach far; the ceiling was indistinct shadow. A few rough ledges followed the contours of the rock that had been heaved and twisted millennia ago. She needed to get to high ground and those ledges might serve. She hurried over to the cave wall and scrambled up to a ledge, her boots hardly making a sound.

The ledge was about eighteen inches wide and it led higher. Soon she had to crouch as she moved forward, her head almost touching the ceiling of the cave. At times she had to cling on with fingertips to negotiate a section without any ledge, but she never feared she would fall. At least she was not visible here in the shadows.

Then the slope eased off a little and she paused, stunned, and held onto the rock by her sides.

Zabala stood about fifty yards away in the center of a huge clearing covered in stone chipped into shale. Beside him were Pointer and Basset and the rifleman Barrou. On either side tier upon tier of rock-hewn catacombs gaped, the vast majority of them still occupied by human bones. Niches next to each tomb were crammed with dust- and dirt-encrusted objects: ornaments and antiquities. A thin beam of light lanced down from a hole somewhere in the roof of this natural cathedral.

Four bulky men, stripped to the waist, chipped at the walls with pickaxes to release marble artefacts that had over time become part of the rock. Four small four-wheeled trolleys were half-filled with their booty: Cat glimpsed brass plates, copper jugs; hammered and chased copper, patterned boxes; silver jewelry—bangles, medallions, brooches. She recalled that silver was highly prized by Berber women, since they could rarely afford gold, and wondered about the three female workers outside. The Berbers didn't use bank accounts, Howard told her; their jewelry was purchased when times were good, and sold when they were bad.

Zabala clapped his hands, caught the men's attention.

They stopped working, straightened up, massaging aching backs, and eyed him. Sweat covered their torsos and glistened.

"Right, men," Zabala barked in slow French, "I want you to load these carts into your trucks and move out."

"But we haven't finished, there's a lot—"

"You can return in a day or so. This stuff isn't going anywhere."

"What about our payment?"

"You will be paid in full at the port, as agreed."

Their spokesman gestured at the others and dropped his pickaxe. He said something in Berber and they all grinned. Then they started pushing their carts up the gradient, the axels creaking.

She was glad she'd chosen this perch. She'd be no match for any of them, she felt sure, Taekwondo training or no. Training was one thing, while a life-and-death situation was quite another. She peered down at Barrou and was thankful that they'd left Oundir outside the cave; Barrou's bull-neck would have proved difficult for her choke hold.

As the sound of the retreating carts and men diminished, Pointer said, "You've got a good racket going here, Zabala. Looting these tombs and selling the finds to private collectors, probably to the highest bidder. Is that it?"

"Something like that." Zabala gesticulated at the nearest catacomb. "This was a surprise find, actually, a horde of Moulay Ismail's possessions from the seventeenth century."

"Luck, was it?" Basset asked.

"Yes, in a way. A few months ago, Maclean, our surveyor, was looking for talc..."

"The local chemist has plenty," Basset retorted, "even after that ovarian cancer scare."

Cat remembered that. She'd studied it. Yet another instance of scare-mongering with inadequate data and a total lack of common sense: volume of talc sales compared to the incidence of ovarian cancer? Before 1973, talc might have contained minute traces of asbestos. Talc miners were tested for lung cancer. For years lawyers have plagued cosmetic firms with lawsuits, fighting on behalf of unfortunate sufferers, but no case has been proven conclusively. Apparently, studies in rats showed lung damage caused by talc; which wasn't surprising since they were forced to inhale talc for six hours per day for six years; she recalled the critics of the tests referred to it as "particle overload". Poor bloody rats. Manufacturers ensure the relatively large, non-respirable particle size in talc powder so it can't be inhaled into lungs. These scare stories run and run, and at one point talc was even taken off a number of shelves, yet there was no significant statistical proof. She hated it when the science was bad science and had more to do with hubris, greedy lawyers, inadequate statistics or commercial competition than saving lives.

Zabala scowled. "For someone whose life is in jeopardy, you're too flippant, Sergeant."

"That's me," Basset said, shrugging, as if she hadn't a care in the world. "Sorry I interrupted. You were telling us about your surveyor looking for talc deposits?"

"I was. He found a large deposit of talc, several thousands of metric tons; its seam is about fifty percent talc, fifty percent calcite. Nowhere near as big as the Nkob deposit west of Ouarzazate. Still, Ananke has permission to mine the talc. Naturally, the Moroccan government gets its cut. Maclean is back in London with his report and all the boring paperwork."

"But instead," Pointer interjected, "he found these tombs?"

"No. He left behind a couple of men to begin experimental drilling. Got the shock of their lives when one of them fell through here." He pointed at the small hole visible in the cave gallery ceiling. "Sadly, he didn't survive the fall. His associate contacted HQ and I scooted here to have a look—and conceal the unfortunate death."

"I suspect you're quite good at that," Pointer said.

Zabala glared. "You remind me of someone else who got in my way in a similar situation." He laughed without humor. "That was underground, as well!"

Pointer folded his arms across his chest. "You're talking about Rick Barnes, I take it?"

Zabala swore. "You *are* well informed, Inspector."

"You won't get away with this—once the Moroccan government gets wind of it, they'll have your head."

"They won't learn of it, I'm sure. As you implied, I'm good at covering my tracks." He half-turned, spread his arms, indicating the sepulchral place. "I know you were talking figuratively, Inspector, but your allusion to losing my head has a strong resonance in here. The murderous beheadings by the Islamic State adherents are nothing new, sadly. Moulay Ismail was a great exponent. In 1672, when he was twenty-five, and simply as a warning to unruly tribes, he sent the heads of 10,000 enemies to adorn the walls of the capitals Fez and Marrakesh."

"It was barbaric then, and it is now!" Basset shouted.

"I agree." Zabala shrugged. "How long he'd kept those heads for that purpose isn't known. His twenty years of bloody pacification—with about 30,000 deaths —accomplished a rare feat at that time, bringing the whole country under a single sultan's control."

"At what cost?" Basset demanded.

Zabala strode up to her, pressed his pistol against her throat and with his free hand stroked her cheek. "Perhaps he needed to control the population explosion which in fact he almost single-handedly caused!" He squinted; his eyes lit with a glow of mischief and he pushed her aside, moved to a dark niche and lifted an ornate chair. "Yes, this is French," he said. "Ismail and King Louis XIV exchanged presents." He chuckled. "Though the Sun King drew the line when Ismail requested to marry the French princess of Conti. Not that he needed another wife—he had anywhere between 300 to 500 wives and concubines already, who gave him about 800 children."

"You treat death very lightly, Zabala," Pointer said, flexing his gloved hands, balling them into fists.

"Life is cheap in the African continent, Inspector. I thought all westerners knew that—and, in fact took advantage of it throughout history."

"You're Spanish, you're part of that history. And that's what it is, history. I have nothing to apologize for."

Without warning, Zabala pounced, slamming the automatic against Pointer's face, gouging his chin, dislodging his hat. "Don't be so arrogant!"

Pointer stumbled sideways and sank to one knee, but didn't utter a sound.

Basset took a pace, as if to help the Inspector.

Barrou stepped forward, leveling his rifle on Pointer and Basset.

Cat had seen and heard enough. She pulled free the Heckler & Koch she'd taken from the dead Aziz Basri.

"Now," Zabala said, "what am I going to do with you two?"

"Let us go?" Basset offered.

"No, sorry." Zabala's face held a pained expression. "You're witnesses to two murders, after all."

"But you didn't kill them," Basset persisted. She accusingly eyed Barrou as she spoke.

"You want me to throw him to the wolves, is that it?"

Pointer got to his feet. "Take away his rifle, take him into custody and we'll try to explain it was all an accident."

Zabala walked over to Pointer, abruptly darted a hand and grabbed Pointer's left arm, held it. "Why do you wear gloves in this heat? Afraid of getting Ebola?"

"That's none of your business," Pointer said.

"Oh, I'm curious. What if..." Suddenly, he snatched at Pointer's hand, tugged off the glove, threw it in the direction of Barrou.

Basset shouted in alarm and took a pace forward, resting a hand on the Louis XIV chair, but stopped as Barrou raised his weapon in a threatening gesture.

Zabala chuckled. "So, your devoted sergeant was right. You've got bad sunburn there. You should be more careful."

Pointer kept quiet and Cat admired him for that, considering the provocation.

Letting go of Pointer's hand, Zabala shrugged. "I'm sorry, I have no choice. With any luck, when the four bodies are found near the burnt-out wreck of the Range Rover, it will be assumed that bandits killed you all."

Sergeant Basset turned to face Barrou, unflinching, one hand on the chair.

"Barrou, get rid of the sergeant first," Zabala commanded, covering Pointer with his pistol.

Barrou raised his rifle.

Chapter 13

"Call me Cat..."

Rick heard the creaking sound of wheels trundling toward the cave mouth. He checked the rifle, rested it on the boulder in front of him and waited. He brushed sweat from his brow and eyes, blinking at the saltiness.

Four men emerged, their bare torsos glistening with sweat; each one pushed a small cart. None of them seemed to be armed. Still, he couldn't shoot them in cold blood. They helped each other to load the contents of the carts in the back of the three remaining trucks and the Jeep. He licked his dry lips. His heart pounded.

The men climbed into their vehicles and started the motors. The trucks swung round and headed in a small convoy to the exit.

Rick let out a huge sigh and eased his finger off the trigger and wiped sweat from his brow. Where was Cat? How had they missed her on their way out?

Oh, hell, do I go in and look for her? *Whatever happens, don't go in the cave.* Those were her instructions.

He glanced at the three women under the awning. They'd stopped briefly while the trucks were loaded but were busy again now.

He peered at the domed structure some distance away on his left. There seemed to be a preponderance of holy men around here at one time. Now the place was full of criminals. And Zabala. God, how he hated that man. If he got the chance, he'd definitely shoot the swine. His hand trembled as wedged the rifle stock into his shoulder and aimed at the cave entrance.

———

CAT AIMED AND FIRED, the bullet hitting Barrou in the left shoulder. He grunted, dropped the weapon and lowered to one knee, clasping the wound. In almost the same instant, Basset lifted the chair and crashed it on Barrou's head; the wood shattered and she was left with a section of the chair in her hands. Barrou fell on his back, groggy.

"My chair!" Zabala wailed and fired at Basset.

The sergeant was hit in her upper arm and shrieked; she staggered but remained standing, a hand covering her wound.

Fists balled, Pointer reached out for Zabala but was clubbed on the chin with the butt of Zabala's automatic.

Holding the pistol to Pointer's head, Zabala squinted at the cavern wall, scanned the shadows and shouted, "Whoever you are, if you fire another shot, I'll kill the Inspector!"

"Leave Pointer and Basset here!" Cat called. "If you do, I'll let you go!"

Cocking his head, pushing the barrel of the gun

against Pointer's temple, Zabala said, "Vibrissae? Is it really you?"

"Yes, damn you!" She was finding it difficult to hold the automatic steady. She'd shot a man. She'd never done that before. Maybe Barrou had been going to kill Sergeant Basset, but that didn't make it feel any better.

"We're in a stalemate here, Miss Vibrissae." Zabala heaved Pointer to his side. "It is for me to break it. I'm going to take the Inspector as my hostage. No harm will come to him if you don't follow."

"No!" Basset screamed. "Leave Alan—you can't take him into that sun! Take me!"

"Such loyalty, but he's more valuable than you, Sergeant," Zabala said, raising his gun.

"Don't think about shooting her!" Cat warned. "This is a very accurate weapon!"

"Alright. We're leaving now," Zabala said. "Don't try to stop me!"

Walking crab-fashion, hauling Pointer at gun-point with him, Zabala moved up the slope, following the tracks of the carts.

When he was out of sight, Cat jumped from ledge to lower ledge and then landed firmly on the ground.

Basset stumbled to her. "Leave me—try to—try to help...Inspector Pointer!"

Pulling her own automatic from her backpack, she tossed it to Basset. "Can you handle this and cover Barrou over there?"

Catching the weapon one-handed, Basset said, "It'll be a pleasure!"

Cat swiveled round and sprinted up the gradient. At each point where there was concealment—boulders, an outcrop, a slight curve in the natural passage, she halted so she could cautiously peer ahead.

Zabala was more intent on getting out, though; each time she saw him, he never checked behind.

What would Rick do? Shoot and ask questions afterwards? *What would I do?* She shuddered, remembering Barrou. Dear God, Barrou had murdered Aziz Basri and the driver. He deserved to get shot. Zabala deserves it, too.

———

RICK'S NERVES were in shreds: he'd heard gunshots, echoing from the cave. Two shots?

He started as he spotted Pointer being pushed from the cave mouth by Zabala. He aimed but couldn't get a clear shot. Where was Cathy? Had Zabala killed her? His chest seemed choked with an unfamiliar sensation. Profound anger, hate, or despair? He fired and was surprised at the harsh kick of the weapon against his shoulder. Cathy hadn't been joking.

The bullet hit a rock to Zabala's right and whined away.

"Oundir, it's me, Zabala!"

"He can't hear you!"

"What happened to Oundir?" Zabala called.

"He's trussed-up like a chicken!" Rick shouted. "Drop your gun, Zabala! You can't get away."

"Is that Rick Barnes?" Zabala demanded, a note of amusement in his tone.

"Yes. So, what of it?"

"You never struck me as the adventurous type. I doubt if you could hit me with that rifle!"

"Try me!" He fired again.

He fired again, accepting the recoil with familiarity now. His second bullet slammed against the rock, very close, rock chippings spattering Zabala's right cheek.

Zabala ran a hand over the small bloody cuts, swore and hunched behind Pointer. "You can't hit me while I hold the Inspector as a shield!" He edged to the left, tugging Pointer with him.

The Inspector's face was now very pale, twisted in pain. Yet he didn't seem wounded. A couple of bruises on his face, but no blood. Why did he have a glove on his right hand? He kept his left hand inside his jacket, and hunched, the jacket collar turned up to cover his neck. "If you harm him," Rick yelled, "you're a dead man!"

Without replying, Zabala dragged Pointer with him and scurried to the marabout on the left. Suddenly he thrust Pointer to the ground and dived to cover behind the ancient structure.

Rick fired a shot but it whined harmlessly off the stone.

Pointer stumbled to his knees, clearly in agony, using only his right gloved hand in an attempt at covering his face with his jacket.

Another movement caught Rick's eye. He was swamped with an upsurge of giddy relief: Cathy ran out of the cave, her eyes scanning the scene, and then she rushed to the shade of the awning. Without hesitation, she grabbed a container and dashed toward Pointer.

Distracted by Cathy's action, Rick missed the moment when Zabala made a break for it and climbed into the Montero and started the engine.

Zabala drove his car directly at Cathy.

Rick fired and a rear window shattered, but the car kept going. He couldn't risk another shot, the angle was wrong, he might hit her.

At the last instant, Cathy dodged the vehicle, dropping the container, rolled away, and sprawled in the dust disturbed by the Montero's wheels.

Hastily regaining her feet, she retrieved the container.

Rick fired at the dust cloud of the retreating car.

As the echo of his shot died with the vanishing vehicle, Rick broke cover and ran to them both.

Cathy was spreading Fuller's earth on Pointer's exposed hand and the sudden relief on the Inspector's face was surprising.

"Thank you," Pointer breathed. "That helps a lot."

"I don't know what ails you, but I hoped it might alleviate the problem. Fuller's earth is absorbent and a good decontaminant..."

"You guessed right—it isn't simply the sun's rays—they trigger something else, a chemical reaction that could easily get out of hand." He glanced at his hand and grinned ruefully, then cast about, concern in his eyes. "Is Carol—is Sergeant Basset alright?"

"Yes," Cathy said. "She sustained a flesh wound, but she'll be fine. Let's get you to shade."

Between them, Cathy and Rick hurriedly half-helped, half-carried Pointer to the welcome shade of the awning. The women had hidden behind the crates, but this time they didn't move or resume their work.

Cathy indicated the boulders she'd hidden behind. "The bodies of your travelling companions—the Gendarmerie—are there."

Pointer trailed his trembling gloved hand across his brow. "Christ, that was a shock. I feared we were all going to die." He massaged his exposed hand, rubbed more Fuller's earth on it.

"Are you suffering from porphyria?" she asked.

"No, thankfully. That's a dreadful hereditary disease I wouldn't wish on anybody. My affliction's a long story, Miss Vibrissae..."

"I'll go check on the sergeant," Rick said, hefting the rifle.

"Yes, do," Cathy said. "But let her know it's you—she has a gun."

Rick swallowed and nodded, then headed to the cave mouth.

―――――――――

"CAN you tell me why you're here?" Cat asked Pointer. "What business has the NCA in Morocco?"

He smiled in spite of the pain he must still be feeling, which reflected in his eyes. She warmed to him.

"How do you know we're with NCA?" he said. "I never mentioned it."

She returned his smile. "I have my sources."

"For a chemist and model, you seem to be remarkably resourceful and well-informed, Miss Vibrissae."

"Call me Cat, Inspector."

"Cat...from the catwalk?"

"Among other things. Are you changing the subject?"

"No, of course not. I have nothing to hide, Cat." His tone and look implied that she had; and he wasn't wrong there. "We were tracking Zabala. He'd set one of his minions on us, attacked us."

"But you haven't said why you're in Morocco."

"We were following a lead on you and Mr. Barnes. A certain incident in Wales..."

"Interpol blue notice?"

"Now you have me really worried, Cat. Who—?"

"We didn't sabotage anything. In fact, we saved a man's life, despite the fact that he was threatening us with a blow-torch."

"I'd be interested in hearing your side of things, Cat. Really, I—"

At that moment Rick exited the cave with Sergeant Basset, who had Barrou's rifle slung over her shoulder. Barrou stumbled ahead of them, his visage twisted in pain or perhaps disappointment, Cat reflected.

"Maybe Barrou here can help you with your enquiries, Inspector?" Cat said. "Rick and I have to be somewhere else."

Pointer indicated the ground near where Zabala had used him as a hostage. "Before you leave, can you go and find any stone chippings with blood on them? Zabala's blood." He thumbed at Rick. "A ricochet from Mr. Barnes' shot cut Zabala's right cheek. I'd like the blood analyzed."

"Why?" she asked. "You know who he is already."

"Just a hunch."

"I'll go with you," Basset said, delving in her jacket pocket with her free hand. "I've lived with his hunches for quite a while!"

"Are you alright, Sergeant?" Pointer asked.

"A graze, sir. I'll be fine."

It didn't take long. Cat found the four shards of

discolored rock and Basset produced a latex glove for her. She picked them up and dropped them in an evidence bag Basset held out.

When they returned to Pointer, Cat said, "I was hoping for a bit more of his blood than that, I can assure you."

Pointer pocketed the bag. "Well, Cat, it seems we both have history we need to swap some time."

"Where does this leave us now, Inspector?"

"Alan. You've saved my life; I think you can call me that now."

"Alright, Alan. What's your next step?"

"Zabala's in the employ of Loup Dante who's presently in Shanghai."

"Interesting," Cat said.

"As far as Interpol and the Moroccan law system are concerned, I never found either you or Mr. Barnes."

"Which is true enough," Basset chipped in, "since you both found us, right?"

Cat eyed the Range Rover; the brain and blood had dried in the sun.

"What about Barrou?" Rick asked, prodding the man with the rifle.

"We'll secure him in the back," Cat said. "He and Oundir will fit snugly into the trunk."

Cat watched Barrou, amused that he didn't know the cramped fate that awaited him. She motioned at the three women who had stopped working; they all looked anxious. "Can you take them as well to Ouarzazate?"

"Yes, certainly." Pointer turned to Basset. "It's my turn to drive, Sergeant, right?"

"I thought you'd never offer, sir."

"We'll be fine," Pointer said. "I'll hand over Barrou and Oundir, report the deaths."

Basset gingerly hefted a rifle. "And I'll hand in Barrou's rifle—forensics will prove it killed Lieutenant Aziz and the driver."

Pointer got behind the wheel. "And I imagine within a few hours this place will be off-limits. Ananke will have a lot more answering to do. It gets worse, it seems. Southampton, Seahouses, Wales, Barcelona..." He paused, glanced around. "But where's your car?"

Cat gestured vaguely beyond the tumbled boulders. "Parked a short way out of sight."

Chuckling, Pointer said, "Can we give you a lift to it?"

"No, thanks. I have a couple of things I need to do here, first."

Chapter 14

Hand of Fatima

Ouarzazate

Zabala cleaned his cheek in the petrol station's toilet, using paper towels; those four cuts would probably become permanent scars. Barnes would pay most dearly for that!

When he felt he was presentable enough, he returned to his car and drove to the hire company at the Mohammed V airport.

He caught a flight to Casablanca and once there had to wait for a connection to Tangier. All the while, he fumed. He needed a woman to relieve his ire—but there was no time.

He'd had the Vibrissae woman almost under his car-wheels yet at the last second the bitch jumped clear. At that time, he hadn't cared that Mr. Dante wanted her alive. He was so furious. In retrospect, perhaps it was just as well. Mr. Dante would have been exceedingly annoyed if he'd killed her.

While waiting for his flight, he dialed Mr. Dante's

number, and dreaded the conversation that would follow.

Shanghai

Loup Dante lounged on the edge of the hotel's roof pool beside a nubile bikini-clad blonde on another sunbed. He had few idle moments like this, and treasured them. He could afford the view, which pleased him. The panorama was striking, the hundreds of strollers crowding the Bund that curved along the side of Huangpu River, its backdrop the grandiose buildings from the past—edifices to banking in colonial style, in contrast to this side of the river, which was modern and almost futuristic.

His contentment was shattered when the cellphone trilled. It identified the caller. He picked it up. "You'd better have a good reason for calling, Zabala. I'm resting."

"I'm sorry, sir. I wouldn't call unless it was urgent."

"Go on, then. But be brief."

"Vibrissae and Barnes are friends with Greenleaf and Kominsky, two of your directors."

"That explains it!" Dante snapped.

"What, sir? Explains what?"

"I've just been notified by the company secretary that the other directors have arranged an EGM to vote me off the Tangier board."

"That sounds like her doing, sir."

Dante sat up, the blood rushing to his face. "So, you're saying that she's there in Morocco?"

"Yes, sir. They both are..."

"What aren't you telling me? Have you harmed her?"

"No, sir. They both got away..."

"You know, Zabala, you seem to be losing your touch. Of late, when dealing with Catherine Vibrissae, you seem to be nothing short of inept!"

"She has all the luck, sir."

"What about the Moulay Project? We're siphoning everything through the plant's books, for God's sake!"

"The Moroccan authorities will be closing it down by now."

He gripped the phone so tight it hurt. If only this were Zabala's neck! "Yes," he managed through grim lips, "you were right, this is an urgent matter." His tone grated now, threatening. "What happened?"

"The project was compromised when one of my men shot...two officers..."

"My God, Zabala, this is a calamity!"

"I know, sir. I called you as soon as I could."

"When did this happen?"

"Earlier today."

"And where are you now?"

"At Casablanca airport, on my way to Tangier."

"Sensible choice. Well, Zabala, you have one opportunity to redeem yourself. Give me satisfaction—or you will cease to be in my employ."

"Yes, sir. I will see to it."

Dante closed the call.

"Was that a problem call, dear?" the blonde asked, turning to face him.

"No, not really." He got up, sat behind her and kneaded her neck muscles. The sounds she made told him she liked that. "As we enjoy ourselves here, it will all be rectified. I have assurances. No need to distress ourselves."

Vibrissae was determined to destroy his business connections and very likely him as well. It didn't seem possible that somebody could harbor so much venom. He dearly wanted to have her in his power again. First, to learn her father's identity; her stubborn ruthlessness suggested she was his own flesh and blood, but he needed definite proof of that. And second, he wanted to punish her for the grief she'd brought him, whether his daughter or not.

"Ow, Loup, that hurt!" the blonde yelped as his thumbs pressed firmly on her neck.

"Sorry, my dear. My mind was on other things." Dark things.

High Atlas Mountains

Pointer and Basset bundled Barrou and Oundir in the trunk of the Range Rover. The blood- and gore-stained upholstery had already started to smell in the heat. The three Berber women managed to wipe down most of it and neutralize the smell with Fuller's earth. Then the three women sat in the rear; the seat was cramped but they didn't complain. They then left for Ouarzazate.

Cat and Rick went back for their car and drove it round to the cave entrance.

It was dark by the time Cat finished collecting an assortment of gold jewelry and chains, coins, and a necklace with the hand of Fatima; the open palm was supposed to protect its wearer from ill fortune: that might come in useful! She put them in her backpack and loaded it in the car's trunk, on top of their two suitcases.

"What are you going to do with all that?" Rick asked.

"It will go to a good cause."

"You're not Robin Hood—or Maid Marian, you know. If we're stopped on the border with that lot, we'll get sent to prison!"

"No, we won't. It would get confiscated and we'd be fined."

"How much?"

She shrugged. "About 20,000 Dirhams—that's £1,500."

"Oh, that's alright, then."

"That fine might be for each item, though..."

"Great!"

"Anyway, this is all academic as I'm not taking it to the border. Honest. Trust me."

"Alright." He seemed to calm down. "I do trust you —with my life, as it happens too often! I'll drive for a while, and then you can take over."

"That suits me fine. We'll stop overnight at Casablanca."

"Yeah, I fancy seeing my bar?"

"Come again?"

"Rick's Bar. *Casablanca*?"

She playfully slapped his arm. "Actually it was Rick's Café Américain."

"Know-all!" He started the engine and switched on the headlights.

It was eerie, negotiating between the high rock

clefts, impenetrable blackness all around, the occasional glare of red in the rear-view mirror as he braked. "A few road markings would be a big help," he quipped.

"It's more adventurous this way, isn't it?"

"Oh, definitely!"

Casablanca

Cat and Rick settled on the Hotel Majestic. Its foyer was decorated after the fashion of the Merenid era; here, she bought a large padded envelope, bubble-wrap and adhesive tape from the shop. The room was comfortable and adequate for their limited needs. After all, it was only somewhere to wash and sleep.

As he padded naked to the bathroom, she said, "Take your time and soak that shoulder. After a few more sessions you'll hardly bruise."

"More sessions? That's not comforting."

"You did well, dearest."

"For a beginner." He went in to get a shower.

Cat phoned Howard and told him what had happened. Glad to get out of her dusty clothes, she stripped to her underwear and sat at the small writing table and wrote a note. She placed this in the envelope together with the jewelry she'd taken from the site. She sealed it with tape and wrote the name and address on the front.

"Posting ill-gotten gains to our Nice apartment?" Rick asked, leaning against the door-frame. Steam wafted behind him. He wore a towel around his waist. His eyes danced.

"I don't know about 'ill-gotten'. We damned well-earned every item!"

"I'd agree if they belonged to Ananke, but they don't, do they?"

"No." She stood, and put the envelope on the table. "But I think some of it can do good. You know, Carthaginians and Romans left their mark not only with roads and buildings; farmers in the Maghreb have sifted their land for gold coins for centuries, despite what the law demands. Their finds end up on the black market. I'm just doing the same kind of thing for a good cause."

He walked over to her, glanced at the envelope. "Whose cause, did you say?"

"Sometimes, you poke that big nose of yours where it shouldn't go." She grabbed the towel, loosened it and let it drop to the floor.

"My nose?" he said.

Chapter 15

Travesty of Jackson Pollock

Tangier

Sitting at a small round table, Howard sipped crème de menthe while Gerard applied the finishing touches to a painting of Cathy. He was quite overcome. "Gerard, the likeness is striking," he remarked. "You've captured her beauty and...something else."

"Thank you." Gerard lowered his brush and stepped back. "Her determination?"

"Yes. That's it, the set of her lips and chin." He put down his glass, stood and walked to his friend and embraced him. "I envy you your skill to appeal to the emotions."

"Why, good sir, I'm overwhelmed."

Howard's phone trilled. He went to retrieve it from the small table.

Caller's number withheld. "Yes?" he demanded abruptly, intent on closing the call.

"Howard Greenleaf, this is Loup Dante."

"Oh." That sounded totally inadequate. His pulse raced and his mouth felt dry.

"I'm calling about the proposed EGM you have called."

He sounded reasonable enough. "You must be referring to the food plant."

"I am. And I am not pleased. I believe you should reconsider. Do that and I will forget the entire incident."

"Monsieur Dante, I wouldn't dream of abandoning our workforce to your conniving mercies," Howard said fervently. "I know that the plant has been used for laundering money and transporting certain historical artefacts from an ancient catacomb. I assure you that these facts will come to light, to the detriment of yourself. My concern is for the plant and the men and women who work there, not the Ananke global empire."

"The catacomb is no longer viable," Dante said, "thanks to your friend Catherine Vibrissae!"

"Catherine who?" Howard queried, winking at the attentive Gerard. "Who do you mean?"

"You may know her as Cathy Gledhill."

"Ah, the model. What has she to do with this historic catacomb?"

"It seems you find all this amusing, Greenleaf. I do not."

"Then I will be quite serious, Monsieur Dante. Let the board members do their work and resign gracefully!"

He closed the connection.

Gerard grinned at him, clearly brimming with joy. "I like it when you're masterful."

Ouarzazate

After Pointer and Basset dropped off the three women on the outskirts of the town, they drove up to the police station near rue de Marché. They immediately caused a stir when they bundled Barrou and Oundir onto the path at the entrance. Pointer showed his ID and explained in French that Barrou was responsible for two cold-blooded murders, and handed over the killer's rifle.

Fortunately, the police quickly referred them to someone in authority who arranged for Barrou and Oundir to be put in the cells.

A hasty telephone call then brought a handsome officer of the Royal Gendarmerie. Lieutenant Wahami was horrified to learn of the death of Aziz Basri. "I will arrange for the site to be sealed until the crime scene officers have completed their examination. Then an ambulance will be arranged to collect the bodies of our comrades."

"This is a portion of their contraband." Basset had carried a small wooden crate from their car's trunk and now plonked it on the desk. She removed the lid to reveal glinting gold and silver, along with black marble, quartz and amethyst artefacts.

"This is most serious, Inspector Pointer," Lieutenant Wahami said. "I will make some telephone calls and the Ministry of Culture will send representatives to safeguard the site, as soon as the crime scene is cleared."

"You'll want statements, I imagine?" Pointer said.

"Yes, sir, of course. But they can wait. You both

need medical attention. My associates in the police will escort you to our hospital."

"Thank you," Basset said.

"Oh, Inspector, one more thing."

"Yes?" Pointer enquired.

"Do you know where the contraband trucks were going?"

"Yes," Pointer said, recalling what Cat had told him. "We overheard one driver mention Tangier. Perhaps they intend to ship the items into Europe?"

"This is possible." Wahami slammed a fist into his palm. "They will have forged authorization from the Ministry of Culture, no doubt. Still, we shall see. I will arrange for Customs to issue an alert. Of course, road-blocks might waylay them before they get there." Lieutenant Wahami lifted the phone. "Excuse me, I am going to be busy."

Tangier

Beyond the Gate of Rest, Howard was waiting for them on the walkway that overlooked the sea. "I came this time instead of Gerard," he said. "It's good to see you, Cathy." He embraced her briefly. "You'll have to tell me in more detail all about your adventures." He nodded at Rick, who carried their two cases, and then grinned. "I know you were successful but I haven't seen anything in the press about Ananke, you know."

"You're a tease, Howard," Cat said, linking his arm. He liked an attractive woman on his arm. Fortunately, Gerard never got jealous in that way.

He glanced behind them at Rick. "Don't dawdle with those cases, young man! We're both anxious to hear what you've been up to!"

Howard's cell-phone rang. He gently disengaged from her, removed it and gazed at the caller ID, which he didn't recognize. His brow creased as he answered, "Hello?"

"You shouldn't have called for the board meeting."

"Who is that?"

"Emilio Zabala. Head of security. I've left a warning, Greenleaf. Remember, the authorities here don't like your sort. You could be sent to prison."

Howard's chest felt constricted and his hand trembled as he gripped the phone. "Piss off! You don't intimidate me!" He closed the call.

Cat laid a hand on his arm. "Howard, is something wrong? Who was that?"

He told them.

"COME ON, LET'S GET HOME," Cat said.

Left a warning. She sensed a creeping unease in her gut, threatening to rise and choke her. What did Zabala mean by that?

Howard unlocked the door and led the way inside.

"Oh, my God!" Howard exclaimed.

The table in the courtyard had been overturned. Every painting had been slashed and thrown to the floor. She shouldn't be surprised: Zabala had circumvented her home's security system in Alverstoke.

Howard's eyes brimmed at the sight of such vandalism. His steps grew more unsteady as he moved forward. Yet he kept walking, as if impelled to learn the worst.

In the lounge, more paintings were cut to ribbons. Oil paints—reds, greens, blues, yellows—were splashed on the ornate furniture, on the walls, a travesty of Jackson Pollock.

"No, no!" Howard cried and dashed over to the sofa, where Gerard lay stripped to the waist and daubed in red paint.

Gerard trembled in a palsied fashion, his tear-filled eyes staring at an empty wooden frame that rested askew on the sideboard.

In the distance, sirens wailed.

Howard wailed, too, and then knelt by his friend, touched his forehead. "Oh, Gerard, your paintings! The swine's ruined all of..." His hand began to shake, his mouth tried to make words but couldn't.

Cat realized at the same instant, and her heart tumbled. It wasn't red paint, but blood.

Chapter 16

Hugs and Nightmares

The sirens grew closer, louder.

"He...he..." Gerard stammered.

"What has he done, dear friend?" Howard whispered as he gripped Gerard's hand.

"He...he took Cathy's...painting..." Gerard let out a final breath and was still.

Now they were very near, those sirens.

His eyes swimming, Howard abruptly let go of Gerard's limp hand and stood. "We must leave now, at once."

"What about Gerard?" Cat managed, her mouth dry, her eyes moist. Lately, she'd seen too much violent death. Petra, Lieutenant Aziz, his driver, and now dear inoffensive Gerard.

"We must leave him," Howard whispered hoarsely. "Don't you see, Zabala wants to get me arrested for the murder of Gerard. He's bound to have planted clues to incriminate me." He shuddered. "I cannot go to that overcrowded, stinking prison with murderers and rapists!"

"Quick, wash your hands, change your shirt!" Cat commanded. "You can't go outside with blood all over you!"

"Yes, yes, of course." He scampered to the bathroom.

Rick held her arm. "If he runs, they'll be convinced he's guilty."

"Howard needs to be free to prove his innocence."

He hesitated and then nodded. "Alright. Where do we go?"

"I've stayed at the Hotel Continental before. We'll go there."

N1 road, Casablanca to Tangier

Police roadblocks had been set up on the roundabout, with several spike strips laid across the access roads; to the left was the road to the airport; directly ahead, Tangier city center.

Sûreté nationale in their gray uniforms flagged down a convoy of three trucks. All the men carried small machine-guns or automatic pistols.

The truck driver at the rear of the convoy must have panicked, for he braked and began reversing rapidly, the engine whining, the safety lights flashing and the truck making an irritating beeping sound.

Two officers shot the front tires with their sub-machine guns and the vehicle slewed to the side of the road and crashed against a hoarding. The men ran to the driver's cab. The driver was conscious, but had sustained a bloody nose. He was ordered to climb out and open the back of his truck.

Meanwhile, the other two trucks braked and the drivers sat in their cabs, sweating, watching the crashed vehicle and driver.

An officer checked the undersides of the trucks with a mirror on a long pole, while the senior officer present demanded identification and papers from the drivers.

The paperwork seemed in order.

The drivers were invited to step down from their cabs and open the rear of their trucks.

At gunpoint, the drivers opened the doors of the trucks to reveal crates that did not tally with the consignment documentation. An officer climbed inside and jimmied open a crate with a crowbar. Inside was a collection of contraband items: silver, gold and earthenware curios.

The senior officer grinned broadly. "Book them!"

Ouarzazate

Pointer opened his hotel room's door to Sergeant Basset. She was beaming, wafting a sheet of paper. "Come in, Carol, tell me the news!"

She strode across the room and sat on his bed.

He shut the door and folded his arms. "Well? Don't keep me in suspense."

"Sir, we've got confirmation through on the DNA from Zabala's blood sample." She handed Pointer the sheet. "It was e-mailed to me and I had it printed at reception. Your hunch was correct!"

"That was fast work, Carol." Pointer read it and whistled. "So, our nasty murderer is Zabala, eh?"

She shuddered. "Yes, sir. Ganix Elizondo is Zabala. And to think he was standing so close to us!"

"He shot you, remember?"

She gently massaged her bandaged arm. "I won't forget that in a hurry."

"I'll pass on this information to the Royal Gendarmerie and whoever else in their law enforcement organization that needs to know. I would hope checkpoints can be set up within the hour."

"Should I inform London?"

"Yes. It's always possible he's left the country already. Arrange to send someone to check Ananke's London HQ."

"Will do, sir." She smirked.

"What's so amusing?"

"We've come all this way to solve a murder in Southampton!"

His face turned grim. "And a lot of places besides. But we still haven't caught the murderer."

"I know, and that's so frustrating. I've also been informed that our flight to Casablanca is in an hour, sir."

He slapped some Fuller's earth on his face. "On with the motley. I'm ready when you are, Carol."

Shanghai

Dante sat at his office desk and glared at the phone—caller ID said Zabala—and reluctantly picked it up.

"Mr. Dante, I have neutralized the millionaire, Greenleaf. He will not give you any more concern."

"I was going to ask you to speak in plain English, Zabala. But perhaps it is best that I don't know what you mean by the term 'neutralize'." He grated his teeth. "I take it that you have been unable to locate Miss Vibrissae?"

"Regretfully no, sir. But I have made it particularly uncomfortable for Barnes."

"I'm not interested in Barnes. He has proved to be a nuisance, but he is small fry. You can 'neutralize' him for all I care."

"That will give me great pleasure, sir."

"Don't bring your pleasure into our conversation, Zabala. I don't know why, but any time you mention it, I come away feeling grubby."

"Yes, sir..."

"Make sure I am not involved in any of your 'neutralizing,' is that clear?"

"Yes, sir. Crystal clear."

Tangier

A welcoming smile on his face, Youssef the concierge stood behind the Hotel Continental's dark marble reception desk; he spoke English to Rick and Spanish to Cat. They registered for a double room, handing in their Spanish passports, which they were assured they could collect later.

Trying to appear unobtrusive, Howard sat reading a newspaper in the foyer, near the stairs; there was no elevator.

The pair of them followed the bellhop. As they passed Howard, Cat whispered their room number and added, "Ten minutes."

They ascended the marble stairs to the top floor and, a little breathless carrying both cases, the bellhop let them into their room.

The colors were muted red and dark wood, with arches seemingly at every opening. It had a double bed, which was a pleasant change from two singles shoved together. There was a red leather settee, and a French window. The orange and brown tiled bathroom was small, with toilet, bidet and shower unit with a curtain. The bellhop put their cases on a large ornate wooden table; Rick tipped him and he left.

Now that they were alone, Cat moved to the double glass doors and stepped onto the balcony which over-looked the patio below. The view was as she remem-bered—the broad vista of the harbor, with motorboats and sailing boats moored; the sky clear blue. She heard the faint sounds of traffic, merely a background hubbub, not intrusive.

About ten minutes later, there was a knock on the door and Rick let Howard in. He appeared drawn, his eyes flat, almost devoid of life. Now, it seemed that his lover's death had finally hit home. "It's all been a waste of time—with Gerard dead and me in hiding, there won't be a board meeting to oust Dante."

Rick shut the door. "I don't agree, Howard. We can

contact the company secretary, tell him what's happened. The revelations at the Moulay catacomb will cook Dante's goose. Ayad El Foukai will ensure that the health food plant is not implicated, only certain individuals—Dante and the notary."

Cat took Howard's hand, the flesh cold. "We need to get you out of Tangier, Howard. Is that alright?"

He nodded docilely as she led him to the settee and sat beside him. She looked at Rick. "What are we going to do?"

"He'll need a fresh change of clothes, a suitcase. At least he brought his documentation."

"But his passport is useless. They'll monitor the ferry port and the airport."

"I'm here, you know," Howard said, jerking his head round at them both in turn. "I've had a bad shock, but I can think straight and contribute to the discussion of my future."

"Well, Howard, have you any ideas?" Rick asked.

"Money talks in Morocco, my friend. I've been here long enough to know that. Scandal is usually buried, especially if it involves government ministers or friends of the royal family. Despite their best efforts, corruption's still a serious problem... But, alas, I don't know if I have enough to buy my way out of this nasty business."

"You have access to your money?" Cat asked.

"Yes, I brought my bank cards."

"But they'll block your account as soon as they find the paperwork at your home," Rick warned.

"That is why I withdrew as much as I could while you came up to your room. The hotel was amenable, since they got a good commission." He fished inside his jacket and produced a wad of Dirham bank notes.

Cat gently touched his hand. "Your card will be traced to the hotel, Howard."

"Oh, shit, I should've thought of that."

"They don't know which room you're in, though," Rick pointed out.

Howard brightened up. "That's true. Even so, I can't hang around here. I'll have to...get away?"

"As soon as possible," Cat conceded. "What had you planned to do with the money?"

"As I said, I don't think I could pay my way out of a murder charge. But I think it will buy silence when I cast off in my schooner."

Cat laughed softly. "Your boat's in the harbor?"

"Yes. We...we usually sailed in her every Sunday." He gazed into space, probably reminiscing about his sailing jaunts, and then he stared at the money in his hands. "It's of little use outside Morocco, you know. It's forbidden to take the currency out of the country." He retained about half and gave the rest to Cat. "Here. You might find it useful. I've kept enough for fuel for the boat, and provisions."

"Thanks, Howard." She pocketed the money. "Can you sail the schooner by yourself?"

Howard stood up. "I should say so! In my youth I took part in many solo races." He looked wistful again. "Of course I was younger then..."

Shanghai

The intercom bleeped and Loup Dante's secretary Peizhi said, "Sir, there's an urgent call from head office.

214

It's your secretary."

What the hell does London want? "Very well, Peizhi. I'll take it now."

"At once, sir."

His desk phone buzzed and he lifted the receiver. "Yes, Malorie, what is it?"

"I'm sorry to disturb you, sir, but I thought you'd want to know straight away, as soon as they left."

"You're talking in riddles, my dear. Who left?"

"The police, sir."

His heart managed a short sharp tap-dance and then quietened to a pounding marathon. He had nothing to fear from the police in London. Or anywhere else. Surely? His operations were all legitimate. Well, not quite all. On the surface, they were, though. "What did the police want, Malorie?"

"They urgently need to speak to Mr. Zabala."

"What about?"

"The Detective Inspector wouldn't say."

"No, I suppose he wouldn't..."

"But as soon as I explained that Mr. Zabala was in Morocco, they left, and I was then able to contact my cousin in the Met."

Smart woman. That's why he employed her, after all. "And what did your cousin find out?"

"Mr. Zabala may be able to help them with their enquiries into one or more murders, sir. He wouldn't go into details, but he did say the deaths were 'especially gruesome'—his words."

"Oh, that doesn't sound nice at all. I'm sure Mr. Zabala is probably just a potential witness and it will all blow over. Don't worry about it. I'll see if I can contact him and arrange for him to get in touch with the police. Leave it to me."

"Thank you, sir. Sorry to disturb you."

"That's fine. You did the right thing."

As soon as he hung up, he dialed Zabala's number.

After the second ring Zabala answered. "Yes, sir?"

"Mr. Zabala, it would seem your thirst for pleasure is muddying the waters. London police are looking for you and want an interview."

"Interview me, sir?"

Dante gripped the receiver tightly, his knuckles white. "Your antics are liable to bring Ananke Corp into disrepute and I cannot permit that."

"Antics, sir?"

Don't play the innocent with me, you worm! Enough! "I find that I cannot be associated with you any further, so I'm cutting you loose."

"Loose, sir?"

"As of this moment, you no longer work for me or Ananke. Is that clear?"

"But, sir..."

"I will brook no argument, do you understand?"

"Y—yes, sir."

"Good. I will inform the London office and your severance pay will be sent to your bank. That will draw to a close our association." He hung up, quite pleased. Yes, Zabala had been very useful over the years, but of late he was becoming a liability, quite careless, even dangerous. That thought sent another scurrying: what if Zabala took umbrage—violent umbrage? A chill shimmered across his skin and assaulted his spine. He lifted the phone, and told Peizhi, "Please get hold of Mr. Song Chong at our Nanjing plant. It is urgent."

"I will do that, sir, immediately."

"Thank you." Song was a good security man, an ex-bodyguard—and he had other attributes that might mean he could replace Zabala. He felt better already.

Tangier

Plainclothes scene of crime officers moved through Howard Greenleaf's home, searching, discarding as they went, not particularly respectful regarding personal possessions, which irked Detective Inspector Farid Ghazzouli of the *Sûreté nationale*. One of them, Ahmed, swore and used the term 'zamel,' an offensive reference to homosexuals. Ghazzouli reckoned that Ahmed's attitude needed to change, but it would take time. He sighed: it was an uphill battle.

"Sir, we found this," said Detective Latifa Badouri. She wore a fitted dark blue jacket and pants and a white blouse. She stood about eight inches shorter than him, and appeared diminutive alongside his overweight, almost corpulent frame. Her dark brown eyes were huge; her black wavy hair framed an oval face with a pointed chin, thick sensuous lips and an attractive rounded nose. She wafted a passport in her latex-gloved hand. "It had fallen behind the sofa."

Ghazzouli pulled on his own gloves and then examined it. "British. Name of Richard Barnes." He turned to her. "This name seems familiar."

"It is, sir. We received a blue notice about him from Interpol."

Chapter 17

Last Sunset

"So we did. Thank you, Detective Badouri." She was bright, one of the new breed. There'd been controversy when female police were sent undercover to tackle the country's serious prostitution organizations. Yet they harvested many offenders and broke up a number of people trafficking rings as well, which went down well with the public. Badouri seemed dedicated and incorruptible. It was several years since the declaration of a clamp-down on state corruption, yet it was nowhere near resolution. Sometimes, he despaired. It only took one high-profile case to have the western press baying at Morocco about "human rights" and all the good was forgotten or ignored; yet the same couldn't be said of western countries that were just as scandal-ridden. Blinkered, some of them!

"The evidence suggests this was a gay murder of passion," he observed, his tone cool, almost disinterested.

"That is what we are meant to think, sir," Badouri replied.

Inwardly, he smiled. He waved the blood-spotted passport. "And this?"

"I find it doubtful that the owner would be so careless. I would even suspect it had been stolen, perhaps to confound us, no?"

Ghazzouli grinned with immense pleasure. "I like the way that your thinking process works, Detective. See that everything is bagged, as usual. Don't release any statement yet. Let us see what surfaces, eh?"

"You think the murderer might reveal himself?"

"Or herself."

"Indeed, I stand corrected. Or herself."

"Possibly."

"What should I do about Richard Barnes?"

"Put out an alert for him. In relation to the blue notice, *not* this murder."

She released a deep gratified sigh. "Very good, sir."

IT WAS SETTLED. Rick would help Howard crew his schooner to the Canaries. Howard contacted Ayad El Foukai and explained about Gerard's death and his imminent absence. Ayad El Foukai agreed to a fresh meeting to appoint new directors amenable to ejecting Dante from the board. "Take care, my friend," he ended, hanging up.

While Rick and Howard went to the shops to buy clothes and provisions for the sailing trip, Cat packed their cases and checked the car's water and oil. She booked the ferry to Algeciras for the next day.

When they returned for a bite to eat, Howard went to the bathroom to change into his new clothes.

In their bedroom, Rick held her close. "We'd better sail this afternoon," he said. "Go while we still can."

"I'm going to miss you," she said. "It will be strange, sleeping alone..."

"Yes, me, too." He hugged her.

She felt warm and secure in his arms. At the beginning of their relationship, hugs invariably became the foreplay for making love. Yet, in the last few months, they hugged just for that special feeling of togetherness. She was going to miss that, too.

"Will you take turns at sleeping at sea, go on watch?"

"I'll let Howard sleep first, if he can."

"That's the best thing for him," she whispered. "Sleep helps the healing process."

"I'm not so sure, love. When you sleep, you get nightmares."

"You haven't mentioned nightmares before. Do you suffer from them?"

"Sometimes. Remembering when I was in that dark tunnel, the water rising, those bloody rats...I wake in a cold sweat; but I don't want to disturb your sleep, as I'm sure it'll go away in time."

She hugged him tighter. "Next time, wake me, and I can soothe your troubled brow...or something."

He kissed her. "That 'or something' might do the trick."

"I'll be looking forward to it after your absence," she purred. "Where can we meet up?"

"Once Howard's settled somewhere safe, I'll leave

him there and fly to Madrid. I'll text you my flight details."

"That should work. Give me plenty of notice and I'll drive up from Nice to meet you."

He kissed her lips briefly. "You could always leave the car here and join us on the boat."

"No, as much as I'd love to. We can't keep throwing money away. And abandoning our car is doing precisely that."

Casablanca

Basset explained that their flight from Ouarzazate had left them with an hour or so to await their London flight connection. The pair lounged in the concourse, perusing the English daily papers. She hated it when a lead went dry on them.

She almost jumped when she received a call on her cell-phone. She listened intently, answered: "Yes, please", closed the call and then grinned.

"Now what's amusing?" Pointer demanded, lowering his paper.

"Tangier police have flagged a passport belonging to Barnes, sir. At the scene of a murder. They wanted to know if we're interested."

Pointer stood abruptly. "Can we get a flight to Tangier?"

"They've booked one for us already, sir. It's all set to take off and the flight will be about an hour."

Tangier

Cat retrieved their Spanish passports from reception and then drove to the quay. Rick carried his suitcase, Howard and Cat hauled boxes of provisions, and they boarded the boat, a gaff rigged 54ft schooner with a rigid life raft supported on davits aft.

The craft looked splendid, most of its superstructure either wood or fiberglass, its name prominent aft: *Life's Good*. "If it wasn't for all the damnable paperwork, I'd change her name," Howard said roughly and clambered down the companionway from the pilothouse through a storm hatch. Rick and Cat followed, descending the ladder, each carrying a cardboard provisions box, and entered the salon where there were opposing settees port and starboard, cabinetry, a small bar, a wall mounted heater that was unnecessary for now, and generator and main engine enclosures. The floor comprised interlocking panels. Howard had explained that the interior was custom built: "Beautiful museum quality woodwork and workmanship is evident from bow to stern."

Cat noticed it didn't get any better inside, though. There were plenty of reminders of Gerard: an easel, a half-finished painting of a sunset. "That was our last sunset," Howard said. "Unfinished."

Gesturing left and right, Howard said, "Have a look around. I'll go and check the engine."

They put the two boxes on the settees and Rick commented that he was surprised there was sufficient headroom for his height of six feet. They then moved forward from the salon and walked along a gangway amidships with private bunk rooms to port and starboard. A ladder mounted on the port wall of the gangway was labeled *Emergency Exit* and went through a deck hatch. Farther forward they found a head and vanity area: "rather essential, no?" Cat said. "You don't get seasick?"

"No, luckily."

Moving aft from the salon there was a dining room to port with a large gimballed table. Across from the dining area was a U-shaped galley with double stainless sinks, counter space, stove/oven, and full-sized Kenmore refrigerator. Cat went for her box and put packs of bacon and beer tins inside.

Aft of the galley and dining area they found the master stateroom with a larger head with shower/tub and vanity to starboard, then aft was the queen bed, and on port a settee aft, and navigation station forward of that. Forward of the nav station was a large pantry with washer/dryer.

"Home from home," Cat stated.

Cat and Rick went back to the boxes and stocked the small bar. "I suspect the spirits will get low in more than one sense," she said, trying to lighten the mood.

"I'll try to keep him from getting too maudlin." Rick clenched his teeth, glanced at the homely cramped quarters, mostly polished wood. "I wish I could've shot Zabala then, outside the catacomb!"

She touched his arm, stroked his face. "You're no sharpshooter, Rick. You could as easily have killed Inspector Pointer."

"I know. But some people don't deserve to tread this earth, and Zabala's one of them."

"Forget about that dreadful man." She hugged him. "Think only of us. I'm going to miss you."

"Sorry to disturb a beautiful relationship," Howard said, standing on the companion ladder, "but we need to get under way. I don't know how long we have before the police discover I've got a boat and decide to block the harbor. We're fully fueled now."

"Right," Cat said, stepping from Rick. "Have a great trip! Oh, how long will it take?"

"I estimate about two and a half days if we keep to ten knots," Howard said.

"I'll text you if I can, when I can," Rick promised, and they kissed briefly, all too briefly.

They went up top and she stepped ashore.

Rick kept the stern line on and cast off the bow line first while Howard motored gently, swinging the bow away from the jetty and then Rick hastened along the upper deck and released the stern.

Howard waved to Cat and hollered, "He's a natural already!"

And then they were motoring a good distance from the jetty.

Cat waved and the two men gave her a thumbs-up sign.

She swallowed and wiped the blur from her eyes and paced back to her car.

It promised to be a long miserable night.

ZABALA CLOSED his cell-phone and stood in the foyer of the Continental. He should go to his room and change. His clothes smelled of a kind of lemon scent, which masked the blood under his finger-nails. He'd managed to wash it all from his hands and fortunately hadn't cut into an artery, so there was no spray; only cut deep and let the *mariposa* called Gerard linger.

He licked his lips. The urge could not be quashed. He hungered for another woman. Very soon.

He turned on his heel, left the hotel, and went downhill through the jumble of streets. He knew a small number of likely haunts where he could pick up someone suitable. He fingered his right cheek; some women fancied a scarred man.

The decision made, he sensed the rising tension ease off. The promise would keep him going until he found her, anywoman.

Then, after he'd dealt with anywoman, he'd be able to think straight. Clearly, this was all the fault of the Vibrissae bitch. Mr. Dante wouldn't have let me go, if she hadn't been on the scene. God, if only he could get his hands—and knife—on Catherine Vibrissae right now!

LEAVING THE PORT AREA, Cat drove the wrong way along a one-way street in order to get to the hotel carpark, thankful that there were no oncoming vehicles. She passed a few pedestrians who didn't seem unduly concerned; she'd heard that tourists did this all the time, which was no excuse, granted.

At least she'd finished the packing. She planned to order a meal in her room and then have a shower and get an early night. The ferry crossing was only ninety minutes, but she'd have a long drive ahead. She intended staying overnight en route to their Nice apartment. When Rick got in touch, then she'd drive to Madrid to meet him.

Already, it felt odd not having him by her side.

ZABALA STOPPED WALKING AND STARED. He couldn't believe his luck. Vibrissae drove past without noticing him. Heading uphill—toward the Continental?

He swiveled round and walked fast, keeping the Toyota Land Cruiser in sight, careful not to be in line with the view from her side-mirrors. He didn't want to alert her, but it was unlikely that she'd use her rear-view mirror since she was going against the traffic.

Warmth radiated throughout his body. It looked like *anywoman* was now quite specific: Catherine Vibrissae.

Chapter 18

"No last words?"

Life's Good ploughed through the Atlantic, wind billowing in the main and jib sails. The fresh smell of ozone filled Rick's nostrils as he sat in the stern, sipping a Flag Speciale pale lager.

Nursing a gin and tonic in one hand, Howard stood at the controls with legs braced, facing into the wind, his cheeks damp and crusted with salt, glistening, long salt-and-pepper hair blowing in disarray.

Rick was glad he'd come along. He didn't want Howard to be one of those depressed sailors who deliberately got lost at sea and was never heard of again.

Howard turned to face him. "Thanks for joining me, Rick. I appreciate it."

"No problem. I wanted to give you space to mourn."

"I must admit the thought did occur, to do away with myself." He held up his glass, sipped the drink. "But it was only for a fleeting moment. I realized that I'd much rather see Gerard's murderer get what's coming to him!"

"That's more like it!" Rick said with a grin, and they leaned forward and clinked glasses.

Swallowing his beer, Rick wondered how Cathy was coping.

CAT STOOD ON THE BALCONY, watching the harbor, all the night lights and boats. So romantic. She felt very alone.

"Room service!" a voice announced in accented English.

"Just a second!" She remembered their stay in Marrakesh, when the intruder who stole Rick's British passport had used that ploy. Calm down, she told herself. After all, she *had* ordered a meal. She dug out the Astra A50 automatic from her handbag, held it behind her back, and then opened the door.

It was her food. She released a breath.

The waiter carried a silver tray and placed it on the ornate wood table. He lifted the lid: kefta and egg, exactly what she ordered.

"Thank you."

He hesitated.

She couldn't tender a tip without him seeing her gun. She offered a smile instead and, casting a dark look, he left, shutting the door loudly.

Her hands trembled as she put the gun in her handbag. She'd hidden Aziz Basri's Heckler & Koch Mk 23 automatic in the car. When she checked out tomorrow morning, she'd conceal the A50, too, and hope for the best. Entering Melilla, she hadn't wanted to risk being caught with a firearm. But now, with the ever-present threat of Zabala, she'd have to take that risk, because she only considered herself safe with a gun in easy reach.

She'd been hungry, yet now, surprisingly, she found her hunger had deserted her. Her mouth was dry. Should have ordered sandwiches, and if she hadn't fancied them she could have kept them for the journey tomorrow. She poured the Vieux Papes red table wine and was surprised that it went down so smoothly. And after the first bite the spiced ground meat was more-ish —or was that Moorish?

When she'd eaten and emptied her glass, she spread on the settee her clothes for tomorrow—fawn chinos, white blouse, white lace underwear, and then got undressed. She poured a second measure of red wine into her glass and padded to the bathroom. She placed the glass on top of the toilet cistern and stepped into the shower base, drew the curtain—not for modesty's sake but to contain the shower-water.

The water spray wasn't too hot; quite pleasant. In the foyer, she'd overheard some guests complain about lack of hot water; maybe the old girl needed a massive face-lift, but she liked the place as it was: somewhere exotic and not modernistic glass and metal with no character.

Feet spread on the non-slip mat, she lathered soap over her shoulders, knowing she'd punish those muscles tomorrow on the long drive.

"I'd offer to scrub your back," boomed the voice above the sound of the shower, "but I don't think you'd appreciate it." Zabala chuckled.

Before her heart could resume its beat, he tore the curtain aside to her right, exposing her to his gaze.

He stood there, a knife glinting in his right hand.

Shower spray splashed his tan suit but he didn't seem to notice. His almost black eyes scanned her body, a leer on his thin lips. His right cheek was pitted with four tiny cuts. How'd he get in? Stupid question, he's expert at breaking in, as she should know by now.

Her heart started to beat again, now hammering. She gulped in air and spluttered as she sucked in water as well. Spray from the shower-head continued to hit her.

Shouting above the sound of the shower, he growled, "I'm going to cut you like I cut Petra." He gestured with the knife. "You won't know what I'm talking about. Still, you knew her, didn't you?"

She felt her legs weaken as images of Petra Grimalkin lying dead in her shower flitted before her mind's eye. He was unaware she'd discovered Petra's body. In mute response, she nodded and water gushed off her head.

"I'm going to enjoy this." His lips curved in a thin line. "It is going to be my finest moment."

Clenching her teeth, she steadied herself, a hand against the tiled wall, the squashed sponge oozing suds. With her free hand she turned the faucet and stilled the shower's flow.

"That's good," he said. "Now we can hear much better."

"There's nothing I want to hear from you!" she snapped, her voice firm, surprising herself.

He cackled. "So brazen, standing there, aren't you? Tempting."

She dropped the sponge. "Give me a towel."

"No, I don't think so. I like what I see, Catherine Vibrissae." He waved the knife, left and right, emphasizing the negative. "Or should I call y
Moreno? Useful, hotel registers, aren't they?

"For stalkers, especially." She wanted t
eyes, go into denial. Yet images of poor
persisted. Stark, uncompromising. She sta
knife. Would it hurt very much? Anot
intruded into her thoughts. Her taekwondo i
Mark: "The likelihood of any of you facing
with a gun or a knife is remote, very rem
wouldn't make a good soothsayer. "Remember,
you cannot hope to use these skills at your leve.
a gunman. But someone with a knife, you might
chance if you're unable to run away. Always ru
if you can." *No chance of running.*

"You're not very talkative, are you? N
words?"

"I have nothing to say to you." She tentativ
reached toward the toilet cistern and picked up th
glass of wine. Willing her hand not to shake, she tipped
it to her lips, swallowed a little. God, that tasted good. If
only she could get so drunk she'd be unaware of what
was going to happen to her.

"You're quite brave, Catherine. I like that in a
woman."

She swallowed a little more. "I don't care what you
like, Zabala."

He chuckled and took a step closer, pointing the
knife blade at her. "I'm going to enjoy this."

"You said that already." One lunge and he'd impale
her, slice and dice her. The kefta threatened to erupt
from her stomach. She tensed, awaiting the thrust, her
left foot firm on the non-slip mat, knees bent, taking the
weight on her back foot.

He ared. "You won't be flippant when I've

finish er sparring, she'd often detect a blow being
before it was delivered, but Zabala's eyes
d nothing. The blade darted toward her, high to
de, past her right cheek, and pulled back as
enly. She hadn't moved, had barely seen it. She'd
ed the swift rush of air at the movement. Had he
ant to cut her face and missed? Or was he playing?
er insides roiled, and she clenched her left fist.

He laughed, touched his knife-hand knuckles to the
ight side of his face. "Maybe I should scar your cheeks
like mine, first, eh?"

Cat shook her head. *Don't let the fear in, that's the
real enemy.*

She breathed in deeply, steadily, chest rising and
falling. *Keep calm!*

His eyes narrowed as he stared at her wet breasts
and he licked his lips.

He's toying with me.

Two can play that game.

Her hand quivered a little as she gripped the glass.
*Not too tight, or it'll shatter. Use it as a weapon? No, it's
too small, and it has limited reach.*

Control the fear.

Eyes wide and glowing, he lunged at her again, the
blade flashing past her left cheek. *No scarring yet, then.*
In that same instant, she deliberately let out a little
shriek and jerked in response to his near miss, spilling
the red wine on her chest and breathed in deeply.

He stared, wetting those lips, the knife held at about
level with his rib-cage. He was distracted by the wine
dribbling over her, dripping from her nipples.

In one swift action, she threw the empty glass into the far corner of the bathroom, simultaneously raised her right knee and rotated her body ninety degrees, and extended the right leg, striking Zabala full in the face with her heel; one powerful *yeop chagi*—side-thrusting kick—delivered with force.

As her foot made contact, she slipped slightly on the mat, and then steadied herself with her left hand gripping the chrome shower hose.

Zabala swore and tumbled a couple of paces backwards toward the doorway, his nose streaming blood.

Still gripping the hose, she jumped out and landed on the wet tiled floor. She steadied herself, tugged at the shower hose and pulled it off the wall fitting. Swinging it round above her, she slammed the shower head on the end of the hose into Zabala's face, cutting his brow. Water and blood trickled into his right eye from the fresh wound.

She snatched a hand towel from the basin, wrapped it round her left forearm and charged at him, swinging the metal hose again.

If she could get to her handbag, withdraw the A50.

Wiping blood from his eye, Zabala braced himself against the door jamb. "You bitch!" He ducked and weaved under the swinging shower head. "I'm going to make you die so slow, you'll..."

His attention was on the hose, not her legs. She launched herself and her right foot slammed into his knee with a side-piercing kick. He shrieked and fell on his back.

She landed on her rump on the wet floor and quickly scrambled to her feet.

Gritting his teeth, he regained his footing and threw

the knife at her, but it glanced off her defensive towel-covered forearm. He fumbled inside his jacket, pulled free his pistol, but the shower head side-swiped his gun-hand and he dropped the weapon. It skittered to the far corner of the bathroom. Ducking again, he backed away, through the doorway, into the room, and hobbled toward the French window.

He fumbled at the catch, flung the door open and staggered onto the balcony.

Cat unraveled the towel from her arm, snatched at her handbag, unzipped it and grabbed the Astra A50 automatic. Must kill him; shoot him for murdering Rick's brother-in-law, for slaughtering Petra, for slaying Gerard. Trembling, she raised the weapon to shoot.

But Zabala wasn't there.

She ran onto the balcony and immediately the cool night air assaulted her wet flesh and she realized she was naked.

Fortunately, nobody nearby seemed to be looking up.

Heart pounding, she tentatively edged to the railing and scanned the patio area. Couples sat around, chatting, drinking, smoking. There were no shouts of surprise; there was no confusion: so he hadn't tumbled down there. So where the hell was Zabala? He had a damaged kneecap. He couldn't run off.

She crossed to the side railing and leaned a hand on it to peer over and quickly withdrew. Stickiness—blood. He'd escaped across the gap to the next room. Yes, she could discern a few dark patches on the floor of that balcony.

Hurrying inside, she shut and locked the doors,

leaned against them, but only for an instant as she was fearful that he would return. Grabbing the nearby chair, she wedged its back against the door-handles.

Her stomach felt like it had been kicked in a taek-wondo session. She rushed into the bathroom and disgorged the wine and kefta into the toilet bowl.

She washed her face and hands in the basin, splashed her chest to clear the diluted dribbles of wine, and then dried herself with a bath towel.

Unsteadily, she padded into the room.

Fresh waves of nausea hit her.

She spotted the bottle of wine, returned to the bath-room and brought out the plastic beaker, topped it up. Sipping the wine, she sat on the bed, surprised that she experienced this physical weakness; it was so frustrat-ing! She'd free-climbed mountains, free-fallen from airplanes, put her body in jeopardy countless times, but she'd never experienced this kind of reaction.

Maybe Rick was right, and it was time to call a halt to her crusade against Dante and Ananke.

But Zabala was still alive, crawling under some rock. He'd bide his time and come after her, she felt sure.

Would she have nightmares now? Zabala with his knife, perpetually thrusting the glinting blade at her face.

She recalled her vow to Papa at his funeral.

No, these people were content to ride roughshod over anyone who got in their way, anyone who didn't buy into their at-all-costs philosophy. Christ, her crusade could extend a long way beyond Ananke, if she allowed it. There was nothing wrong with big business

—providing those responsible didn't eschew common humanity. Responsibility: sometimes she suspected that was considered to be a dirty word.

Hadn't she done enough already? Razed the Angers plant, exposed the Southampton outlet, seriously imperiled the plant at Seahouses, exposed the project in Wales, effectively dismantled the sordid business in Barcelona, virtually stolen the Tangier plant from under Dante's nose, and also exposed Ananke' grave-robbing.

No, it wasn't enough. Never enough. Dante and Zabala must pay for what they'd done.

She shook her head, stood up, and finished the wine in the beaker. I'm not going to sleep right now, am I? Yet I've got a long drive tomorrow. Not necessarily. Cross on the ferry to Algeciras and then find a hotel or pension to rest and recuperate.

Yes, that made sense.

She poured another measure and stared at the closed French window, wondering if Zabala would attempt a forced break-in.

Shanghai

"Mr. Song Chong, sir," Zoo Peizhi said and ushered the man into the presence of Loup Dante. She retreated with dainty footsteps.

Song was an imposing Chinese man. He had a golden complexion, with an inscrutable gaze from almond eyes with gold-flecked irises. His nose was pug, with high-cut nostrils. He wore his black hair close-cropped to a bullet-head. His lips puckered above a round firm chin. He was tall, about six feet four, muscular, broad-shouldered and barrel-chested.

As Song walked in, Dante noted that the man's arms were longer than normal, more like a gibbon; the hands at the end of them were huge, and calluses were visible on the knuckles and edges.

"You sent for me, Mr. Dante."

"Yes, I did." Dante stood behind his desk and extended his hand in greeting.

Song approached. His hand was warm, strong, and hard. The man's eyes glinted and he smiled, baring pointed teeth, two of them gold. "I got here as fast as I could, sir."

"Commendable. Now, can you find a replacement for your post in Nanjing?"

Song's face betrayed no puzzlement. "Yes, sir, I have a reliable deputy."

"How would you like to be Head of Security for Ananke?"

"For Shanghai, sir?"

"No, worldwide."

"I understand that you have someone in that post." He gazed into the middle-distance, and finally came out with a name. "Zabala, isn't it?"

"It was, Mr. Song. Past tense. He has retired. It was sudden."

Song smiled again. Dante supposed he could get used to those teeth.

"I accept, sir. When do I take up my post?"

"You can start now." Dante sat and gestured for Song to sit opposite.

The man's chair protested but at least it didn't collapse.

Dante opened his drawer and withdrew two photographs. "These individuals are proving disruptive to our worldwide concerns. I want you to find them."

Soong took them but didn't look at them. "What do I do with them when I have found them?"

He liked that, too. No conditional response. Song *would* find them. "Bring the woman here, to me. Try not to harm her. I reserve that pleasure for myself."

That smile again, though a little twisted this time. "And the man?"

"Neutralize him."

"Neutralize?"

"Isn't that the term?"

"Do you mean I should dispose of him, sir?"

"Yes, that is my meaning."

Song nodded his bullet-head and finally read the stickers on the photos: "Catherine Vibrissae, Richard Barnes."

"Can you do that for me, Mr. Song?"

"Oh, yes, I'm sure it can be done. Do you have any more information to go on, other than these photos?"

"I have." Dante pulled a folder from the drawer. "You'll see the extent of their nefarious activities when you read this. And, in addition, there's a man in Morocco who has been in touch with my office. I've asked him to fly here. He has interesting information to divulge."

Tangier

At 3:15am Cat woke with a stiff neck and an aching back, the wine bottle empty. She shivered naked on top of the bed.

Bleary-eyed, she set her alarm, and then snuggled under the sheets.

Later in the morning, when she settled her check at reception, Cat apologized for the broken shower, explaining that she'd slipped on soap and tore it free by accident.

They seemed more concerned about her. Was she alright? She wasn't going to sue them? She offered to pay for the repair, but they waived that expense, and hoped that she would return soon.

She promised she would be glad to; though she wasn't sure. It depended if she could exorcise the association of those images of Zabala standing in front of her with a knife, intent on butchering her.

She loaded her luggage and set off.

Car windows open to let fresh air clear her head, she drove down to the port.

ZABALA HAD BEEN fortunate to fall onto the balcony next to Vibrissae's. The woman staying there was a widow who liked her whisky too much; she lay unconscious on her bed. He had sneaked into her bathroom and undressed to examine the damage Vibrissae had inflicted. The pain in his head emanated from his nose, which was surely broken. His brow was cut, and bruising around his eyes showed already. His knee-cap was badly swollen. He washed his face and hands and ripped one of the woman's blouses into strips, wet them and used them to bind the knee. Every step was agony as he hobbled out of her room.

He cursed the hotel for not installing an elevator. By the time he'd descended the stairs one floor, he was lathered in sweat. Not so long ago, he'd been a fit man, good with a knife, good with women, and now he felt like an octogenarian.

It took him a long time to get to his room. Here, he poured a glass of brandy and swigged it down.

He eyed the portrait of Catherine Vibrissae executed by that homosexual, Kominsky. He studied it, admired it. He possessed it, but he wanted to possess her—if only to hurt her, and then to kill her. And Dante as well, he vowed. If Dante hadn't wanted her spared, in the deranged belief that she was his daughter, she'd be dead by now.

He packed quickly but methodically, making sure the painting stayed flat. He kept fainting, pushing himself too hard, and lost track of time, and slept.

Finally, when he woke, it was daylight. Over his suit he put on a djellaba with hood.

Eventually, he went to the foyer to settle his account. The receptionist was too professional to comment on his garment. He suspected he gave the appearance of an old man, hunched due to the insidious pain in his knee.

Vibrissae. The name hissed from his lips every time that pain lanced up his leg.

He bought a Bowie knife and sheath in the gift shop.

Then he hired a taxi to take him to the ferry port.

Hobbling painfully, he milled about with dozens of other travelers, and boarded the ferry for Algeciras.

Chapter 19

End It Once and For All

Beni Ansar, Morocco

Abdel sat with his family. Their gaze never left him as he opened the package and unfolded the letter that accompanied the bulky bubble-wrap.

His hands trembled as he read it.

Dear Abdel

I know you have contacts who will be able to convert the enclosed into money. I ask that you give the money from the transaction to Nora and any other deserving mule women and their families to ease their financial difficulties.

My love to your family.

Go with God,

Cathy

Abdel carefully opened the bubble-wrap and stared in amazement. His chest filled to overflowing. A woman had achieved this munificence. He looked up. "My good friend Cathy is a true benefactress, dear Amina, dear Sheera. I must do her bidding first thing tomorrow."

"It will not be dangerous?" Amina queried.

He held up each item of jewelry and scrutinized it. "There is a little risk. But the good that this can do outweighs that, most certainly."

"Take care in your dealings. You truly are a good man, Abdel. I do not want to lose you."

"I am good because I have you and only you, Amina. I cannot comprehend why a man needs more than one wife!"

"Perhaps the other men are dissatisfied?" she said and then flushed and glanced at Sheera; but the girl seemed innocent about the variations "satisfaction" could offer.

"I am exceedingly content."

"That is good to hear, my husband."

Tenerife

By the time they approached the Canaries, Howard had recovered some of his bonhomie, primarily because he was the master of the schooner and though Rick was keen to learn, he was no sailor. The daily navigation and yachting requirements occupied much of Howard's attention.

Rick thought Howard used the sextant like an ancient mariner, his cast of features serious as he took readings. After a short period of instruction Rick was able steer to whatever heading Howard decreed. Rick was also given the responsibility of completing the boat's log, filling in the columns: time, course, speed, log reading, log difference, wind speed and direction, water temperature, barometer reading, barometric trend, engine hours, sails and comments. "You could be born to this, a mariner in the making," Howard declared. "Gerard was hopeless at filling it in regularly." After that comment, Rick reckoned his new friend had surmounted the first phase of accepting the death of a loved one.

On the starboard they passed Fuerteventura, skirted round the north of Gran Canaria, its central Pico de las Nieves in contrast to the relatively flat Fuerteventura. Their journey here was aided by the acceleration zone, winds that could move the craft roughly ten or fifteen knots faster. Howard sailed past Punta de Roque, the northern tip of the island and passed shallows on the starboard.

Howard pointed to the golden sands of a beach beyond. Playa de las Teresitas: "It's supposed to be the best beach on the island; and so it should be, the sand's imported from the Sahara complete with harmless scorpions by all accounts!"

When they approached a long breakwater, Howard set to with Rick to haul in the sails and start the motor. Finally, they entered a gap at the south end: "Dársena Pesquera!" As they sailed through into the fishing harbor, Rick saw a group of oil tanks at the north end. Rounding the breakwater elbow, Howard pointed to a small marina of pontoons, with many boats berthed. "We'll tie up there."

As they fastened the lines, Rick asked, "What about paperwork?"

Howard shrugged. "Our boat's a regular visitor here —admittedly not every Sunday." He faltered, and then continued: "You have your Spanish passport, so you'll be okay. The harbormaster, Fran Acosta is a friendly chap; he knows me. I've already radioed him on channel 9."

"Won't there be a problem when the Moroccan authorities broadcast...the murder?"

Howard gently slapped a hand on Rick's shoulder. "No need to be so delicate, my friend. Gerard's dead but we must go on living."

"You never said. Where are we going to stay?"

"Well, first we have a long hot walk round the head of the basin before we can meet my friends Sara and Gene who are waiting for us. I radioed ahead to them, too."

So they locked the boat and started their walk. And on the way Rick asked, "Does Cat know your friends Sara and Gene?"

"No. Sara's a linguist and Gene's a conservationist. They're presently agents working undercover for CITES."

"CITES? What's that?"

"Convention on International Trade in Endangered Species."

"What, endangered species here in Tenerife?"

"Tenerife seems to be a conduit, one of many, for transporting forbidden items derived from endangered species."

"Sometimes, Howard, you talk in riddles just like Cat. What do you mean, "forbidden items"?'

"CITES banned trade in more than eight hundred —yes, eight hundred—species. And the trade in another 30,000 items is supposedly controlled worldwide."

"So how do you know Sara and Gene?"

"They're staying in Santa Cruz. Sara Whitney, a Brit, and her partner, an American called Gene Brin. They were introduced to Gerard and me a while back by their predecessors, Laura and Andrew Kirby."

Howard waved to the two agents who stood beside a dark green Toyota Yaris. They waved back. They shook hands and made their introductions.

"Pleased to meet you, Rick," Sara Whitney said in a soft lilting tone. She was in her mid-twenties, Rick estimated. She had an attractive tanned complexion, bright blue eyes and long blonde hair that reached her narrow slightly sloping shoulders. Her wide mouth smiled in greeting. Her multi-colored blouse and tight-fitting white shorts showed she had curves in the right places and wasn't reticent about them. His well-trained nose caught the scent of Miss Dior, he reckoned, hints of Lily-of-the-Valley, centifolia rose, wood and musk. It suited her openness.

"Sorry to hear about Gerard, my friend," Gene told Howard. "A terrible business." Gene Brin was Rick's height, probably in his mid-thirties, at a guess. His black hair was thick, and curled down to the lobes of his ears. He, too, was tanned. His hazel eyes sparkled and skin crinkled at the corners. He had a hooked nose and a cleft chin and leathery cheeks. His tropical short-sleeved shirt displayed a muscular body. He had a firm handshake and a resonant voice.

Gene's cell-phone rang. He excused himself and answered it and turned his back. "Yes, Ruben? Oh, that is bad news. Then Sara and I will drive directly." He closed the call and then faced them and pulled a face.

"A problem?" Sara queried.

"Yes. Pablo's dead."

Sara glanced at Howard and Rick. "What do we do?"

Howard stepped forward. "Look, if your work needs you, we'll simply catch the next bus into Santa Cruz."

"There's no need for that, Howard," Gene said. "Besides, it will be quite a wait in this heat. Where we're headed isn't far. If you're happy to stay in the car while Sara and I speak to the police, we can then take you on to the apartment we've rented for you."

PABLO'S CORPSE was sprawled on the concrete floor of an empty warehouse. His mouth was stuffed with rotten banana and his eyes had been gouged out. Scattered on the floor were the discarded brown speckled skins of many bananas. Blood was splattered all around the body.

"Careful you don't slip," Estrada, a member of the SOCO team said as he scratched his bulging belly.

Ramos, his partner, scowled. "Very funny." Despite having a love affair with junk food, he was not overweight.

Ramos was *amargo*, bitter; while Estrada was *retorcido*. Ruben Salazar, Inspector *Jefe del Grupo de Homicidios de Canarias* sighed. He dreaded it when "Bitter" and "Twisted" pulled the SOCO duty. They forever complained and continually exercised inappropriate black humor.

"You know bananas are high in potassium," said Estrada. "You should try them sometime instead of junk food."

"I know. And they come ready-wrapped. So, what you're you suggesting," Ramos replied, "the guy must've died of an overdose of potassium, is that it?"

"That's enough, guys," Inspector Ruben Salazar said. "Show a little respect here." He cocked his head, heard a car engine outside. He strode to the open door and walked past the Civil Guard officer on duty.

Sara Whitney and Gene Brin got out of their vehicle and moved toward him, their faces grim.

As they joined him Ruben pointed to the Yaris: "Who've you got with you?"

"Howard and a friend, Rick Barnes," Gene explained. "Staying here for a short while."

Ruben nodded. He knew Howard. "Where's Gerard. Aren't that pair joined at the hip?"

"They were." Gene shook his head. "Gerard was murdered in Tangier a few days ago. Howard needs time to get over it, I guess."

"Sorry to hear that."

Sara peered through the open warehouse door and pulled a face. "I see you've got Bitter and Twisted. Lucky you."

Ruben shrugged. "They're a pain, but they're good at their job. What can you tell me about the deceased?"

"Pablo was working with a group of smugglers. The last he told me, they were about to ship out a consignment of rhino horn powder. He was hoping to find where they processed the horn."

"Not bananas then?"

"Eh?" Sara said.

"Follow me." Leading them past the sentry, Ruben entered the warehouse and Sara and Gene acknowledged the two SOCO men and left them to it.

"I see what you mean," Sara said. "Do you reckon he was choked?"

Nodding, Ruben added, "I think he lost his eyes while alive. Torture to make him talk. And then he didn't know what to expect next." He stroked his narrow mustache. "I wonder if the banana signifies something."

"Maybe," Sara suggested, "he discovered something was being smuggled with the fruit?"

"That is a possibility. But of course there are dozens of legitimate banana farms on the island. We couldn't possibly search them all."

Bitter walked up to them, said, "Nothing in his pockets, Jefe."

"Thank you, Ramos."

APPROACHING FIFTY, Anton Belofsky was a Russian oligarch who took pleasure smuggling in his luxury cruiser *Mara* desirable women into Tenerife, mainland Spain and Morocco. The majority of the women were willing, being recompensed generously for their high-end services. A small number of them had been kidnapped and with the assistance of drugs, brutal coercion and the dubious promise of riches, eventually acceded to the demands of their mistress, Jacinta Ortiz.

To all intents and purposes, Belofsky appeared to

be a playboy with a stable of attractive women. Yet he was a realist and knew it was only his wealth that attracted the opposite sex. He had wide-set grayish-brown eyes, and long tawny-brown unkempt hair that reached his earlobes. His corpulent belly pressed against his waistcoat.

He was also a financial partner in another smuggling operation masterminded by cruel twenty-eight-year-old Alita Lopez. Now the pair of them stood on the Santa Cruz dockside, watching the longshoremen load crates of bananas on the cargo ship destined for Shanghai.

"Another cool transaction completed," Alita said in her sensuous throaty voice. She linked her arm in his. Quite inappropriate for the dockside, she wore a slinky split thigh-high cream dress, which emphasized her deeply tanned complexion and breasts like melons. She was marginally taller than Belofsky in her brown leather high heeled shoes.

"Yes." He fiddled with his Chinese silk cravat. "Most satisfying, my dear." His voice had a nasal twang.

"When do you sail?" Alita asked, stroking his high Slavic cheekbones with a manicured hand.

"Later tonight, with Jacinta for company."

She chewed on peppermint gum, wondering what he saw in Jacinta: the woman was slim, true, but with no definable hips and preferred to wear trouser suits. "The brothels will miss her firm hand."

"Don't be catty, my dear." His smile was like an alligator's, broad and menacing. "Now tell me, what are you going to do about Brin and the Whitney woman?"

"Pablo told me everything I needed to know. I will take Vito and we will pay them a visit tonight."

"And?"

"Oh, we'll deep six them."

GENE DROPPED off Sara at their apartment on Calle de Juan Padrón and then drove Howard and Rick to an apartment on the other side of town, Calle Dr. Fleming, one down from Pasteur. "It's all I could get at short notice," Gene said, handing Gerard a set of labeled keys.

"Thanks for getting us this, my friend."

"What will you do tonight?" Gene asked.

Rick grinned. "Howard's talked about introducing me to the casino after a meal."

"We don't do gambling but we'd both like you to join us at our place for a bite to eat, if you want?" Gene suggested.

"We wouldn't want to put you to any trouble," Howard said.

"Sara thought of it, actually. She likes entertaining —when the job allows. I can pick you up at 7pm."

"That would be good," Howard said. "It gives us time to freshen and change."

"See you at seven then." Gene drove off.

The apartment was on the third floor, with two bedrooms, each with an attached bathroom. There was a spacious lounge, a dining/kitchen area and French doors that opened onto a balcony that overlooked bungalows, lush green gardens and swimming pools.

Rick yearned to share the view with Cathy. He was tempted to phone her but she was probably already driving on to Nice about now, though naturally she'd stop somewhere on the way.

THE SPANISH OMELET—EGG, potatoes and onions—bubbled in the pan. Sara had overturned it once, revealing the blotchy browned surface. The smell of onions was strong even with the extractor fan blowing.

Movement caught her eye and she turned, about to say, "You're earlier than I expected" but halted when she realized she was confronted by a man and a woman who had entered the door from the hallway. Shock, alarm and anger vied with her emotions. She settled on anger: "Who the hell are you and what are you doing in my home?"

"You can call me Alita. We've come to see you and your man, Gene Brin." The woman had a whiskey voice. She was deeply tanned and had umber-colored eyes, high cheekbones and short black hair swept behind her ears. She was chewing gum and smiled to reveal bright white teeth. She seemed over-dressed in her split thigh-high cream dress that showed a lot of leg and breast. She had a black leather shoulder bag.

Alita eyed the set places on the dining table. "Expecting company?"

"Not you. How did you get in?"

The woman pointed to the shorter man, who was thin in features and build. "There isn't a lock that Vito can't pick, Miss Whitney."

Sara glanced toward the dining table. The strap of her bag dangled on a chair back. If she could get her cell-phone out... A sizzling noise from behind drew her attention. "Damn!" She swiveled round and turned off the gas burner under the omelet.

"Smells nice," Alita said "First course, is it?"

"Yes." Making a fuss about wiping her hands on a towel, Sara moved nearer the table and her bag. "But you're not invited!"

"How inhospitable!"

Sara lunged for the bag, which was unzipped, but as her fingers clasped the cell-phone Alita pounced and slapped her face.

Sara grunted in shock, her cheek inflamed, and dropped the phone to the tiled floor where it broke into several pieces.

"What a pity. Hope it's insured," Alita snapped. "Where's Gene?" she demanded, tugging at Sara's colorful apron, drawing her so close she could smell the woman's strong orangey perfume combined with the cloying sweetness of the chewing gum.

"He'll be here soon—with two friends."

"Good. We'll wait."

Vito lifted a bowl of potato chips from the table and began eating them.

Alita didn't seem bothered, four against two.

"Then we can all go for a little boat ride." Alita withdrew a revolver from her shoulder bag and waved it at her. "And don't get any ideas, eh?" So, that's why she wasn't too bothered: a great leveler, a gun.

GENE UNLOCKED the front door and stepped into the hallway. Rick and Howard followed and Gene shut the door. "Ah," he said, "smell that—tortilla!" Clutched in his arms Howard carried a brown paper bag holding two bottles of wine, a red and a white, which they'd purchased from a supermarket on their way here.

Abruptly, Rick grasped Gene's arm. "Wait," he whispered with urgency.

Gene saw the concern in Rick's face reflected in the hall's wall mirror. He turned. "What?"

"There's another smell, quite strong." Rick's nostrils dilated and he sniffed. "Noir Extreme—yes, I get a hint of mandarin, neroli and sandalwood." He eyed Gene. "Does Sara make a habit of changing her perfume?"

"No," Gene replied. "She swears by Miss Dior. Makes present-buying easy for me, I can tell—"

"Somebody else is here," Rick murmured. "And you're not expecting anyone, are you?"

Gene shook his head and then bit his lip. "Oh, shit. Pablo talked..."

Howard hovered, anxious, and then lifted a bottle of red wine from the paper bag. "Red or white?" he asked Rick.

Rick nodded at the red. Gene smiled and took the white.

"I'll stay well back," Howard whispered. "I'm not in a party mood."

Gene then approached the slightly open door into the apartment's kitchen-dining room. "Honey, I'm home!" he called. "The tortilla smells delicious!"

There was no response, which was worrying.

Gene pushed open the door wide and took in the scene in one swift heart-sinking appraisal.

A woman stood partially behind Sara and held a revolver pointing at Sara's head. A thin man lounged to one side, eating potato chips, apparently unarmed and unconcerned.

"Welcome!" the woman said with a sneer that contradicted her sensuous throaty voice.

With all his strength Gene threw his bottle of wine at the woman's head. It was a good pitch, maybe not quite Major League standard, but then again maybe worthy of the Yankees.

The woman attempted to duck and hastily fired her revolver, but the bottle still hit her on her cheek. The shot went wild, shattering a wall mirror in the hallway. The bottle smashed on the floor, white wine spilling seemingly everywhere.

As the woman had ducked, Sara pivoted round and grappled with the gun-hand. The pair of them bashed into a dining chair, it toppled over and they unbalanced and tumbled to the hard unforgiving floor.

At the same instant Rick had charged the thin stranger and clubbed him with the bottle of red. It remained intact but a couple of teeth were dislodged and fell to the tiles with the half-filled bowl of potato chips; the bowl shattered. The man groaned, lifting a trembling hand to his mouth, and slumped against the wall, all fight deserting him.

Suddenly there was another explosion, a second shot.

The strange woman screamed, and red discolored her cream dress.

Sara rolled away, clasping the revolver in her right hand. "I shot her—I shot her!"

SUFFERING from a gunshot wound to her midriff, Alita Lopez was taken under police guard to hospital and, after an emergency operation, eventually transferred to Hospital del Sur in the center of Las Americas, away from the capital and the prying eyes of journalists and gang members. Vito was arrested and revealed the details of the smuggling of rhino horn. A radio request to the cargo vessel resulted in the skipper turning back to Tenerife where the crates of bananas would be impounded.

Inspector Ruben Salazar explained that the SOCO pair, Bitter and Twisted, had identified several finger-prints on the squashed banana flesh. They tallied with Alita Lopez's.

"As soon as she is fit," the homicide inspector said, "she will be transported to the penitentiary to await trial."

"At least we've broken one smuggling gang," Sara said.

"Just the tip of an iceberg, I'm afraid," Gene added. "Our work is never done, I'm afraid." He clapped a hand on Rick's shoulder. "Thanks for the assist."

Rick's chest swelled with pride. "Glad to help. And the wine tasted even better, knowing what the bottle did!"

Howard chuckled. "So much for relaxation!"

Rick grinned. "I bet Cathy will be jealous when I tell her—I'm seeing all the action this time, not her!" He wondered how she was getting on.

Two days earlier—Tangier

Pointer and Basset waited in the Tangier airport concourse. He had bought a new hat and another pair of gloves.

"How are you feeling, sir?"

"Better, thanks. That Fuller's earth did the trick. It seemed to neutralize the dye-solution."

"It's a cure, then?"

"Hardly. It neutralizes. It's better than my golden liquid vial, because with that I'm left with scarring, but Fuller's earth seems to effect slight repair, too. Bottom line, Carol, it is still the same: if I'm exposed to direct sunlight and don't have Fuller's or my golden liquid handy, then I'm a goner."

"But can't someone analyze the properties of Fuller's earth, apply it?"

"It's beyond me."

"Me, too. I really think you shouldn't go out in sunshine, sir."

"It's what I do—investigate. Yes, I can constrain myself, only go out at night. Some shift workers rarely see daylight." He squinted at her. "Enough about me. What about our little ray of sunshine, Zabala?"

"I've heard from London. Their report tells us that Ananke HQ has said Zabala isn't in the UK, and our sources say he hasn't entered Shanghai either."

"That's annoying. I suppose the notices have gone out?"

"Yes. But that's the problem, sir."

"Indeed. He did it before. So what is he calling himself now?"

At that moment they were paged and were soon

met at the information desk by Detective Latifa Badouri of the *Sûreté nationale*. She was a good six inches taller than Basset. Her dark eyes and dark hair complemented her complexion.

She led them outside and they all got in the back of the police car and she urged the driver to go straight to the port. "I've been authorized to give you this," she said, handing Basset the British passport of Rick Barnes.

Pointer removed his hat, rested it on his knees.

"And this was at a murder scene?" Basset queried, holding the passport daintily between thumb and forefinger.

"Yes. We have dusted it for fingerprints, photographed and copied it, but we believe it was planted to distract us." She showed them a half-dozen photographs of Gerard Kominsky. "This is our murder victim."

Basset studied each image and passed it to Pointer.

"The knife-work is familiar," Pointer observed, "but not the same."

"My thoughts, too, sir." She glanced at Detective Badouri. "We think this murder was committed by Emilio Zabala, otherwise known as Ganix Elizondo."

"Intriguing." Badouri produced a Samsung Galaxy tablet and flicked through, touching keys. "Yes, I remember the name. Arrested for ETA offences, escaped and then vanished."

"I don't suppose you've been able to put out an alert to the port security?" Pointer asked.

"Yes, we did that. I am pleased to inform you that Zabala boarded the Algeciras ferry."

Pointer smiled. "That's terrific news, Detective Badouri!"

"If we are quick," she added, "we can still get aboard."

They arrived at the port in time to catch the ferry. Detective Badouri instructed her driver to return to the police station, while she would accompany their guests on the ship as foot-passengers.

As THE FERRY left the harbor behind, Cat wondered if she'd ever come back. Knowing her next destination, she had to consider this: would she even live to return?

She stood overlooking the stern, the wash of the propellers churning a trail from the African continent to Europe.

The agitation reflected the churning in her stomach; she should have eaten something for breakfast, but hadn't been able to face it.

She was convinced that Zabala would haunt her waking and sleeping moments. Her latest confrontation with him made her realize that her death was a real possibility. Could she continue her crusade against Dante and Ananke? Lives had been lost. She thought of Rick and her mind overlaid the image of Gerard's cut body with Rick's face. For a split second her heart seemed to immerse itself in a freezing lake and she gulped involuntarily, breathed in ozone. Rick had faced death at the hands of Zabala more than once.

No, she couldn't put him at risk anymore.

She let out a sob as she made her decision. Tears trailed over her cheeks; the sea breeze dried them.

She must go to Shanghai without Rick, and end it once and for all.

Algeciras

Having completed her passport and immigration forms on the ferry, Cat awaited the call on the public address system for car owners to go to the vehicle deck; it came when the ship was about thirty minutes from the harbor.

Cat went down to the deck and worked her way past several vehicles, and then used the remote key-fob to unlock her car. She climbed in and sat behind the wheel.

An instant later, Zabala swung open the passenger door and sat beside her, a huge knife-blade pressing against her side. He held the knife in his right hand, his arm across his body. His door remained open.

"Drive off when the time comth, Vibrithae."

He sounded different, nasal. Not surprising, since his nose was askew and bruising showed under both eyes. She'd done that. In any other situation, it might even be amusing.

"Underthtand?" he snarled.

Oh, she understood alright. She nodded, not trusting herself to speak. Her voice, her tone would transmit to him her fear. She gripped the steering wheel and realized her knuckles were white. *Ease off. He won't try anything here, will he?*

He could stab her, kill her, and leave before anybody noticed.

So why didn't he do that?

Then she got his answer to that thought. "I want you to drive to a thecluded thpot," he said, "where I can

260

deal with you without witnetheth." *Secluded spot. No witnesses.* Yeah, I get it.

She wasn't going to play his game, no way! "If...if you're going to kill me, I might as well stay here. Your risk is greater here."

He sighed and called her bluff. "If you wish."

Chapter 20

Nine Lives

Zabala pressed the blade into her side, and it cut her blouse, pricked her skin. "I will make it thlow. And I will thtill get away."

Stay alive, you fool! She nodded, a little too hastily. "Alright! I'll do as you say."

"Very thenthible."

They were momentarily distracted as someone walked past the car, swore something and slammed the passenger door shut.

The slam made her start and she felt the blade dig in. She was sure there was now a sticky wetness at her side. Had he cut her?

"I'm going to cut you more than thith little nick," he promised.

Paradoxically, her mouth was dry and her palms were damp. She wanted to lift her hands from the wheel, wipe them on her thighs, but she feared that any movement she made would be interpreted as an attempted escape or a martial arts attack and he'd slide that blade deep into her. The knife seemed at least twice as large as that one he'd used last night. *Was it only last night? Oh, God!*

"I'm going to cut you into little piethes and send them to Dante. He can run his DNA tethts on them, if he likes!"

And she was sure he meant every word.

The ship maneuvered to the dockside and within minutes the massive doors in front of them opened and the ramp lowered.

Ahead, the vehicles started moving.

Switching on the ignition, she put the car in gear. She glanced at the knife. "I need to release the hand-brake."

"Alright. Do it." He moved his arm and the blade back, slightly beyond the brake lever. She noticed the tip of the blade was discolored with her blood.

"No thudden movements," he warned.

She slowly lowered her right hand to the brake lever.

The van in front of her motored forward.

"Go on!" he urged.

She released the brake, and then pressed the pedal, and the car slowly passed across the metal plates, the racket of all the vehicles quite loud.

Usually, it never ceased to enthrall her, driving off a car-ferry, passing through the massive mouth, out into sunlight. Today, though, she wasn't enthralled at all. Simply scared. Frightened for her life.

She kept her right hand hovering above the gear-shift. He hadn't pressed the point of the blade against her. He must feel secure, now they were moving.

Gently toeing the foot-brake as the car moved down the ramp, she noticed a group of people over on her right. Something familiar about them. Especially the man with the hat and the gloves.

POINTER SPOTTED them first and shouted, "He's there —with Cat!"

Basset tapped Detective Badouri's shoulder, pointed at the Toyota Land Cruiser.

Whipping out her Beretta 92 automatic, Badouri took up her stance, legs braced, both hands on the raised weapon. "Stop!" she yelled above the din of rattling metal, aiming at the Land Cruiser's windshield.

IN THE SAME INSTANT, Zabala heard and saw the threat and swore; while Cat clenched her right hand, swiftly swung it backwards into Zabala's face, knuckles slamming into his damaged nose.

She unlatched the door and tumbled out, the sound of her blouse being cut and Zabala's screams in her ears.

She hit hard metal and smelled oil and petrol fumes.

Vehicles behind her made screeching noises as they suddenly braked.

Horns honked.

A single shot was fired. Glass shattered.

Her car veered to the left, and the front wheel jarred against the raised metal edge of the ramp, thumped, juddered and leapt over it, the axle grating loudly, then the vehicle stalled and hung there.

Cat struggled to her knees and stood shakily. Her

left shoulder was sore, and her pelvis. Her hand went to her right side, and she wasn't surprised to touch flesh, for a portion of her blouse had been cut away. Her fingers came away smeared with blood.

A couple of Spanish police from the port hurried over, their pistols drawn. A woman in plain clothes held a badge in one hand and kept her automatic trained on the passenger window of the Toyota. She was shouting, telling Zabala to come out. Interesting: she used his name.

Seconds later, both Pointer and Basset ran up the ramp to her side.

"Are you alright?" Basset asked.

She covered the cut flesh with a hand. "I'm a little bruised, thanks, but I'll live."

Pointer pushed his hat off his brow. "One of your nine lives, Cat?"

She rubbed her shoulder. "Something like that."

He glanced at her car. "Detective Badouri only wounded Zabala."

"Oh," Cat said, "that's a pity."

"Don't worry," Pointer said, "he'll pay. He'll be tried for several murders—in Spain and England, at least. They'll throw away the key."

"That's good, Alan. But I suspect that his arrest won't affect Ananke."

"No, I suppose not."

They watched as Zabala stumbled out of the car, a hand to his face, blood dribbling from his nose and shoulder. Hastily, the police handcuffed him and led him away.

Putting a hand on Cat's shoulder, Pointer said, "You know, we need to see about clearing up a few things for you and Rick Barnes. You've both been instrumental in helping us capture a serial killer. We should be able to wipe the slate clean regarding international warrants and so forth."

"That would be a huge help." She'd text Rick, once she had confirmation that the heat was off. Perhaps he could go back to a normal life, whatever that is.

"By the way," Basset said, "where is Mr. Barnes?"

"Sailing to the Canaries." A heaviness descended on her, constricting her chest. He'd declare his love, she knew, but she couldn't ask him to risk his life anymore because of her obsession.

"Lucky blighter," Basset said.

"Too much sun for my liking," Pointer moaned. "And are you joining him there?"

"No." Cat eyed her car ruefully. "Once the insurance has been sorted on that, I'll be flying to Shanghai."

A Look At Book Three:

Cataclysm

An action-packed thriller with exotic intrigue and vengeful tendencies...

A cataclysm is a political or social upheaval, a disturbance that must be thwarted. And that's what Catherine Vibrissae is determined to do.

Some months after her and Rick Barnes' adventure in Morocco, Cat receives devastating news—news that is about to change her life forever. Still determined to face down her archenemy Loup Dante in Shanghai and end her vendetta once and for all, Cat impedes an ambush by Ananke's new head of security, Mr. Song. Too bad oligarch and people smuggler Anton Belofsky is also in Shanghai...with a devastating new agenda.

While Cat plays cat-and-mouse with Song, she uncovers a conspiracy that she fears will lead to all-out war between China and Japan and wonders if she has what it takes to end true evil before it begins.

Book three in the Cat's Crusade series, Cataclysm follows a strong female character who is on her final crusade for vengeance.

AVAILABLE MAY 2023

About the Author

Nik Morton has sold over 100 short stories, edited periodicals and contributed to magazine articles, chaired writers' circles, run writing workshops, and judged competitions. He has edited many books and was sub-editor of the monthly magazine *Portsmouth Post* (2003-2007) and Editor in Chief of a U.S. Publisher (2011-2013). He has had 32 books published —including 3 books in the psychic spy *Tana Standish* series and 8 westerns—and co-written 4 books in the *Floreskand* fantasy series. His *Write a Western in 30 Days – with plenty of bullet points!* is a best-seller. With his wife Jennifer, Nik lived in Spain for several years (2003-2019). They have since returned to England, residing in Northumberland—near their daughter Hannah, son-in-law Harry and grandchildren Darius and Suri.